SWEET TEMPTATIONS

MARY TILLING

authorHOUSE

AuthorHouse™ UK
1663 Liberty Drive
Bloomington, IN 47403 USA
www.authorhouse.co.uk
Phone: UK TFN: 0800 0148641 (Toll Free inside the UK)
    UK Local: (02) 0369 56322 (+44 20 3695 6322 from outside the UK)

Published by AuthorHouse 12/15/2021

ISBN: 978-1-6655-9018-1 (sc)
ISBN: 978-1-6655-9020-4 (hc)
ISBN: 978-1-6655-9019-8 (e)

Print information available on the last page.

Edited by Nichola Evans

This book is printed on acid-free paper.

The Profile

The front door gently clicks as it shuts behind me. My work kit thuds as it lands on the tiled floor. What I once considered my cosy cottage entrance doesn't feel so cosy at all anymore. A deafening silence surrounds me in the chilly hallway.

"This cottage is bloody freezing," I declare to my cats as they come to greet me. I step into the tiny lounge and stare into the cinders of my open fireplace thinking about the life ahead of me. "Come on now, sort yourself out," I tell myself.

I go downstairs to my quirky little basement bedroom to change out of my work clothes. I love my little upside down four-hundred-year-old cottage, despite what I said when I walked in.

Back in the lounge, I arrange the kindling, coal and logs and light the fire. I need warmth. The only other heat is from the storage heaters, and I've never figured out how to work those.

I go to close the lounge curtains and see my pale reflection staring back at me in the window, alone. I feel myself begin to well up unspent tears, but I hold them back. I'm so used to the noise, laughter and bickering of a loving, crazy, family home. One I'd spent my entire twenties building, nurturing and loving completely. I did this alongside my love, my best friend, my husband.

This was, of course, until I didn't. It wasn't something that happened overnight. I didn't wake up one morning and decide 'yup, we're done.' I wanted, needed, this marriage to work. The usual reasons to stay kept me ploughing on, lost in the routine of daily life. I told myself so many times:

'We have three beautiful girls. They deserve both of us.'
'My family have accepted him. My brothers count him as another brother.'
'Who will help me if the car cuts out?'
'Everyone will hate me.'
'The girls will hate me.'
'How will I afford to get by?'
'How can I be 'Kate' without him?'
And worst of all, the most terrifying: *'If I leave there is no coming back.'*

This was the rhetoric that played in my head daily. I had decided I had to be there 'til I was forty. The girls would be old enough to understand and I'd still be young enough to start a new life. But who was I kidding? I began to realise that my girls deserve the love of two stable and happy parents. They don't deserve being witness to the silent treatment, the tension, the snide comments, the full-blown temper tantrum that would erupt when everything just became too damn much. Or the sobbing when once again my birthday was forgotten.

I realised that the voice inside me saying, *"You're not worth remembering Kate"* was crushing my spirit little by little, and was in fact, a bit of a fuckwit. I decided the way he behaved when he got home from work, all absorbed in his own little fantasy world within his computer instead of me, instead of us, was just plain rude. I'm a delight! He should want to be absorbed by me and the girls!

Now, don't get me wrong. I love the bones of this man. He is funny. He is spirited. He is absolutely the best father my girls could ask for. But we became more like friends than husband and wife and lovers. Both our eyes began to wander. I didn't want that. Walking through the front door to our home made my mood change instantly. A black cloud would appear over my head, bringing me down and filling my mind with anger and resentment, until eventually hatred began to bubble. No, this was definitely *not* what I wanted.

It broke my heart that however hard I tried to fix the cracks, however hard I tried to make it work, deep inside I just knew we couldn't go on like this. I also knew that I had to be the bad guy. He wouldn't leave me. He was oblivious to the fact he had rendered me invisible and that I sobbed in the bathroom, thinking of a way out. As far as he was concerned, we loved each other, and I did love him, just more like a brother. So I did it. And now here I am. Alone.

I know he still loves me, and I know it would be easy for me to pick up the phone, tell him I am over my midlife crisis, and we could begin again. The noise would fill this cottage. The girls would be ecstatic to have us all together again. I also know that it took a huge amount of courage to get here and once the initial joy at seeing them all together again wore off, I would be back living in turmoil. I simply cannot let that dark cloud engulf me and kill my spirit.

I tell myself to stop being so melodramatic. The girls will be back tomorrow. I worked bloody hard to get to this point, pulling myself together and carving out my career as a mobile hairdresser to support my family. And me and the ex are nailing co-parenting too. So, I've got this.

Earlier today a client had asked me, "Why don't you give online dating a whirl?" I'd laughed at the time. I'd been complaining about the lack of men in my tiny seaside village. And the lack of time to go out. And the lack of energy to get off my sofa after standing and chatting all day. But after my initial dismissal, it was like a niggling worm in the back of my head. Try it! Why not? Everyone does it now! But I guess that is it. I'm arriving *now* when my dating time was *then*.

When I began dating my husband, it started with a good old-fashioned, simple night out with the girls, ending with a drunken snog. That's how we did it back in 2004. But now, suddenly I am in a world where it's the norm to date via online apps. So maybe it is something I should try? I give the cats their dinner and I have a firm talk with myself. I should do this! It will be OK. In fact, it will be fun. And if not, I can just delete it. It's only an app.

Aaargh! Here we go! I'm *actually* doing it. I'm in my now cosy lounge, the fire burning brightly, and a throw over my lap whilst I get to grips with setting myself up online. I'm downloading POF (Plenty of Fish). Add email address, password, blah, blah, blah. Oh God. I feel sick! I'm a thirty-one-year-old woman, mother-of-three, putting myself on a dating app. Holy fuck! What on earth am I doing? I must be losing my mind!

Verify using Facebook. What the actual? No thank you. I don't want my friends and family seeing this. Ah no, my bad. No one will see this information. They just want to check I'm me. OK. Verifying.

Right, pictures. Oh man, this is uncomfortable. I don't have many pictures without my girls. Ah, found one. Yep, my hair looks nice, cute dress, not too sexy. Not that I can do sexy, but I do try.

I need wine. Where is the wine? Why on earth hadn't I poured myself a glass of wine for this job? I chuck my throw on the floor and jump up from the sofa, disturbing the two cats curled up by my side. I wave the third cat off the work surface in the kitchen, collect the red wine and get back to the job in hand. I pour a very large glass of wine and realise that wine is very much a necessity for this moment in my life. I need Dutch courage, or I won't complete this.

OK, a few more pictures. One with curly hair, fuller makeup, nice black dress, taken on a night out with The Nine, my best friends, my girl gang. Lily, Lemon, Kimberly, Jessica, Lottie, Penelope, Bambi, Sophie and I are The

Nine. I met Lily and Lemon first, through drama classes when we were ten, then Lottie through secondary school. The rest of the gang were Lily's friends who she'd also met at secondary school. We've grown up together and I love these ladies! Yes, at thirty-one you still need a girl gang.

Next picture: straight hair, not much makeup. I don't wear a lot of makeup so I can't be selling myself as something I'm not. I'm totally putting a filter on it though, a natural one, 'dramatically cool'. If asked, deny filter. Nice top and jeans. All good. A couple more. Jeez, I feel like I'm putting myself on eBay or something. Highest bidder wins.

Oh my god. What if no one likes me? No bidders at all? Oh, this is a hideous experience. I am so glad I have a bottle of red right now.

My gender: Female

Seeking: Male

Height: Five feet three inches. I'm actually five feet two-and-a-half inches, but that's not an option for this box.

Looking for: So, the options are 'hang out', 'friends', 'dating', 'long term'. Oh man! Dating, I guess? I've only just separated from the husband so I can't say I want long-term. I really need to find myself, have fun, relive my twenties. But who doesn't want their Disney prince to run off into the sunset with, happily in love? If I'm honest, I do want that eventually. Oh, heck. I can't put 'long term' though. Nope, dating it is.

I have some serious issues with relationships! I can't close doors. I'm friends with almost all of my exes, no matter how badly I've been treated. At the same time, in new relationships, I struggle with bringing down my walls. It all stems from my childhood, I guess. I stop myself dwelling and crack on with completing my profile.

So, hair colour: Brown (well, brunette if you want the correct description from a professional!).

Body type: Oh, dear God! What do I say here? Big thighs, mum tum, wobbly bits, breasts that fed three babies? Erm, nope, better not. Options are:

- 'Athletic': Hmmm, that's not me. I have gym membership, but I hate going. I only go so I can get away with eating pizza and chocolate without becoming obese.
- 'Average': What's that supposed to bloody mean? What size is average?
- 'A few extra pounds': Oh great! Now I'm wishing I loved the gym and went more often.
- 'Big & Tall': Yeah, not me. I was *not* blessed in the leg department.

OK, OK. Google can help. I type in 'average size for a thirty-one-year-old woman'. Well, average height is five feet four inches, weight is twelve stone, dress size twelve. I love Google right now! I'm a size ten / twelve. Winning at life! Yay me! Average it is!

Do you own a car? Yes (my little run-around for work. Nothing posh, but it gets me from A to B).

Describe your personality in one word: Wow! This is a long drop-down list. Adventurous, Animal Lover, Arty, Athletic, Beach Bum, Blogger, Blue Collar, Bookworm, Chef, Class Clown, Club Kid, Coffee Snob, Comic Nerd, Crafty, Daredevil, Design Snob, Diva, Fashionista, Film/TV Junkie, Free Thinker, Foodie, Geek, Gamer, Hedonist, Hipster, Hippie, Homebody, Hopeless Romantic, Humanist, Intellectual, Maker, Music Snob, Night Owl, Nomad, Photographer, Player, Poet, Princess, Professional, Rockstar, Starving Artist, Straight Edge, Traveller, Techie, Tree hugger, Tattooed/ Pierced, Vegetarian, Vegan, Yogi, Yuppy…

I don't even know what half of those are! Right. Well, I'm an animal lover, a free thinker, tattooed and pierced. I'll go with free thinker.

Second language: No, I'd love a second language. I should learn one!

How ambitious are you? Very.

Education: College level.

State/Province: England.

Do you want children? Oh my god. I'm having to think about children! I have three children. Do I want more? Would I be open to more? Do I definitely *not* want anymore? I have absolutely no idea. Erm. I'll go with 'prefer not to say'. I'll cross that bridge another time.

Do you have children? Yes.

Would you date someone who has children? Yes.

Do you smoke? No.

Would you date someone who smokes? 'No' or 'Yes, I only date smokers'. Ugh. I hate the thought of being with a smoker again, but do I want to eliminate the love of my life because he smokes? Maybe not? Nope. I'm saying no. I know I won't date a smoker through choice. My ex-husband was a smoker and I hated it. I always begged him to stop.

Do you drink? Jeez! Can't I just say yes? Apparently not. Options are 'No', 'Socially' or 'Often'. OK. Socially it is. Selected whilst drinking a glass of red wine from a bottle opened for one. Oops.

Religion: Hmmm, more spiritualist, but there's no option for that. Catholic it is.

Do you have pets? Cats. Three (I embraced impending singledom and got three cats).

Eye colour: Brown.

Your Profession: Mobile hairdresser.

When it comes to dating, what's your intent? 'I want to date, but nothing serious'… Erm, *nope*! I'm not clicking that option. It makes me look like I only want sex! 'I am putting in serious effort to find someone'… No, that makes me seem desperate. 'I am serious and want to find someone'… Well, I am, and I do, but I need to take this all slowly. 'I want a relationship'… Yep, that's the one. I do want to meet someone and in time I would like to turn it into a relationship. I will just explain I need to take things slowly.

What's the longest relationship you've been in? 'Over ten years'… I'm feeling a bit sad now. This is all very real. How am I here? I had a husband, a beautiful man who loved me, wholly and completely. I had a man who stood by me, who I grew up with, became a parent with. Reality check Kate: A man who grew apart from me, drank too much, ignored me and escaped life by playing computer games. A man who became addicted to an iPad. A man who forgot my birthday and Valentine's Day, never took me on a dinner date, ignored my existence and then questioned why I was leaving. Yep, that's how I got here.

I'm looking for a man who sees *me*, who wants to get to know *me* and walks side by side with me through life. I want a man who buys me little gifts just because they happened to think of me, who pays attention to the little things I like. I'm fired back up. Next question.

First Name: Kate.

Income: Less than £25k.

My birth father and mother are: Divorced.

Siblings: I am the youngest of four. The only girl.

Headline: What the fuck? What do I put here? Erm, a headline. Headline, headline, headline. Can I come back to this? No. OK. Be casual, something breezy. I couldn't be further from breezy! I'm now thinking as Monica from 'Friends': *"I'm breezy"*. I know, 'Single mum looking to meet someone to have adventures with.' Nailed it! Done! I'm laughing now. I'm a little giddy with excitement and wine, but nervous all at the same time. Oh my god. I am now an online dater.

Let this new chapter in my life begin.

Boost: First, First Date

It's nearly 11.30pm. I'm tucked up, all alone in my king-sized bed, looking through the dating app on my phone. I'm quite surprised by just how many strange men are out there, and it seems ninety percent of them use this app. But what's this? Oh, this is exciting. I really like this profile! He is hot! Nice arms, dark hair, dark eyes, kids, non-smoker, works for himself: he looks yummy! I'm so happily surprised.

> Hello

Oh my god. A message! He has just messaged me! Had he seen me checking him out? OK, I can do this. Shit, I am actually having to do this. Come on Kate, pull yourself together. Text him back.

> Hi. How are you?

I'm totally doing this!

> I'm good thanks. Yourself?

> Yeah I'm good. Where do you live?

> London. You?

> Well, I live in Kent. Under a rock it seems. I'm new to all this.

How long have you been single?

Haha, under a rock!

A year. You?

6 months. You're the first man I've spoken to on here. Unless the persistent, gormless guy who sent me four separate messages and doesn't seem to take the hint that I don't wish to chat back counts?

I only joined last night.

😩 Nope he doesn't count! Wow you really are new here. Freaked out or enjoying it?

A little of both TBH.

Well, I'd just like to say that I think you're gorgeous. I'd love to chat more and get to know you.

Awwww thank you! You look gorgeous yourself!

I'm off to bed now, I really must sleep. Hopefully we can chat tomorrow.

Yes definitely!

Oh my god! This is crazy. Could that have been the first conversation with my future boyfriend? I'm ever the optimist! How ridiculously exciting. OK I need to screen shot his profile and send it to Chit Chat, (that's The Nine's WhatsApp group). I want to show them how gorgeous he is. Such nice arms. Nice build in his second picture. Nice haircut. At five feet seven inches, he is slightly shorter than I would normally go for, but yep, this man is definitely my type.

We have spent a week messaging back and forth, getting to know each other, establishing what we do and don't like, what we have in common. I get so excited when his name pops up on my phone. I check the time whilst replying to one of his chatty texts. Its five past eleven. Time for elevenses! I fancy a bit of chocolate and a cup of tea. But not the kids' small bars. I need the good stuff. Forget the diet regime for the moment. It's time for the top shelf, the 'mum stash', the chocolate tin, my candy box. Such sweet temptations. Hmmm, what have I got? A Dairy Milk, a good old favourite of mine. I do like those, but… oh, what have we found here? A Boost? I haven't had a Boost in years! I love them. How did that get in here? Then I realise Lily had brought a few different bars of chocolate for my girls when we had a movie night last week, but one seems to have found its way into my box. Yay for me!

My mind wanders. I think about my girls (probably because I feel guilty for pinching their chocolate). I don't really want them knowing I'm chatting to different men. I don't want them to see the names in my phone. I need a code. I dip the Boost bar into my tea, enjoying how it melts and lasts longer. I make the most out of my chocolate treat moments. Oh my god! That's it… chocolate bars. I will make the most out of the men who ping into my life. I'll enjoy them for the treats they are during my search for the perfect one. I laugh and nearly spill my tea. Yes, the phone book code is chocolate. The name might need to change as I get to know someone, but it is fun thinking what bar each guy might personify.

What would this one be? Is he Nestlé, Cadbury, Galaxy, Lindt? What others do I like? Thinking about it, Boost is very fitting. He's certainly given my life a boost this last week. I take a sip of tea, giggling to myself. Boost it is.

What about my ex-husband? I wonder. He's a good sturdy bar. Solid. I knew what I had with him. After all, there was no way I would have had children with anyone other than a reliable chocolate bar. He's not a novelty bar with lots of things going on. (What on earth are those bars with popping candy all about?) No. He's a classic bar. One you can eat when you're happy or sad. He's a bar that you can count on to always be in stock. He is a great father. He has the girls half the week and never lets them down. He does everything they ask of him. And he continues to be a great friend to me. It's just a shame we didn't have more in common towards the end. Yes. A good, reliable, solid bar of Cadbury Dairy Milk.

After a second week of texting and a couple of phone calls with Boost, we have arranged to meet for the first time at Thorpe Park. This is going to be such fun. This is such a random first date and I absolutely *love* it! At least we can talk about the rides if conversation runs dry.

I'm nervous. I haven't had a 'first date' for so long and deciding what to wear was a challenge. My hair is up in a messy side bun. I have strappy sandals on and a pinky-orange dress. As I get out of the car, I begin to doubt myself. *What was I thinking wearing a dress? It's Thorpe Park for fuck's sake! Oh Kate! Really? Well, I'm committed now. Tough.* I call him to see where he is.

"Hellooooo," he says in a sing song voice. It's cute and I smile.

"I'm just paying for parking. I'll meet you by the gate."

Oh gosh. There he is. He looks just like his pictures. I like his hair – dark with a low fade that's styled well. I hope he thinks I look like my pictures. *Oh my god.* This is really happening. I'm going on my first date.

"Hi Kate," he says, and kisses my cheek. "It's great to meet you."

He smells good, nice cologne. I smile. "You too."

I'm so nervous I'm almost shaking. This is exciting and I can feel the adrenaline pulsating around my body.

"Let's go," he says. "I've been really looking forward to this – with a bit of luck we won't have to queue too long with it being a school day!"

We hurry through the entrance behaving like a pair of teenagers. He was right. The park is pretty empty. I had thought we would have time to chat in the queues, but the longest wait is only ten minutes. Despite this we laugh and chat all the way round the park, ride after ride. I feel so comfortable, as if I have known him for years. I'm glad we'd been texting for a couple of weeks before we met. It makes us feel more familiar with each other.

Towards the end of our day out, we grab a cup of tea before we leave. It's gone so fast and it's five o'clock already.

"I feel so sick from those rides," I say, laughing.

He sighs with relief, agreeing he has had enough too. Reality has hit home. Though we really enjoyed behaving like teenagers today, we are not actually teenagers. We're in our thirties. I try to stop my mind wandering back to the things waiting for me when I get home. The kids, the laundry, the bills to pay. I shake my head. *Surely I'm still young enough to enjoy this moment? I should allow myself a little bit of irresponsibility.*

We stroll back to the car park, flirting all the way. He walks me to my car to say our goodbyes. Then he goes in for a kiss. This is new. Exciting and nerve-racking at the same time. It's a perfect ending to an awesome first date. In fact, the best first date I could have asked for.

My connection with Boost strengthens every day and we are going to meet again. This time in London. He's taking me to see 'Wicked' and I absolutely cannot believe it. I have wanted to see the show for years! So many birthdays passed when Dairy Milk (my ex-husband) had promised he was going to take me but didn't.

"Are you sure about going to see a musical?" I asked Boost when he told me, not convinced he really wanted to.

His reply was just perfect! "I booked it because you told me you used to love going to the West End. I wanted you to go again and I wanted to be the one to take you. That would mean a lot to me."

"You are lovely. Thank you! But how much do I owe you for the tickets?" I asked. Over the last few years, I've become fiercely independent.

"Oh no, they're on me."

I froze. I very much want to pay my own way. I surprised myself at how much I wanted to fight it, to assert my independence. But I also realised I have to choose my battles wisely. We are still early in our relationship. I need to let him know how I feel about that over time. I offer one last time, then let the matter go. For now.

We meet in central London for a couple of pre-show drinks. Boost doesn't disappoint and is as hot as he was on our first date, smelling good, once again. The show is everything I could have wished for. We sat holding hands, resting them on his thigh. It was so comfortable. We chat away in the interval and the feeling of familiarity is reassuring. Boost is breathing life into me. I feel like a woman again. Not just a mum, or a forgotten wife.

After the show we go for a couple more drinks before I head for my train home. I'm so happy. I'm excited about how this will progress and what our future could hold. And at the same time I'm freaking out that at some point we will take this further than kissing and hand holding. And this guy will see me naked. *Holy shit*. Retreat! I'm way over-thinking this now.

OK. So, tonight is the night. We've been dating for five weeks now. I want to take this to the next stage, but fuck, fuck, fuck, I am completely freaking out. How am I going to get naked with this man? Oh, Dairy Milk. He knew my body. He understood my body, what to do, how I worked. I could find no fault with Dairy Milk here. Sex is what helped us stay together for ten years. Now I'm going to be having sex with someone else.

Oh my god, I need to change my mindset. This could be fun. It is actually rather exciting, Kate. Snap out of the nerves and get on board with excitement.

Waxed, shaved, bathed, big bouncy hair, all good to go. Sexy new underwear (well, sexy on the model on the shop's website anyway, but I'll try the best I can to make this work). Yes, classic, sexy black French knickers and a black push up bra to match. I need all the help I can get with my mum boobs. Maybe he will leave my bra on? Cunning plan. Well done, Kate. That could work. Just leave the bra on.

I'm going to drive over to his place for dinner and drinks, and we've planned for me to stay for the night. Obviously, we don't have to have sex, but I know we both want to. *Note to self, Kate: Give yourself a gold star. You just said it. You want to. You're starting to feel the excitement. Just enjoy the evening. What will be will be. For fuck's sake, I feel like a virgin again.*

Boost's flat is homely. I feel comfortable here. Two spacious bedrooms, lounge/diner, kitchen, bathroom, a little balcony. *Clean. Thank God it's clean.* You never really know what someone's like until you see their home. I breathe a sigh of relief.

I wander round the lounge looking at photos of his kids. *Cute.*

"Wine?" he asks.

"Yes please." *Down the wine, Kate. Down it!* I scream to myself in my head as I gulp at the wine. *Oh shit, no, slow down. Classy Kate. Think classy. Not piss-head!*

A couple of hours fly by. I'm really loving this. I knew I was overthinking things before. I'm enjoying the evening, the chat, the flirting, the curry he cooked. I like this man. He makes me feel so at ease. The wine's helping though! I'm now on my third glass. He doesn't know I'm lighter than lightweight when it comes to wine, or any alcohol for that matter.

Moving to the sofa from the table, he leans in for a kiss. Mmmm. He's good at this. His hands move up my thighs to my waist. He pulls me onto his lap, facing him. We're kissing the entire time, while his hands make their way to unbutton my jeans. *Shit. This is happening. Keep calm,* I tell myself. I'm pulling at his top, he pulls at mine, exposing my lacey black bra.

I feel at ease about my body now. I know the attraction is mutual and I feel more confident. He stands up, takes my hand and we make our way to the bedroom, kissing all the way. I really want him. I want this to happen. I'm still nervous about him seeing my whole body but I don't care. I'm excited. This is going to happen because we want it to happen. But the bra is staying on!

I wake up crazy early, feeling well and truly boosted! It's a weekday. I need to get back to collect the girls from Dairy Milk so he can go to work and they can get to school. I leave Boost's flat at six and arrive at Dairy Milk's place just before seven thirty. It's a long drive, but this man's worth it. Now back to Mum mode.

Boost and I continue dating, hanging out in London's bars and restaurants, which is far more exciting than what's on offer in my sleepy coastal village. Plus, I don't want to bump into friends. Dairy Milk would be heartbroken to see me out with someone new. We're trying so hard to be friends, to respect each other. We're just not at that space yet where we can talk about new dates. We need our friendship to grow and develop as we transition from husband and wife to friends and co-parents.

All the while, Boost and I are loving our time together. I feel so lucky to have met him. And how lucky am I that he's the first man I started talking to online and he's not a crazy loon. He seems to be amazing. It feels like fate.

I'm nine weeks into this all-new way of life. This weekend I am out in Soho with Lottie. She has been my bestie for twenty years. Her girlfriend, Sarah is here too. Boost had said he'd join us when he finished work, but it's getting late and he still hasn't arrived. I'm confused. It was all going so well. Eventually he calls and makes his excuses. He apologises, saying he has been caught up with work. I can't help but feel suspicious. Something doesn't feel right.

"We can meet tomorrow if you are free?" he asks.

I say no. He's let me down. I would understand if our plans had been last minute, but we'd arranged it a while ago. I'd thought as I was in London, he would want to see me and would make sure work couldn't get in the way. Oh well. I give myself a shake. *Don't let him put a damper on my night with Lottie and Sarah,* I tell myself. In the end, I really enjoy letting my hair down, drinking and dancing in Soho's eclectic bars. We have a great night without him.

Later that week, Boost and I meet for a drink near St Pancras station. It's full of commuters talking loudly. I need to be close to him to talk properly, but something feels off. As we talk, I realise he is making dig after dig about the gay bars. I brush them off to begin with, but he doesn't let it drop.

"Why do you keep going on about the gay bars?" I ask.

"I don't like them. They're not natural. I mean, you're Catholic! Surely you can't be fine with them?" he says, taking my hand. "I mean…"

I take a large gulp of wine. This isn't the guy I have spent such happy, fun and carefree time with over the last few months or so. My cheeks flush and tears sting the back of my eyes. I blink rapidly, reminding myself of fun times with my girls, to force the tears away. They retreat. I realise I am still holding his hand. *What the fuck do I do? How the hell did I get this so wrong? How did I almost introduce this pig to my best friend and her girlfriend?* Lottie is like family to me. I'm filled with rage, wondering how I can get away from this prat.

So, I do what any thirty-something people-pleaser would do. I pretend that my phone is vibrating in my pocket. I release my grip and let his hand drop away from mine. "Sorry," I mouth, pretending I have an urgent call.

I turn away. "What was that? The girls? Oh, for God's sake! I'm in London… OK… You feel terrible? It's not your fault, it can't be helped. I will get the next train back. Leave them with Mum for now. I'll be there soon."

All those years attending my mum's drama club as a kid have finally come to fruition. *Come on Kate, you can do this.* I walk back to him and take a deep breath.

"I'm so sorry. I need to get back to the girls. My ex has developed man-flu." I roll my eyes dramatically. "He can't have the girls, and my mother has a church do tonight so she's not available either. Sorry."

Please believe me. Please believe me, I say repeatedly to myself.

"Oh, er, OK," he replies. "Maybe next weekend?"

"Absolutely. Sounds great." I smile. *Thank you, Mama!* I think to myself. I turn and walk briskly away. If he texts me, I'll just respond with short non-committal messages then ghost him. I'm not very good at the old block and delete tactic. Closing doors is not a strong point for me. But this door will most definitely be closed.

I can see now that it was all too good to be true. I see Boost in such a different light. I replay every conversation we had, questioning how I missed his narrowmindedness. There's absolutely no way on earth that I would bring someone like that into my girls' lives. He wouldn't fit in with my friends or family. Not one bit. How could I have him as my 'plus one' if my Lottie gets married one day? I mean, what the fuck would he do? It's barely worth thinking about. No *fucking* way. I just don't want to be around him. He's not the one after all. Just a boost to bring me back to life.

Wonka: Falling in Love with A Phone

I decided it was time to try a new dating app and was introduced to the world of swiping on Tinder. It's brilliant. Who knew how much fun having an online shop of catalogued men would be? Now I can just swipe left (no) on the men I don't like the look of and swipe right (yes) on the ones I do. My god, this is so bloody shallow, but so much better than the last app. Anyone could message me before, but now we can only message each other if we both match. I feel a lot more comfortable.

But why on earth am I turning down so many guys? I wonder just how many men I swipe left to, before I find myself swiping right. I mean, what am I looking for? What is my type? I seem to fancy guys with dark eyes, dark hair. Men with a happy looking face, or a sexy as hell face too. I realise I swipe so quickly now too. That's bad. I laugh out loud to myself at this whole process. Why am I judging myself for having a type? Tall, dark, handsome and happy looking. Yep, that is my type and I'm sticking to it. Why shouldn't I swipe quickly? At the end of the day this is online shopping, and I don't buy shoes unless I like the look of them. That is the point of this boy app. I guess if I was involved in an evening of speed dating that would be different because I'd be face to face with the men and it would involve chemistry and personality, as well as looks. Swiping on the other hand, well, that's all about looks. And as shallow as it sounds, that's how it works!

I kind of see Tinder as a night out. Imagine, you're out with the girls, keeping an eye out for potential hot dates. You can walk by hundreds of men and only two or three of them might catch your eye, but that doesn't mean you'll catch theirs. Of those three, you might chat to one, have a quick natter, then never see them again. After a few nights out you might only have exchanged your number with one man. At least swiping is time efficient! Yes, online dating is great for the single, working mum. Besides, if I'm out with the girls I want to gossip and put the world to rights with them, not think about dating.

I decide to count how many lefts I swipe. One, two, three, four… one hundred and two! Now. Wait. Who is this? He's *definitely* a right swipe. Very handsome indeed.

I'm running late, as usual. I rush across the near-empty school playground towards my girls. "I'm so sorry. I was held up."

Their teachers usher the girls towards me, as they all talk together loading my arms up with their book bags. "Mum, can we pop into the shop? Please? Just a packet of sweets or something. *Please?*"

A 'hello' would have been nice, but that's life as Mum!

"Urgh, OK." I reply, rolling my eyes dramatically, hoping the incessant nagging will cease. I smile at them and adore their happy faces beaming back at me. Those knowing smiles. They won so very easily. We walk down the road to the corner shop.

"Hello," we chorus together as we walk in manoeuvring the cramped aisles towards the confectionary section. The little ones (they're three and five) take their time choosing what treats they might like. My eldest (she's nine) makes her choice quicker, hands it to me and tells me she's going to wait outside with her friends.

I decide to restock my chocolate stash. Hmmm, what do I fancy? I want something a bit different. Something I haven't tried before. I'm craving something new and unique and can't see anything here that I particularly want. The youngest two pick their treats, I pay and then hesitate as I leave the shop. I wish I had a treat for myself now. Serves me right about having such high expectations of chocolate. But then it is a treat, so I should be choosy. I should truly enjoy it when I get the treat I crave. Hmmm, maybe I'm not so much thinking about the chocolate bars in the shop, but the options available on my phone. I chuckle to myself as we continue our walk home.

So, back to the swiping. Oh, a match! This guy looks so sweet. He doesn't look like a poser at all. Hmmm, honestly, he seems so cute. This is exciting! Average build, gorgeous, dark hair, kind-looking face. He seems like a down to earth kind of man. *Yes Kate, of course you know that from pictures,* I say sarcastically to myself. I'm laughing and giddy, checking out his profile again.

I hope he likes me and that I get to meet him. *Ah, his Instagram is at the bottom of his profile. I'm totally going to do some stalking here. Oh, my goodness. Look at this. What a marvellous moustache! This man looks like such fun.*

And it's a match people. *Whoop whoop. Mini wave to me. Yay!*

> Kate, thank you for the mutual like. I'm both flattered and humbled. What did you want to be when you were younger and what do you do to finance your fun times?

What a brilliant first message. Not the standard and boring, 'Hey' or 'Hi, how are you?' that most of us send as our opening line. It's safe to say, I'm hooked!

> Well hello there. Great question. I wanted to be a farmer 😄 Now I'm a hairdresser, and a passionate one at that.

> A farmer? I wasn't expecting that!

> So which hairstyle do you wish you had created and dubbed 'the Kate'?

> Yep all true. I love animals! 😄 I would totally have loved working the farm but I couldn't have killed the animals cos I would love them too much. I'm a veggie.

> That's another awesome question! The ombre. I'd be rich! 😄 No, in fact I love playing with bright colours. So much fun.

> If you created the ombre you'd be rich and you wouldn't be messaging me on here, so count your lucky stars or we wouldn't be having this conversation. 😄

The main things I look for when I'm dating online are that prospective dates have a job, they have kids and they have good dress sense. This gentleman is a photographer (job, tick); seems very creative (tick); has kids (tick); six feet tall (tick, tick, tick); wicked dress sense, kind of retro vibe (tick, I like it a lot); handsome (tick). This is a great start.

After a couple of days chatting on the app, we exchange numbers. That was quite quick for me. I am so excited to receive messages from him and a big grin fills my face whenever I see his name appear on my phone. *Sugar, I need a code name. Hmmm. Something different. This one has something no one else has. He's quirky, not the usual high street brand. I need something spectacular for this guy. Oh, I know. He's a Wonka Bar! This is brilliant. Come on, the moustache and the retro vibe, his way with words. Perfect!*

Well, that was short lived. Wonka hasn't messaged back in nearly a week. He just stopped. I keep looking at his profile and he always seems to be online. He must have started chatting to someone else. I'm totally deflated. This guy was Disney all over I'd created a real Prince Charming in my head. Ah well, I know I can't win them all, but I had thought he was awesome. The way he wrote his messages was unusual. They were so well written yet seemed effortless. I totally believed this was the beginning of a great romance. But there we go. Back to earth with a bump as I land flat on my now scrunched up face. Apparently, he's *not* my Disney prince.

Three more days go by. It feels like weeks. I toy with the idea that he might text me again, then slap myself back into harsh reality. The gem just wasn't into me. Not only that, but the last time we had a text message conversation it concluded with me sending a double text to which he didn't reply. There was no way I could triple text (although I had been trying to talk myself into that, for one final attempt to win back his affection).

My phone pings.

> Morning Kate! How's your Halloween weekend treating you? Hope you're good. xxx

Yay! I'm so glad I didn't send that third text message. I do a little dance. *Whoop, whoop, mini wave!* This is what I'd been hoping for. And not secretly either. I've been telling anyone who'll listen just how much I clicked with this sweet treat and how much I hoped he would contact me again.

"Mum, Mum, Mum," my youngest shouts from the bathroom.

Why is it always the most inappropriate moments that kids need your attention? They know, I'm sure of it. That one moment I might just be being 'Kate' and the girls need me to remember my name is Mum. I know it's not just me. I reckon it is probably every mum on earth. They need to chat to you while you're having a quick wee, or the third world war breaks out between siblings the moment you answer your phone. Heaven forbid that you might have a relaxing bath. No way. You must be mad. That's the moment they need a poo! Jeez, give mama a couple of minutes, won't you? The love of my life is texting. Well, a love you have never met and who I've only known a week. Yes, that's just quite long enough to count and I'm sticking with it. I laugh. *Oh my god. Calm down and compose yourself Kate. Breathe. Text.*

> 😂 dude you baffle me...you send me nice messages then don't reply but you're on Tinder a lot of the time.

Tinder shows when you were last online. I've absolutely been stalking. And I've just told him I've been stalking him. *Bollocks.*)

> I know and you're absolutely right. Grateful for your honesty and apologies for not replying to all of your messages. I think we had a great connection and want to get to know you more. Yes I'm on Tinder a fair bit but I can honestly say I've had no conversation in the same way as we did previously. If this offends you then I'm sorry and thank you for simply being you.

Holy shit. This guy is smooth.

> I haven't got a problem that you are on the search for the right woman, but I don't want to feel at the bottom of a long list. That just makes me feel stupid for giving you my time and sad because I thought we had a connection too. I am happy to start again if you are? xx

I don't want to start again… I'd rather pick up from where we left off, if that's possible?

I don't have much time myself and I just don't want to feel like an afterthought.

I've actually missed you. No one and nothing compares to the connection that we had/have xx

You're way too cute! I hope you're not just saying that mister, cos that's how I feel.

I have no need or personal gain to say such things to you. It's the absolute truth. I want to call you right now.

Oh my fucking god. No, no, no, don't call. Oh shit, he's calling. He is actually calling. I don't want to answer. Why is he calling? We are happy texting. *Oh shite.* OK. OK. Answer.

We speak on the phone for a few minutes, for nine minutes and thirty-six seconds to be exact. Oh wow, this guy sounds so yummy. I am so excited. I need to get the diary out and organise a date. This man is too damn good to let him pass by. He texts me after our call ends:

Kate, you sound ridiculously delicious. Have a great day with the girls and I'll try to call you again in the next couple of days. Xxx

Wow. The smile on my face is so big my jaw aches.

We now message each other every day. I truly can't get enough of this beautiful man's words. Every day we learn more about each other. He's Catholic, like me, but not a church goer. Two daughters, close to my little ones' ages. He is the youngest sibling, same as me, loves his work and works long hours, just like me! This man is just what I'm looking for. I found him. Maybe he is my handsome Disney prince after all. Now I just have to meet him.

> So, you married? Were you married?

Nope, not married. I would like to get married one day though.

> How long have you actually been single? Oh, and who left who? Sorry got straight to the point then, didn't I?! 😂

Kate! Honestly, no bloody filter at all. I must try to think for at least a couple of seconds before I text. This is awkward. I chuckle nervously as I await his reply.

We have been apart for a couple months now, I left, but not sure I should share this all with you over text. Let me call you at some point. Not now, I'm just leaving a show that I have been working on. I will explain though.

> Hmmmm. OK. Sounds scary. One last thing though. Would you go back?

Again this would be better with a call but the truth is that it is not just about me anymore. I have my daughters to think about. We will talk about it.

Ok, well my head is saying run away now. But I'm not going to listen to that just yet.

I honestly don't want to do anything to mess you around or hurt you. That kind of thing doesn't help anyone. Must pack now. Heading to Paris tomorrow. Good night beautiful Kate xxx

Good night xxx

Fuuuuuuucccccckkkkkk. Why am I sad about this? Why does my heart hurt? I don't even really know this man. *Get a grip Kate! What will be, will be,* I tell myself. I have built Wonka up to be untouchable and the reality is that he is actually *unreachable.* A beautiful soul, wonderful words, fun sense of humour. But really, he isn't mine. Yep, it's true. Fairy tales do set us little girls up to fail. How ridiculous. I guess I must let this all play out. Sleep. Tomorrow is another day.

I talk to my friends and family about this wonderful man who lives in my phone. I tell them how much I adore receiving messages from him. I have never known someone I haven't met who has ever said such sweet things to me. He inspires me to be the best version of myself. And *hope.* Wonka gives me hope in this new world of dating.

Everything I know about him so far leads me to believe that he is a true gentleman with a huge heart. I truly believe we have only just begun, that this is going to be a wonderful journey. I feel like we are a modern-day, but old-fashioned couple who write letters to each other while courting. I just wish we were, in fact, doing the courting part.

Wonka's back from Paris and we've been having fun, sending picture messages of toys from our childhoods. Retro toy after retro toy. We're sparking memories and laughing at each other's tales.

We still haven't talked about his ex. I don't want to keep on at him about it. I really don't want to push him away. I get a rush in my belly when I see his name pop up on my screen. I'm on such a high with this man.

A few days later I'm enjoying a quiet evening, snuggled in a blanket on the sofa. The girls are tucked up in bed and I'm hoping Wonka will get the chance to call me after he finishes his latest job. I sip my tea and crunch on a biscuit. Waiting.

There it is. My phone rings, his name lit up on the screen. My heart leaps. It's as if he heard me willing him to call. It means so much that he has made the time to call me. I know how bonkers I seem to the real world. To fall in love with a phone is extremely strange. Let's face it, I can't love a guy I've never met. But the phone world understands me. It's safe. I'm willing to open up here, and I want to enjoy it forever. It *would* be better to have the phone world expand into this universe and be physically available to me, but right now, I'm happy to get any time he will give to me. The pull towards this man is overwhelming.

We chat for over an hour. Oh, his voice. I adore his voice. We talk about so many things: careers, schedules, the long hours we both work, but how we love our careers so much that it is not a chore. We speak briefly about our exes, respectfully, but honestly. We both share the same thought that although love can fade and change, you don't need to hate the person you were once with. In fact, you can love them in a different way and eventually grow and develop a friendship with them.

We are (finally) revealing ourselves to one another. We speak about close relatives that have passed away, about our families and our childhoods. We are so similar, even down to our spirituality. We both enjoy having our cards read. We believe our loved ones who have passed walk with us in this life. I even share with him the visions I have had, about dreams that then happen, and tell him I receive messages through my dreams. He doesn't judge me or make me feel silly. Instead, he completely understands my soul.

My god, I really hope the universe steps in so we can arrange a meeting soon. I want to know this man physically, to look him straight in the eyes. It feels so intense now with such a strong natural pull between us. I can't explain how I am feeling to anyone because no one can understand. They just get frustrated that I haven't met him. I can't even explain why we haven't met, because the truth is I don't understand that either.

I dream about Wonka now. Every night he fills my head. It's been seven weeks and four days since we matched. *Why haven't we met?* I ask myself over and over. I don't mind getting to know him through my phone, but it's really starting to bug me that we haven't even met once. I wish he would make some space for me, but he is so busy.

I'm catching up with Adira at a quaint little café in the village today. She's one of my oldest friends in the world and is actually more like a sister to me. We've made time together whilst she's here from London visiting her parents. A handful of customers sip their drinks and nibble on delicate cakes whilst I tell Adira all about Wonka. I show her lots of pictures and share my frustration that a real-life date hasn't yet come to fruition.

"Is he not curious at all? Does he not want to see if he fancies me in real life? To find out if there is true chemistry between us?" I ask.

"Maybe he is a catfish?"

"What the heck is that?"

"Come on Kate, haven't you seen the programme on MTV? It's someone who pretends to be someone they're not and hides behind an online profile."

"Oh, wow, yes. I have seen it," I exclaim. "Oh my god. He could totally be a catfish. Let's just look at the facts here. No video calls, just a handful of voice calls."

I pause, and say, "But we have pictures?"

"You can just use someone else's pictures though," argues Adira gently.

Oh no! The realisation hits me that this could all be fake. Just like a Disney prince. My heart is still, my face pale, but adrenaline pumps through my body.

"My phone love life could just be some spotty teenage boy, or a big butch lesbian!" I cry. "Oh, why am I not a lesbian? Then we would be so happy together. Goddamn it!"

We start laughing hysterically, a little too loudly for the quiet café. We can't stop and I feel relieved to be making light of the situation I have got myself into.

As I walk home an hour later, I am now completely convinced that my Wonka Bar is indeed a catfish. Despite, this, I want to meet him (*or her*) more than ever. There's so much depth to him that I don't think I could ever reach the bottom. I almost don't even mind if it was all a scam. Well, I do, but ultimately, I just want to look this person in the eyes, to *know* them. I want to know who this person with the kindest, most beautiful words is.

I can't contain my desire to see him any longer, so I continue to ask him to meet with me. It's so frustrating that he can't commit to meeting, and I have a feeling it might push him away, but what can I do?

Then, just like that, almost inevitably, my heart is sunk once more. Wonka texts and explains that now is just not the right time. He says he is sorry, but that he needs to take a step back. He can give no more than text messages and it just isn't fair to keep my attention.

I'm numb. I can't convince him. I know I must let him leave and I head to a box to hide away.

It's coming up to Christmas and I'm trying so hard to be upbeat. I normally crave this time of year. The Christmas spirit, the laughter, the excitement, getting together with friends and family. Every day I put on my happy, cheery mask for all to see, but inwardly I am despondent and downhearted. And I don't think Christmas movies are helping. *Give up the Christmas films Kate. Especially bloody Love Actually!* I tell myself.

Oh, so very many tears have run down my cheeks. I feel silly for allowing them to fall. I'm in love with an imaginary man (or woman) who lives in my phone. *I must be crazy,* I think. *Oh God, and I have cats.* I'm all alone in my emotions too. I wish I could talk things through with my friends, but I know just how ridiculous I would sound.

My heart is so heavy, my mind consumed with what he may be doing. How can you miss someone you have never met, never truly *known*? And it's only been a week. How can I feel like this? Have I lost my mind? I read his messages over and over. I miss his words so very much that reading those from the past helps me.

Today is Sunday and we always used to talk on a Sunday. I know I have become infatuated with him and have such a strong habit of texting him that now my phone feels dead. I find myself unable to resist any longer. I need to bring my phone, and me, back to life. I send my Wonka Bar a message.

> Hello X

A reply, almost instantly.

> Hi Kate x

> Just wanted you to know you are still on my mind. Happy Sunday xx

> Feeling the same my love, sorry. When is your birthday? It's this week isn't it?

> The 28th December, yes.

> Have a gorgeous day with the girls xxx

Oh my heart. It leaps back into life. He remembered my birthday is coming up. No one remembers my birthday.

My birthday falls on the worst week of the year. I don't even want to celebrate it myself half the time. Dairy Milk had forgotten it many a year. He never had any money and always left buying me a gift until the last moment. I'd receive the obvious: supermarket flowers, chocolates, wine. Such a cliché. I believe a gift for a loved one should be considered. Something a person wants, not needs.

For Dairy Milk's thirtieth birthday, I saved for a whole year. I had organised for all our friends to join us for dinner and drinks in London, and we stayed in a posh hotel. I bought him a Supercars Racing Day. I gave him £400 to put towards doing up his old white banger of a sports car too. (I loved that Supra, but it needed a heck of a lot of work.)

My mind wanders back. I only had a part-time job working around the girls and Dairy Milk's full-time job. I remember just how hard he really did work to support our growing family, never complaining, never grumpy. He saw the money he earned was for us all. *Damn.* Now I feel bad for complaining to myself.

I cannot help the way I feel though. I was never celebrated or remembered.

For my thirtieth, I had asked for an iPad. I'd never asked for something so expensive, but I was working more and thought that if he knew well in advance (a year and a half to be exact) he could find the money and buy me one. He had said he could. I was so excited. Now we no longer had babies in our bedroom I had a sanctuary. I loved the idea of being able to relax in bed watching streamed films and sitcoms, or just playing a massive game of Candy Crush.

Two weeks before my birthday, he apologised. He had messed up. He couldn't get me the iPad because the money was gone. I was shocked. I had a tantrum. I had asked for it for this birthday before I had even had my last one. Eighteen months and he couldn't find the money? I mean, come on! We weren't well off, but we both worked. If he had put real effort into it, he could have easily bought it for me. Instead, *nothing.*

Our daughters, but for one, all have their birthdays between November and December. So, with the most important birthdays and Christmas all at that time, I don't normally expect much. Just a gift with thought. But this was my thirtieth and he had had eighteen months to save. His lack of desire to do this demonstrated to me just how low on his agenda I was.

One year, he forgot altogether. I gave the girls a bag of bits to wrap up for me. They were upset that I had bought myself gifts and that I would know what was under the wrapping. I told them it was no problem and that I had already forgotten what was in the bag anyway.

Anyway, back to the iPad. To make amends, he bought one on contract for me. He came home really pleased with himself. I couldn't believe it. The contract was in *my* name and it wasn't even a full-sized iPad. It was a mini one, just slightly bigger than a bloody mobile phone. How would I watch programmes and play that massive game of Candy Crush? He got me a £15 monthly bill, for twenty-four months (for something I didn't want) and the very massive realisation that he truly took no notice of me. And nor did he really seem to want to. *Bastard.*

So yes, Wonka Bar remembering my birthday when he hadn't even met me, was very impressive.

I feel amazing. Wonka and I have reconnected. We want back in. We've been texting again for a week. Unfortunately, my friends can't understand why I would want to continue to speak to him when we haven't met. They think he must be up to no good if he won't meet me. They may well be right, but what can I do? Walk away? I don't want to do that. How would I even start to do that? If I walk away then that's it, the end, no Wonka at all. But allowing him the time he needs without pressuring him means I still stand a chance. I still receive his texts.

And then, finally, we have a date to meet. Tomorrow. Wonka is in the country, working locally to his home. I had already planned to join Adira and her house mate to dance the night away in London and he has said he can join us if a colleague of his can cover for a few hours. *Wow.* I can't contain my excitement. I buy a new dress online. My heart is pounding.

> Kate?

> > Yes?

> Kate…I'm truly crazy about you and there hasn't been a day that's gone by where I haven't thought of you.

> Just thought you should know that xxx

> Good night beautiful Kate xxx

> I feel exactly the same…

> I adore you…

> Let's hope someone covers for you and you get to see me and my new dress tomorrow. Eeeeek, I am super excited 😆 xx

Oh God, I am *so* very much hoping that this plays out and I meet him in the flesh. Everything is aligning. Adrenaline and excitement are building up. I cannot stop smiling. It's amazing to think that in just a few hours I will meet my Wonka Bar. This may not be the most ideal first date, but I'll take any moment of his time I can.

He cancels. He explains he just can't get out of work. Certainly not early.

Of course. I don't know why I'm so surprised. Am I really so naive? Am I bonkers to think he would be true to his words?

I feel foolish and upset. I'm disappointed. This man simply does not want to meet. Maybe he's just not capable of meeting?

Wonka, Wonka, Wonka, what is a girl to do?

After a few more texts he decides it's time to walk away. Again.

He isn't ready to commit to a new relationship and he truly doesn't know how he can make it work around his job and family commitments.

> There just hasn't been enough time between my last relationship and a possible new love. It would be unfair to you, my children and to me to become involved with someone I could have a real connection with at this moment in time. It just isn't right.

I respect his outlook. If it is, of course, a true one. I so desperately want to put the catfish doubts to one side and believe what is being said to me. It can't possibly be a butch lesbian, or a spotty teenager sending me these messages. Time will tell, I guess. Or in fact, maybe it won't.

> Well, we can leave it there, leave it to fate. I will continue to live my life but if I am the girl for you then you will find me when you are ready. See you around. I will miss you more than you could ever understand xx

In hindsight, I should have been wary of the man who woke my heart but had no intention of loving me. All the signs were there. I just didn't want to see them. My heart pounds a slow and heavy beat, acknowledging that Wonka has walked away. As the waves of complete devastation roll over me, I cry into my pillow until I finally fall asleep. I long for the day he might return and meet me. There's a supernatural pull to this man, almost some quantum cosmic connection. It's almost dreamlike, as if he isn't even real. Like a Wonka Bar.

Wonka Bar chocolate is of course not your regular corner shop chocolate bar. It's completely extraordinary, unique, individual. Finding the ticket to the factory is damn near impossible. I won't give up though. Not until the completion of the competition to find the golden ticket. I want to find the factory and enjoy the whole world that awaits inside. The world that is slightly wild, dark, magical and bonkers. Imperfect in a completely perfect way.

Nana had Some Stories

Thoughts of Wonka Bar are disrupted with a devastating blow when my dad calls to tell me my nana is dying. She has terminal cancer and only has a few weeks, maybe a month or so, to live.

Nana is an amazing woman. Unbelievably, when she was eighty-two, she decided to pack up her life in the UK and emigrate to Canada to be close to my auntie, uncle, cousins and their kids. I guess she knew the end was near and wanted to spend time with those she hadn't seen much of in earlier years.

I've never met this side of my family and as Nana wants us all to be together, I am flying across the Atlantic to meet this wonderful bunch with my two older brothers, Luke and Anthony.

This trip is so bittersweet. So many firsts for what may be the last time I ever see Nana. I'm flying with them for the first time, meeting members of my family for the first time, going to Canada for the first time, all for the chance to see my nana to say goodbye for the last time. This absolutely, bloody well, sucks!

Knowing I'll be seeing Dad together with lots of family has brought back tragic memories. My eldest brother John died when he was just nineteen. He drove his motorbike into a tree on his way home one evening. We don't know how it happened, but it was the worst thing we have ever been through. My family split apart, a bit like an orange when you peel the skin off. Still joined at the bottom, still a part of the same orange, but all separate, individual segments held together by the pith.

I was eight. Over the next few years, the sadness broke my mum and dad. When I was ten, Dad moved to Romania and me, Mum, Luke and Anthony also left the family home. This meant I had to leave Adira, Sadie, and Emily. I had grown up with them since I was just two. These girls were my honorary sisters and their family had become mine in the grief of the years that followed John's death. We spent practically every waking moment together before my family moved away. Leaving them behind was another loss I had to give in to, on top of John and Dad, and life as I knew it. For eight-year-old me the loss was… How was the loss? I still don't have the words nearly thirty years on.

My dad is an amazing human, but he lost his way for a while after John died. He had a breakdown but came out of it stronger. He decided to dedicate his life to helping the homeless. I am extremely proud of him and how he moved to that new way of life, but I had to work through a lot of emotions to get to this point. We both did. We've had many a drunken evening putting our relationship to rights, and I am so glad we reached the level we are at now. I had been so angry.

While my dad moved away, I had to watch Mum suffer the torment of losing a son. She woke every day, dragged herself out of bed to make sure I was fed, kept me safe and did the best she could to give me a proper childhood. Imagine having to do this after you have died inside. I will always hold the utmost respect for my mum. I will always be grateful that she held it together enough to keep going every day for me, Luke and Anthony.

I'm so proud of my brothers. They moved to London to pursue their careers when I was a teenager and since then have travelled and seen so much of the world. They've made good lives for themselves.

When I was nineteen, it was my turn to fly the nest. I got my own little place when Mum moved to Birmingham for a job opportunity. She really enjoyed the time she spent there. I think she grew in herself, found a side of her outside of being a mum. In many ways, it brought her back to me.

Even though my family are now based all over the world we are unbelievably close. If I have a problem, I can call any one of them, or all of them, to talk through any issue. They have all bailed me out more times than I would like to admit. I am so grateful to have them. *Ah! Look at me getting all mushy and sentimental because I'm spending a week with Luke, Anthony, and Dad. I must slap myself out of this and remember to mock both brothers on the plane,* I tell myself.

I think, despite how close I am to my family now, my experiences have given me abandonment issues. I know I push everyone away. I expect everyone to leave. Then, when I have pushed someone away, I tend to make a lasting friendship with them, so they aren't gone completely. Honestly, if a man I meet is broken, with one foot out the door (like Wonka), I will absolutely fall in love with him. I run away from all the regular guys. They don't make sense to me. I know it's not healthy and I need to fix it. I am trying. I'm trying to not self-sabotage, trying to understand that it's OK not to please everyone, that if someone is going to leave, that is OK too. It is also OK for people to stay.

Gosh, it's so easy for me to say those things, but I'm not quite there yet. One day, Kate, one day.

Eight hours after we left England, our flight landed in Canada. Dad met us at the airport in a huge 4x4 truck. It's so cool. Everything seems bigger here. I'm so in love with the truck. I can but only dream of owning one. Music plays quietly and we chat about the flight over.

Dad turns the music off as we get closer to his sister Sue's house. He warns us, "Nana looks extremely frail and has lost a lot of weight. I just want you to be prepared as you haven't seen her in a long time."

We pull up outside the house and are greeted by Auntie Sue, Uncle Bob and two of my cousins, Nathan and Dave. As we make our way to the lounge where Nana is waiting, I take in the family photos on the walls. It's such a lovely, warm house. And there she is. Nana. Oh, love her. Dad was right, she is tiny. Drawn in the face, but with the biggest smile I think I have ever seen her wear. I rush over to hug her, hold her hand and kiss her cheek. Then we talk, and talk, and talk.

As the evening draws in, I sit quietly looking around the room. What a truly amazing experience to be with these people. I look like these humans who I have never met before. We have so very much in common. It's brilliant. We are all laughing and joking. Telling stories. Nana is so happy that we are all together.

"Tell everyone what fun we have had, how much we have laughed and know just how much I love you," she says.

God, love her. It must be so heart-warming to look around a room and see all the people within it are part of you. She's tired, a tiny shell of the strong lady we waved goodbye to a few years earlier. She grew, matured and raised a family in very different times to me. With this, she is straightlaced and very regularly puts her foot in it by saying completely the wrong thing.

"Have you gained weight?"

"What have you done to your hair?"

"Oh no, she doesn't look like your father. He was all teeth when he was little!"

Hmmm Nana, I'm sure there are a million different ways to say those things. I laugh with my cousins as we recall stories about these times.

Nana tells us so many stories we have never heard before, and some that maybe as grandchildren we should never have heard.

"When we were in Zimbabwe, we had a lovely time. Parties, working, making new friends. I made the most of my time there. I actually ended up spending quite a lot of time with a wonderful man. His name was Bert, such a beautiful man. But…well…Little Bert!" she tells us, performing a shocked face as she raises her hand and wiggles her little finger.

"*Nana!*" we call out laughing along with her. It's hilarious. We never knew Nana had been like that. Her stories are just too funny. It was brilliant to see her having so much fun with her family. The time flies and before long it is time to say goodnight.

We're staying at Nana's apartment ten minutes down the road. I think about Nana as I walk around her apartment. She is smart, always well dressed, her house well-kept, but homely. She loved to knit and made wonderful teddies, blankets and jumpers in times gone by. She collects little toys too, like cats and puppies. She even has toy hamsters, love her. It's so cute. I smile as I pick them up from around her apartment, looking at them, seeing them through her eyes.

The next day, we sit together in the lounge at Auntie Sue's house, telling our stories of loved ones who have passed away. Dreams, feelings, clairvoyant messages we've had. I ask Nana about how she feels about things. She is so calm and the family being together comforts her.

"I am very much at peace. I don't believe in anything, Dear. When I die, that's it. Nothing. I wish I could just pass away now, surrounded by you all. Just fall asleep in this chair and never wake up."

"Well, please don't, that would scupper our dinner plans." I tell her, joking to lighten the mood. "Do you really believe that when you die then that's it, Nana? Nothing at all? Just dead? I dream about loved ones that have passed. I sense when they are close, and I smell perfumes. Have you never had an experience like that?"

"Grandad did kiss me."

"What? When?"

"Well, we always promised each other that whoever dies first, would come back and show the other one that there is something after you die. He woke me, one week after he passed away, with a kiss. Two days in a row."

"Aww, Nana, see?"

"We shall see, Dear. If it is true, I will show you. OK?"

"Deal!" I tell her.

I spend the next few days filling Nana in on my life over the last couple of years since I last saw her. We talk about the reasons I left Dairy Milk, the tales of Wonka and all the dreams, the feeling of needing to know this man, regardless of any kind of relationship. She takes my phone to look at his pictures.

"Oh Kate, he looks wonderful, truly gorgeous. Sad though. Such sad eyes. Kate, can I ask you something?"

"Of course, Nana." I look at the picture of Wonka and realise Nana is right. There is something very sad and heavy in his eyes.

"Would you mind if I see him?"

"What do you mean Nana? He won't even meet me," I laugh. "How can you talk to him?"

"Well, that's just it. If what you believe is correct, I will be able to visit anyone I want to. So, I would like to see him and let you know what I think. He is yours, you know Kate, if you want him. He is yours. I decided Grandad was mine and I got him."

Oh, I love her. Smiles fill our faces. I squeeze her hand as we share this lovely moment together.

"Yes, Nana. You absolutely can see him. Then definitely tell me!"

A week after we return to England, Nana passed away peacefully just before her eighty-sixth birthday.

All the family are telling stories about their encounters of feeling Nana close to them. Me? *Nothing.* And it really sucks. Having always been so aware of spirits close to me, I had thought I would see her in a dream, maybe feel her presence. But nothing. I'm so disappointed.

A few more weeks pass. As I dry the dishes and put them away, I turn to take a mug from the draining board and *boom.* There she is. Standing in front of me just by the sink. Beige trousers. White top. Hair done. Beautiful. I scream, startled. And then she is gone.

Wow. It is the sharpest I have ever seen anyone. I'm shaking, in complete shock. Maybe this happened because I willed it to. I wanted to see her so much. Maybe she was right, there is nothing but silence when you die. Or maybe there is a whole lot more than we can ever comprehend. What I do know, is that we all die, and only then will we truly know what awaits us.

My nana, the atheist, passed to the next world with a mission. If nothing ever happens with my Wonka Bar, I will be forever grateful that Nana passed with faith in her heart and a mission in mind.

Milky Way Crispy Rolls: Breaking The Diet

I have decided to go back on the dating sites. I'm still a little deflated, but I feel like I may as well get back out there. All is lost with Wonka Bar. Nothing is ever going to happen. The entire situation is clearly pointless and spending my time wishing for romance won't make it happen. I have now accepted it's time to move on. Or at least pop him back on the shelf for now.

This time around I've decided to use both sites I used before. I'm swiping on Tinder and scrolling through the catalogue of men on Plenty Of Fish, the one where anyone can message anyone. It's best to keep my options open.

I'm wandering across the playground with my best friend Lily. It's home time. My girls drop their bags at my feet, expecting me to carry them, as I do every day with my octopus-like arms. My youngest hands over some sweets and chocolate she's been given. It was a classmate's birthday. "I don't really like this chocolate, Mum. You can have it," she says and runs off to play in the park.

"Thanks for that." I laugh. I look down at what she's handed me and see a Milky Way Crispy Rolls bar. Oh my god, I haven't eaten one of these in years. They are *yummy*. It's lightweight too. I'm sure I can eat it without gaining too many Weight Watchers points. I laugh and tell Lily that Milky Way Crispy Rolls should be the name for my next online match. I give Lily the latest on my decisive action to get back into the dating world.

"Try to find a man close to home this time," she tells me. "Surely that way you can build up to it and see the man more? And I don't want you to meet a London boy either. You'd move away."

I laugh. "Aww, love you! I won't be moving anywhere. I don't want to live with anyone anyway so don't you worry about that. I just don't want to confine myself to the limited number of single men from here. Besides, I kissed the best ones when I was a teenager. I think collectively the nine of us must have kissed all the decent men in our age bracket back in the day."

We both laugh and reminisce about the days gone by. We regress to our young gossiping teenage selves again. Oh, drunken teenage nights have a lot to answer for.

"I want to get to know new people with different ways of life, new stories to tell me. I doubt very much I'll find that here, where everyone knows everyone," I say wistfully.

There's not been too much to report lately. I've shared a few random messages back and forth with a few men, but that's it really. That was until I started chatting to an attractive man from London who, by the way, I've named Milky Way Crispy Rolls. Another London boy. I think back to mine and Lily's earlier conversation and the fact that I really enjoy dating in London.

A few messages have been sent back and forth and he is truly deserving of his nickname. He's a little younger than me (only thirty, but younger all the same). He's lanky. He has a trendy blonde hair cut and is very yummy to look at. I laugh. Quite fitting! Yes, Milky Way Crispy Rolls he is. A light treat. I smile to myself and chuckle as I text Lily to tell her about him.

I've decided I would like to meet up sooner rather than later. I think it would be nicer to get to know him better in person rather than through weeks of messages. Milky Way Crispy Rolls is more than happy with this and is as eager as I am to arrange a date. Note to self. I will not be informing him that my heart has just been broken by a man who lived in my phone. No. Best not to share the full extent of my crazy self just yet.

Our first date is drinks in a trendy... *there's that word again! Jeez Kate, middle-aged alert. Please don't say that out loud!*... bar in Soho and before we know it, we are enjoying date after date after date. Lunch, dinner, drinks... we really enjoy ourselves. It is refreshing to get to know a man in real life, rather than just over the phone. We learn all about each other and tell our work and relationship stories.

He works in marketing, Aries, no kids. Milky Way Crispy Rolls is very down to earth. He's grounded. He works hard and is saving for a house. He wants to get married one day and is looking for the right partner. He isn't concerned about me having three daughters and even declares he is looking forward to meeting them one day. Oh, and my cats. He likes cats, thank God.

He does seem quite conservative for me though. I feel a little out of my comfort zone with him wanting the two-point four family, the straight-line lifestyle and the forward planning that I'm just not accustomed to. Perhaps this is a good thing. It would be good for me to date someone who knows what he wants and plans ahead. I think I need to grow up a little with that. I just hope he has some kind of wild and playful side. I might get a little bored if my crazy nature is too suppressed.

Another refreshing fact is that Milky Way Crispy Rolls isn't pushing to get into my knickers. A real gentleman this one. Though I don't want to rush anything, we have definitely got chemistry. We flirt and kiss and I'm feeling more relaxed around him every time we meet. Maybe he's amazing in bed? Yes, that might be where his wild side is. This might be where the fun can truly be found. The more I think about it, the more I'm sure that is it. Well. I'm hopeful of that anyway.

So, plenty of dates later, two months' worth in fact, we have decided to get a takeaway at his and I will be staying over. I am feeling excited, nervous, but overall confident that this is just what our budding relationship needs. I'm hoping for Chinese. I really fancy a mushroom Chow Mein. I chuckle to myself on the train, aware that I have more concerns about what to have for dinner than I do about getting naked with Milky Way Crispy Rolls. I don't even really know why. Normally I'm all flushed and food is the furthest thing from my mind. Maybe I just feel really relaxed around him now.

I arrive at his apartment with a bottle of red wine and some crisps and dips for us to share. I love crisps and dips. A little too much, I think. If I could eat them for dinner every night, I probably would. *Kate, stop thinking about food! What is wrong with you?*

Milky Way Crispy Rolls' housemate is out this evening so it will only be us. The apartment is a great size. I don't really get a homely feeling. It doesn't appear to be much of his character in the front room. But then I guess it wouldn't as he isn't the only one who lives here.

We open the bottle of wine and order Chinese. *Yay.* I chuckle and celebrate inside as we make our order. We enjoy our food and wine and flirt the evening away. Hands touching. Lots of gentle, sweet kisses. I accidentally yawn. I'm shattered. "Sorry," I say, apologising to him for the yawn. "It has been such a long day."

"Let's go to bed. I'll just wash this lot up quickly and meet you in there," he says.

I offer to help but he's having none of it. Bless him. He's either super sweet or a bit of a control freak. Time will tell.

I head to the bedroom. It's clean, neat and tidy, a man's type of room with a TV on the chest of drawers at the end of his bed. His shoes are paired neatly against the wall and a few toiletries are in the en-suite bathroom. I'm happy to have a few minutes to myself to freshen up then hop into his bed and await his arrival. I have my new sexy black French knickers and lacey black bra on.

He walks in, freshens himself up in the en-suite and joins me in bed. He's only wearing boxer shorts now. Milky Way Crispy Rolls is slim built and six feet tall. Just my type. And yummy to look at. I'm so excited now. I knew this was what we needed. Some bedroom fun to spice things right up. He kisses my mouth and explores my body. Then his fingers find my place. I am turned on and hoping he will replace his fingers with what I really want. Then he starts rhythmically moving against me.

Hold on. I thought this was finger time. What is going on? I nearly blurt out that I am ready for him when I realise that I think I am already receiving him. My eyes are open and huge. I'm glad the lights are off. Unsure what to do, I put my hands down under the covers to feel around and realise I was right. Oh, this is tricky. I have never been in this situation before. All I can think about is my nana and Bert. *Oh my god.* I am trying desperately hard not to laugh, but the vision of Nana, wriggling her little finger at me saying, "Poor little Bert" is too much. I lean into the pillow and fake the orgasm he has been hoping to give me. I wait for him to finish, tell him it was great, then go to sleep.

I know it seems shallow, but this is a problem for me. After all, I have had three babies. This coupled with our incompatibilities, has made it blatantly clear I need to walk away. I should have realised this when I was more excited about food than I was at getting the chance to be naked with him.

I call Milky Way Crispy Rolls a week after our encounter and tell him I'm sorry and that I just don't think we are compatible. He understands and says he feels the same. We walk away and wish each other well on our continuing search for love.

I consider my Milky Way Crispy Roll. They are tasty, but there's really not very much chocolate at all. Just the thinnest of coverings. They're mainly wafer with a creamy filling. If I'm going to indulge and take time out from my diet, then I definitely need substantially more chocolate to make it worthwhile. Unfortunately, this bar is just not enough to satisfy my sweet desires.

Yorkie: Man on The Moon

I am off to the O2 Arena to meet my brothers. Luke is working on a band's tour. I'm in awe of him. As a sound technician he tours with lots of different artists. It's such an awesome experience to get to see him at work. Anthony is flying in from Italy for work in London. He travels all over the world for work. His job is like Chandler from 'Friends'. Nobody fully understands what he does. I know it's working to improve teams within companies, but I am not entirely sure how. He tries to explain to me, but it goes straight over my head. He's very intelligent, academically and emotionally. My brothers really are so cool. I find myself daydreaming about one day travelling for work like they do.

Back in the moment and feeling incredibly excited that we are all meeting up, I check the time. Quarter to five. *Shit.* My daydreaming means I am now rushing about in desperation to catch my train. I have half an hour until it arrives at Ashford and I still need to get to the station and park. Oh, and I want to run over to the village shop for a snack and a drink for the train.

I rush into the shop to grab a Diet Coke from the fridge. As I wait behind a couple of teenage girls paying for their shopping, I browse the slim snack shelves on the counter and check out the chocolate bars. I know full well that I really don't have time for this, but... *hmmm, what do we have here? A Snickers, a Mars, a Yorkie. Oh, I haven't had a Yorkie for years. I remember when Yorkie sold themselves as the man's bar. Too big for girls? Well, Yorkie, let me tell you, I enjoy chocolate, and you're certainly not too big for me.*

"Can I help?" I hear from behind the counter.

I look up. "Oh yes, sorry. I was lost in thought there."

I place my Diet Coke on the counter. *Oh screw it, I want a Yorkie now, diet or not.* I pick up the bar and place it next to my drink.

"I thought you were a Cadbury girl. I remember a time when all you would buy was Dairy Milk."

The cashier smiles and laughs lightly. My eyes widen. I feel exposed by his jest. I'm wondering now just how many times he has clocked what I've purchased.

I laugh back, feeling flushed in the cheeks. "Well, I think it's time to try something new. You never know, I might love Nestlé."

I take my change and snacks then hurry to my car. I'm flustered now and catch the train just in time. As I take my seat, I pop my earphones in, sit back, relax and indulge in my snacks.

Luke is waiting for me when I arrive at the O2. I give him a huge hug and we go find the bar to meet Anthony. One of Luke's best friends is there too, already enjoying some drinks with Anthony. He looks familiar and I'm sure I've met him before, but I'm not sure where. As we chat, it dawns on me he is one of Luke's oldest friends. We have a couple of hours to spare before the concert, so we make the most of our time. Luke and Anthony tease me about not buying any drinks so I climb down from the high stool to get a round in. Luke's friend joins me at the bar.

"Wowzers, you're so tall," I exclaim. *Oh Kate, really? Must work on not blurting things out,* I say to myself.

"Yeah. I'm six feet four inches. And you're short," he jokes. "Now that that's cleared up, how have you been? It's been years since I last saw you."

"Yeah, I'm less whale-like than when I was a teenager. Less spotty too!" I can't help it. I have no filter.

He has fair hair and blue eyes. I take in his looks. This guy is not really my type. *Just because he's heading to the bar with you doesn't mean you should automatically size him up for boyfriend material,* I say to myself. I can't help myself these days. I size everyone up, checking them against the boyfriend criteria tick chart. There is something about him though. I think it's his light-hearted chatter, mixed with an air of arrogance. And the glasses. I have a weak spot for glasses. Plus, I love that he's a family friend. It's safe. Or do I like that? I know Luke wouldn't. I decide to see how things go this evening and consider what chocolate bar he might be. I think about the Yorkie I ate on the train. That's it. He's so tall and masculine, he has to be *the man's bar.*

After drinks we go to one of the restaurants inside the arena for dinner. Yorkie doesn't want to eat. I find it odd as the rest of us are eating so order extra chips just in case he wants something when it comes. Maybe he will have some.

When our food arrives, I push the bowl of chips towards him. "Here, I ordered extra chips so you can have some too."

"Aw, no thank you. Really, I don't want any."

"Why wouldn't you want a few chips? We're all eating. Help yourself. Snack on a few."

"I'm actually OK with just drinking this evening," he says, a little short with me. "But thank you anyway though."

I don't get the message and press him further. "Don't you like chips?" The vodka and coke is starting to go to my head. Why am I bothered by how many chips this guy is not eating? I can't help myself though. It is ridiculously frustrating. *Just eat the goddamn chips,* I think.

He ignores me. He doesn't even have one chip. Not one. Strange. *Strange? Strange is also how you are acting over him not eating chips. Get over it Kate. This guy doesn't want to eat any chips.*

After dinner we say goodbye to Yorkie and go to the gig. It is incredibly cool to have a brother who can take you backstage. Anthony teases me about Yorkie. He'd seen me eyeing him up and wondered why I hadn't asked Yorkie out for a drink.

"He's not my type," I declare. "And besides, Luke would murder me if I even contemplated it!"

This only spurs Anthony on. "You totally fancied him," he teases. "You were even trying to feed him up. I mean, what was all that about the chips? Foreplay? Yep, you should definitely tell Luke you're into his best mate."

"I just didn't want to eat around him if he wasn't eating," I reply, pushing him away.

"You just don't want to be seen stuffing your face in front of him because you fancy him."

"Sod off!" I tell him, playfully.

Four days pass and a friend request pops up on Facebook. It's Yorkie. Interesting. I don't know him that well. I accept him though. Being friends on Facebook is fine. Luke won't mind that.

A week later, Yorkie messages me through Messenger:

> So why haven't you messaged me yet?

> I didn't know I was meant to be messaging you?

> I thought you would have said hi by now.

> Oh really? 😂 Well as you're Luke's best friend that wasn't going to happen.

> Why? That is all the more reason for it to happen. I already know your family.

After a few days and what seems like a million Messenger texts, we eventually exchange phone numbers. Weirdly, Yorkie already has my number from a few years ago when a gang of us had helped Luke move house. He hadn't saved me under the correct name though.

> I knew I had met you somewhere before.

> I had you saved as Chloe. I was confused when Luke told me you were Kate the other week.

> Awww you have a little half crescent moon next to your messages when you text me. I don't understand how it's there.

> Well, that would be because I actually live on the moon, did I not tell you?

> Bloody hell! This is a really long distance romance eh? Awww, the moon is there every time you send a message. I don't know how or why but I am keeping it. It is too damn cute! x

The next day I feel my phone vibrating in my pocket. I answer and the voice at the other end says, "Hi. Is that Chloe?"

"Hello, there. Why yes, it is Chloe. How are you up there on the moon? Up to much?"

"Nah, not a lot. Just having a spot of lunch and thought I'd look down from up here and have a little nose about. See what you were up to."

It seems my phone hasn't been alerting me to his messages so he thought he'd give me a call instead. We talk for a short while before he has to go. I Google this moon thing next to his name. *Ah, that's why the moon symbol is there.* It turns out I have somehow turned off notifications for his number. I haven't a clue how I did it though. I decide to keep it like that. The man on the moon. I love it.

Yorkie and I have been texting and calling intensely for a week or so, learning all about each other. It has become all-consuming. He is so much fun to chat to and he is a human Google. He knows absolutely everything. His knowledge is ridiculous. How can one man's brain hold so much information?

Yorkie has gone to Bristol to see Luke who is completely renovating his entire house and everyone who visits has to get stuck in to the decorating. It's very exciting, but it's tiring, taking a lot of time, and help is needed by all. Yorkie tried to persuade me to go but I couldn't. Now he keeps calling and sending drunken texts, saying I should have gone to join them. I wish I could have. I love seeing my brother. And this guy? Well, this guy is really funny.

As the texts continue it turns out that Luke has told Yorkie that under absolutely no circumstances are we allowed to meet up and that we are most definitely never to date. Oh my god. Does Luke not know me at all? If I am told I can't have something or mustn't do something, I am absolutely going to do the opposite. Luke has now made Yorkie the forbidden fruit.

Not one to do things by halves, a few days later Yorkie and I have a frank conversation about where we are with our lives. There's no doubt we are going to date and I want to be honest with him.

"I don't know if I should date a man who doesn't have any children, but wants them," I tell him down the phone. "If I'm honest, I'd say I'm done. I have my three girls and that's enough for me."

He jokes about being the one who could give me a boy. We laugh. "Oh, the arrogance. You may know many things my dear Yorkie, but you absolutely cannot be sure which of your millions of sperm would get to my egg and create a boy. Boy or not, I don't think I want more."

"We might not even get that far into things," Yorkie tells me, bringing me back to earth. "Let's just have a date, have some fun and wait 'til further down the road before we talk about children."

It's date night. I got ready in the madhouse after the school run and have done surprisingly well. I'm bathed, I've straightened my hair and am fully dressed (black Bodycon off the shoulder dress, above the knee, black heels). I need some date night dresses that aren't Bodycon or black. I had never thought I would wear these types of dresses. I didn't think that this tubby little body would work with them, but I think I look OK. I have a small waist, so the Bodycon style makes me look good.

Everything's going well, and all is calm. Until, that is, I am ready to leave and realise I have lost my car keys. *Oh shit, shit, shit. How has this happened? Why, why, why? Oh, for fuck's sake.* I am royally pissed with myself. I stop thinking clearly now, catastrophizing the entire situation. Even if the keys were staring me in the face, in fact, even if they were in my hand, I doubt I would be able to find them. *Bloody hell.* I have now missed the 18:16 train, which means I will have to catch the 19:16. That might not be such an issue if we weren't only meeting for a few hours. I have to catch the 23:37 train home, so now we won't have very long together at all. I'm stressed out and annoyed with myself.

I text Yorkie to cancel. We can meet another day.

No. Just jump on the next one, we can still meet up another day as well. Plus I'm in the pub now with some guys from work so I can wait until you are in London and then I can head over to the bar where we are meeting.

Oh, fuck it! Alright then. See you in a bit. Well as long as I find my sodding keys! x

I search for my bloody keys for a further fifteen minutes before I find them hidden in the bottom of my bag from when I dropped the girls at Dairy Milk's. I calm myself down, laugh and give myself a good talking to about how silly I am. *You should have calmed down and looked properly in the first place.*

I pop to the corner shop to pick up a tiny bottle of rosé and my bag of crisps for the train. *Date night special, got them, yay,* I sing to myself and make my way to the station for the train. I absolutely love this part of my evenings in London. Anticipation of the fun the city has in store, time to myself, some great tunes playing through my headphones, a cheeky rosé, and a nosey peek through people's lives on social media. Yep, I really love this.

I walk into the bar in Piccadilly and clock Yorkie standing by the bar. We say our hellos and he tells me I look lovely. I can tell by his face that he really does mean it. It's nice to hear. Yorkie buys the first round, a large glass of red for us both, and we head over to a high table with stools.

I like the look of this bar. It's a little bit posh, but not aloof posh. It's friendly, with bar-like decor. I chuckle to myself. *Bar like? Yeah, Kate. As it's a bar. Funny that, you div!* There are some good tunes in the background too. Nice. Anyway, enough of that. Time to get your date face on.

Our body language is good. We both ease in and relax as the evening progresses. I have seen pictures of Yorkie's ex and she looks like Selina Gomez. I'm not this guy's type at all, other than being a brunette. All his exes are skinny with big boobs. He describes a woman's boob-job boobs as *big fakies* and we chuckle away at our blunt conversation.

As the evening continues, we take it in turns to buy the drinks. In fact, we drink quite a bit. *I might regret this alcohol in the morning. And red wine too.* We're in the flow of chatting, drinking, chatting, bar. I find Yorkie so damn easy to talk to. He is just so clever, creative, and funny. And the glasses.

I adore his glasses. When they slip down his nose, he nudges them back up with the side of his index finger and it's the scrummiest thing I've ever seen.

Yorkie tells me about his new job with a sound company. He is a sound engineer and although I don't understand exactly what he does, I'm enthralled with his stories of time making music.

"So awesome! I love creative people," I tell him, repeatedly. I'm getting quite drunk now. I know my head will be sore tomorrow morning.

I hear all about his search for places in London to live as he has been living with his mum since the break-up. At the weekend he is moving into a house share in Notting Hill as a stop gap.

"I love spending time with my mum, but I am keen to be back in London. I need my own place."

This guy is so awesome. We can chat away comfortably for hours. We haven't stopped talking this whole evening. In fact, we haven't stopped talking for the last few weeks on the phone. I look at his glasses. They are making me want to kiss him. *Shall I try? He isn't making a move, but he is flirty with me. Should I?* I ask myself. This could be embarrassing if he isn't feeling it back. *Oh fuck it!* Stoked with red wine bravery, I go in for the kill. Flirty eyes. He engages. Right, time for 'the Kate' moves. *Yay! He is kissing me back. Mmmmm. That was nice.* We kiss again, longer this time.

Then it's back to earth with a bump. Yorkie needs to check his train times and I suddenly remember I don't live here either and panic about the time. It's almost midnight. *Shit, shit, shit!* We have missed our trains. Oh, holy fuck. This is bad. We are both stuck here. I start planning in my head. I'll just have to get the 6:00 train home in the morning. I can still do the school run. Dairy Milk will need to drop the girls to me on his way to work, rather than me collect them from him. I will call him in the morning when I get the train and explain. *Oh, fuckity fuck. He's going to kill me.*

Yorkie suggests we should stay at a hotel just around the corner and books it on his phone. As we are here now and getting on so well, we decide to make the most of it. We continue kissing and drinking. It's going to be a messy day tomorrow, but I'm not worried at all right now. We're having a laugh. I just love being around this guy. Who knew this could happen? We're not each other's types at all. I am the complete opposite of his in fact. I have no butt and I certainly don't have big fakies. I'm just tubby with mum boobs!

Urrrggggghhhh. What's that noise? Where am I? Oh God, it's my phone. Shit. What's the time? Half seven. *Oh fuck.* I answer my buzzing phone.

"Hello" I say croakily.

"You're alive then?" It's Luke. *Fuck, fuck, fuck.*

"With my mate I presume?" he continues.

Fuck.

"Yes, I am. I'm safe. We just got a hotel because we missed our trains home," I reply sheepishly.

He continues to tell me off. "And forgot you have kids who need you to take them to school, an ex-husband who has got to get to work and a mother who is freaking out that no one can reach you and nobody has any idea where you are."

"Shit, sorry. Honestly, we just drank way too much." I start to explain, but he cuts me short.

"Yeah, I guessed. Maybe call Mum." He says a short goodbye and hangs up. I'm not used to Luke telling me off. Ugh, I feel really bad.

As soon as the call with Luke ends, my phone rings again. It's Dairy Milk. Before I can say anything more than hello, he starts ranting down the phone.

"Where the fuck are you, Kate? I have been out of my mind. You can't just take yourself off to London and not let anyone know that you are staying. What the fuck is wrong with you?" he shouts.

I tell him about missing my train and that I'd planned on getting the first one home in the morning but had far too much wine and passed out in a hotel room with Yorkie. I feel stupid saying it out loud.

Dairy Milk is angry. "You're old enough to know your own limits, or at least you should be. You've let me down. How on earth am I supposed to get the girls to school and go to work on time."

This is about way more than school runs. It's also because I've spent the night with a man. It's extremely hard to be friends with your ex, especially when they were the one to leave you. He's hurt. I know. It doesn't matter if he is dating someone else or not, he still gets hurt when he knows I am dating. And now he knows I've spent the night with another man. I start to make excuses, but he hangs up on me, furious.

Within seconds my mum calls. She tells me how happy she is that I'm OK and that I obviously must have needed a break. "I'm heading up to Dairy Milk's flat to get the girls ready for school and have asked Lily to pick them up and to take them in with her daughter. Why don't you move your clients around and take the day off to spend it in London?"

I graciously thank her for all her help and the fact that she isn't screaming down the phone at me. I still needed to get home, sort myself out and get to work though.

"I cannot just get pissed and take the day off, letting clients down. Plus, I only have last night's clothes here. A tight black Bodycon dress and heels is definitely not daywear for me!"

We laugh and I say I will call her later. Yorkie is awake now. I can hear him chuckling behind me on the bed. It lightens my mood.

My phone buzzes again. It's Lily this time. We laugh about everything, but she tells me not to do it again. She's more than happy to help with the school run and will call me later for the debrief. *Thank God for Mum and Lily.*

What a metaphorical walk of shame though. Big brother, ex-husband, mother and best mate all on the phone. All of them know that you got smashed and went to a hotel room with a guy on the first date. *Oh, the shame. Did we even do anything though? I'm naked.* I roll over and Yorkie is looking at me laughing about the sequence of phone calls. He is naked too.

As I look at him it all comes back to me. Well, not all, but a hell of a lot of it. The important stuff. I start chuckling as I remember something which was really quite a find. *Am I remembering correctly? I need to check this out again to be sure.* I start kissing him. No tongue. It is morning after all, and we are seriously hungover. While I kiss him, my hand plays under the covers, exploring his body. I reach it.

"Yes! I was bloody right!" I blurt out accidentally. He laughs. He knows exactly what I'm talking about. No wonder he is so arrogant. Yorkie is huge. *Fuck me. I am having that again.*

Somehow, I manage to get through a day of work, school pick-ups and sorting dinner out. Yorkie calls me as I settle down after the girls have gone to bed. He tells me he is meeting up with Luke and his other best mate and will ring me later to will let me know how it goes. *Eeeek! My brother told us not to hang out with each other in the first place. Now we have been caught out spending the night in the hotel.*

"Good luck," I tell Yorkie. "You'll need it."

Out with Luke now. His mate, she's a bit of alright, isn't she?

You can't say that to me now!

Why not? I'm not doing anything with her.

And you better not!

Why not? Are you jealous?

Just know this now, Mr. If you do anything with her, you won't be doing anything again with me.

Oooo you are jealous?

I'm just explaining to you how it is.

I have a great connection with Yorkie. It's ironic we didn't meet online and that I have known him so long through Luke without realising it. It feels like he's a really good friend too. We understand each other. There are no games with calling and texting like the online daters of my past. We can double text, triple call and it's not weird at all. We hang out every weekend, usually going on pub crawls. I stay over at his place in London but it's not ideal. If I stay on a Friday night whilst the girls are at Dairy Milk's, I get home in the morning and start work a little later. If I go on a Saturday night and leave the girls with Mum, I miss out on some of my weekend time with the girls. I feel deflated at the thought of this, but I can't change it. It is what it is.

I really enjoy hanging out with Yorkie. I can't really describe it as dating though. The more I want to be in a relationship with him, the more he pulls back physically. It seems he is happy to have an emotional relationship with me rather than a physical one, despite our first date together. He just doesn't seem to be into me. He flirts a little with words, but not with body language. We kiss sometimes and we do sleep together too, but that's usually when we are smashed on red wine. I think we drink a little too much together. I don't know how he does it. I can't drink like Yorkie. He goes for work lunches, dinners and work events. He drinks at everything. I don't try to keep up with him now. I know how much alcohol I can handle and that is nowhere near what Yorkie drinks. I don't always get the levels right, but I'm definitely better at knowing my limits these days. I laugh to myself. *Kate, you know full well you get this very wrong, very often.*

This Saturday we've been out in the bars of Notting Hill. As we walk home to his flat, I turn to kiss him. It's a shorter kiss than we've had before. There's absolutely no emotion. It's awkward in fact. I try to take his hand and that lasts for all of a minute. Feeling courageous from the red wine running through my veins I ask him gently, "Why don't you want to hold my hand or kiss me?"

I'm lost and confused. I want an honest answer, whatever that may be.

He answers simply, "I'm just not that kind of man."

I start to feel my heart sink and my belly fills with anger and disappointment. I sit down on some big old steps leading up to someone's front door. He asks me to get up and continue walking home with him but I'm not sure I even want to go back to his home, especially without having this conversation. I stay seated. "I will not be walking on until you explain to me what we are doing."

He starts to walk off down the street, frustrated with me and presuming I will follow. What he doesn't know is that I have spent many a time on a doorstep, pissed, refusing to leave until I have the answers I need. Yorkie continues walking down the street until he realises I won't move unless he returns and talks to me. He sighs and walks back down the quiet road towards me. He explains that he does like me but he's confused. We kiss, but once again it's short and sweet. *This man just isn't hot for me at all.* I think about his type, the big boobs and butt.

It's not that though. It's his ex. She-who-shall-not-be-named. He tells me that after the way she treated him, he just isn't ready for a full relationship. That's why he doesn't initiate kissing me, or us sleeping together. He doesn't know if he can be more than friends at this moment in time.

"I just want to enjoy our time together. Can we do that? I love spending time with you, but I am just not ready for anything more."

I am actually OK with this. He isn't ruling it out, is he? He's just explaining that he isn't ready to give his heart away just yet.

The next morning, we walk together to Ladbroke Grove and decide to stop off and have a cup of tea before I catch the Tube. We find ourselves in the café opposite the station and sit down at a table in the window. We chat away about random things, none of which are of any significance to anything, when Yorkie freezes. He is staring outside, beyond me. And he is freaked out. I look behind me, out of the window and there she is. She-who-shall-not-be-named. The bitch who treated him like crap and used him to get what she could out of him. There. Right outside the café window. And with a guy. *Bollocks.*

"Are you OK?" I ask. *Well, that was a stupid fucking question, Kate! Oh God, what shall I say, what shall I do?* I am gutted for him. This is crap. Looking like he is about to cry, he composes himself and manages to hold it together. We see her walk away and he excuses himself. He goes to the toilets, clearly to take a moment for himself. I feel awful for him. He was obviously completely devastated seeing his ex with another man. And now I can see clearly. Yorkie is in no way over her. However much he wants to be. Yeah, this man needs time.

Our friendship continues. Neither of us talk about what we had seen from the café window. We are both watching 'Game Of Thrones' at the moment. We like to start the episode at the same time so we can talk about it on the phone together or on FaceTime. We do so much FaceTiming it feels like we see each other a lot more than once a week. He knows absolutely everything about me, and I know a hell of a lot about him, although I wouldn't say everything. He is still slightly guarded about certain subjects. I do know he is a composer, a musician, a singer. He's so damn creative. I love hearing him sing and sometimes we sing together. OK, not sometimes, just twice so far, but I loved every time. Singing is fun for me again.

I used to sing when I was younger, but the industry broke my heart too many times for me to want to sing in front of people anymore. I used to be what they called 'a big girl'. Being a bigger girl and a successful singer just wasn't a combination that worked back then as far as the powers that be were concerned.

Anyway, yes, singing. He's made me want to sing with him. Just when we are in his flat, not in front of anyone else or anything like that. God no. Yorkie teases me about the fact I can't harmonise. Not nastily, just like a brother would jest with his sister.

"Harmonising was always Lemon's job," I explain. "When we sang together, she harmonised around me, always a perfect ear."

I adored singing with Lemon. I think back on those times fondly.

"Oh my god," I say. "I am going to FaceTime her!"

"Why are we FaceTiming Lemon?" he laughs.

"To tell her that we are singing together and that I need her to harmonise of course."

Lemon answers our FaceTime and through lots of drunken giggling I tell her I need her to harmonise to a song. She laughs at us in our red wine haze. "No way, you mad woman. One, I don't even know the song and two, just no!"

Denying the request of two drunken fools, Lemon says her goodbyes and we end the call.

After spending three months in Notting Hill, Yorkie has found a new flat. I am helping him clear out his old place. As we are moving his things, he tells me She-who-shall-not-be-named has called. Clearly battling with his thoughts, he says, "She was asking for her TV back."

"Are you joking? Why are you giving it back to her?" This pisses me right off. She is taking the piss. The deal was that she kept his bigger TV as it was mounted on the wall. He would take the smaller, older one, that was originally hers.

We're carrying the TV down the stairs as we have the conversation. "Should we drop it?" I ask.

He laughs. He says he should just send the smashed TV back to her in the taxi with a sticky note on the front. *Sorry, dropped when moving home.*

"Too bloody right we should," I agree, both of us laughing at the thought.

They've agreed he will send it to hers in a taxi so he doesn't have to endure going to the place they once shared happily. I think that is by far the best idea, especially after seeing the way he reacted when he saw her through the coffee shop window. She had messed him up so badly.

The next weekend Yorkie invites me for dinner at his flat, a gesture to say thank you for helping him move and also as a celebration on moving in.

This is going to be a really enjoyable, chilled evening. I arrive at his flat and he welcomes me in. Everything is unpacked. It's homely yet boy-like. I can tell he loves living here. While he opens the bottle of red I brought over, he says, "Only one bottle, Kate? Good thing I've already bought another," and nods his head over to the bottle of Merlot on the side.

Yorkie's making a veggie version of cottage pie and is very much enjoying mocking me over it. He is extremely pleased with himself for making the dinner. He isn't really the best chef, which I now very much enjoy mocking him over, but he gets points for effort.

As we settle in, I notice his phone keeps pinging. Quite a lot. He isn't taking the time to read the messages, just ignores them. Then the phone starts ringing. He cancels the call and I ask him about it. He's acting strangely, quite on edge. I haven't seen him like this before and it's weird. It turns out She-who-shall-not-be-named keeps calling. I'm shocked and ask him why. I ask if he sent the TV round as planned and he tells me he took it round himself in the end.

"Why didn't you just send it in the taxi?" I ask, surprised he would take it to her.

"I just thought it might seem a tad pathetic, so decided to just take it round."

Bullshit! Kate, call him on his bullshit.

"I went round, dropped it off, and left. We have texted a bit over the last few days, so I think that's why she is calling."

Yep, I am calling bullshit again. Obviously not saying that to him. I bet they slept together, or at the very least kissed.

"I have been that girl, at the end of the phone, obsessively calling my ex and I think you should just answer the call and hear what she has to say."

I stand up from the kitchen stool, walk over to my bag. "I think I should go. You guys have so much history, baggage, hurt. It's not nice to be her or you right now. I know too well. I've been both parties at different times. It's my first time being this one though. The girl ending the date early. But I think it's for the best."

He tells me he doesn't want me to go and that he's happy spending the evening with me. All the while the phone is still ringing. I look him straight in the eyes. "You should at least take the call. Let her know you can't talk now, but you will call her tomorrow."

He goes outside to answer her twenty-odd calls. He's only gone five minutes, but I feel stupid. I feel like the other woman, not the leading lady. *Urgh.* I just want the world to swallow me up, or at least find a way to be able to leave. If he hadn't only got the one front door I would have left. When Yorkie returns, he assures me he wants to continue with our evening. She won't be calling again. I feel uneasy to begin with, but the calls do stop. We enjoy our evening in the end.

A week later, Yorkie calls me and says he needs to talk to me about something. He and She-who-shall-not-be-named have been in contact quite a bit and she wants to get back together with him.

"Do you know what? I'm not even shocked. I'm sad. Sad because I don't want you to stop hanging out with me. And sad for you that you're falling for the same shit again."

I continue, "I know there's nothing I can do. You can't keep someone when they want to leave. You shouldn't beg someone to want you. I learned that lesson over a long time. If someone wants to walk away, you need to explain to them that they will be missed and then let them go. If there is doubt, set that person free to eliminate it. If they leave and never come back, well then, at least you know they were never yours. But she has come back, so you should at least see what happens if you are unsure."

Yorkie is surprised I'm telling him to go, to see how the path pans out in front of him. He says I'm being very understanding about it all.

"There is no point in being anything else. You were never mine to begin with."

I don't tell him I doubt very much She-who-shall-not-be-named will stick about. She will just spend his wage packet and any savings he has got together. Once that's rinsed, she will be gone. The tears fall down my cheeks and I quietly sniff, my heart heavy and sad. We've been seeing each other for eight months and I've grown to love him. He can tell I'm crying and pleads with me to stop.

I am grateful that I am on my own at home right now. I don't want to be around anyone. I really love this man's company and I have absolutely no doubt that he loves mine too. I don't want to go back to a time without it. I will miss talking to him so much.

Then he tells me he doesn't want to stop talking to me or hanging out with me. He really would still like to be friends. Ouch. This hurts like hell. I was hoping in time he would be free of her and be ready to make something with me. The fact is I was just the paddling pool, the holiday, the weekend break from their fucked-up merry go round, that Luke was right to say he would never get off.

Feeling these emotions for a man I've realised I completely adore, knowing that the only way I can keep him in my life is as a friend, is going to take time. I need to mourn the life we could have had. A marriage full of unconditional love, days full of laughter and evenings spent enjoying each other's company. A beautiful home with a music room. Maybe another child. I would have made a life with him because he would be there as the most supportive wonderful father for that child. To be married to my best mate would have been an honour.

Yorkie made it clear to me that friends is all we can be. I need to get my head and heart to meet with his on the same page. My friends say I need to accept this for what it is. They want me to walk away completely as they lived this last eight months with me. They saw just how confused I was with the entire relationship, how negative I felt about my body, all my insecurities exposed because the man just didn't fancy me. But that was the sexual relationship.

As a friend he made me feel fantastic. If I can find a way to step back and accept that he will be with other women, we could have a really good friendship. There will be other men for me. Men who fancy me and want to see me naked. Not ones that have to get pissed to do so. I miss *lust*. Yes, this way I get the best of him. Friends, a wingman, a drinking buddy. I just have to mourn all this first. I've been listening to 'Let it go' by James Bay. On repeat. Crying. Yeah, a whole lot of crying. There are so many songs to lose myself in while I heal. I need to have hope though. Once this is done and I am through the other side, I hope to God we will be friends.

It has been five weeks since Yorkie friend-zoned me. Of the two hundred and sixty-five available episodes of my newest love, 'Grey's Anatomy', I am on episode two hundred and sixteen. I have ploughed my way through hours of it and it is most definitely get-over-that-boy material. I mean, they all fall in love, break up, then move on instantly. Bloody brilliant stuff. I am going to continue binge-watching them all, back-to-back around work and the girls.

I'm using it to fill my head with anything other than Yorkie. We've got such a strong habit of calling, texting, FaceTiming. It's all way too much for a friendship. Upon reflection, we weren't ever really lusting after each other beyond that first night we spent together. I think he realised then he still wanted to be with his ex. He was trying to get over her and was hoping I could help him achieve that. But he wasn't ready.

I had clung on for dear life too. Why did I do that? He said it's because I'm like a kitten and I wanted the string. I think he might be right. When I can't have something, or someone, I keep going until I can get it. I was blinkered, focused on the string, and unable to see what I did have. A bloody good friend. One of the best.

She-who-shall-not-be-named is back out of the picture. Yorkie saw sense and moved right back out of the bad head space. We start meeting up again. We play retro games, eat pizza, and drink red wine at his flat. We have the best nights in and on nights out we are each other's wingman. He's been dating a few other girls. I've met up with a couple of guys too, but nothing more than a first date.

At first, I used to be extremely jealous of the women he would flirt with and date. We laugh about how I'm really a stalker and there's no way I'm going to let any other woman near him, even though I can date other men. He jokes that he knows I camp out on the skylight above his bed, watching him like the little stalker I am. I play along with it. It makes us laugh.

We have the same silly humour. The texts we send each other are abusive and rude now, but only in jest, as if we're brother and sister. I love that he calls me Butt Face, Shit-for-brains. I call him Butthole, Poo Face and a whole lot more. We chuckle at the absurdities that show up on our phones. The longer the list, the more we laugh.

This is way more fun than trying to get in his pants. This way I can check out other bars of chocolate and still have a drinking buddy, retro gamer pal, and emotional support through life from someone who gets me.

Lots of people don't understand how we can be friends like this, but we are. We make much better friends than lovers and this way we can keep each other forever. We just don't fancy each other and that's the bottom line. I never loved him like I thought I did. He wasn't what I wanted him to be.

The classic Yorkie bar is a strong solid bar of Nestlé chocolate. Some versions have raisins, and it turned out my Yorkie had a crumbly biscuit centre. That completely confused me. I thought he was a strong solid boyfriend material chocolate bar, but really he was a chocolatey biscuit, firmly in the friend zone, lovely with a cup of tea. In stock, dependable when called upon.

I've said it before, I have always been a Cadbury girl and maybe that is what I'm attracted to. Cadbury is my type of bar, the bars I always reach for, but Nestlé? Well, Nestlé proved to make a great friend and has opened my eyes to try new things.

Bournville: Model Man

I love life at the moment. I'm enjoying shopping online for men, focused on Weight Watchers and back at the gym. I'm on my way back from there now and I'm in a quandary. I'd forgotten milk at the supermarket so need to go to the corner shop to grab some, but there are just too many temptations. I don't want to tempt myself with chocolate at the moment, not with my weight loss going so well. I climb out of my car, determined not to give in.

I fail. As soon as I walk in, I remember the corner shop doesn't sell small individual or multipack bars. Just the big bars. I'm already thinking about my options. What to do? Maybe I could have some dark chocolate. It's not as naughty as other bars. I could buy a big bar and keep it in the fridge instead of my candy box. Hmmm, yeah. I think that's a great plan. Bournville. Intense and full in flavour so I will only want a couple of squares. I won't use up too many diet points. Exciting times.

I make my way to the counter and the shop keeper's eyes widen with a confused expression as he looks at me. "Are you in your pyjamas?"

I laugh, unscathed by his question. "I am, yeah. I've been to the gym and hate having to put work stuff back on after the shower, so I just head home in my PJs."

Neil (*well done me for taking note of his name tag*) laughs and scans my shopping. I joke about my chocolate before he gets the opportunity. "I've gone back to my old faithful Cadbury. It turns out Nestlé isn't for me. It's nice and all, very satisfying to be fair, but the taste isn't quite for me. I've decided to go for the healthier, fuller flavour option!"

Now that I've returned to shopping online for my future husband, I have become very picky. I am always swiping left. No-one looks good enough. Sometimes though, I like to try my luck with extremely sexy hotties, swiping right then realising they are out of my league. Fuck it, they might say yes. This time though I think a man has accidentally matched with me. There is no way on this earth he would fancy me. We're in totally different leagues.

I have to be realistic about this. I think that maybe he is just being polite by sending me a message. It's unbelievable.

> Hello.

> Hi Ya. How's you?

> I'm good, you?

Yep, see Kate, just being polite. He will ghost you soon, but it's nice he is saying hi.

> You have a very nice smile.
> I'm glad we matched.

Oh my god. Are you fucking kidding me? Wow! How did I do that? Go with it Kate! He is the most gorgeous man you have ever been able to chat to. Don't bloody well stop now.

> Aww thank you. You are gorgeous!!

Two exclamation marks? Cool. Real smooth, Kate. Sometimes think, or at least re-read before you press send. In all fairness though, he is twenty exclamation marks gorgeous. Those eyes! I look at his topless picture. He's the hottest man. Slim, but muscular arms that could scoop me up and make me feel tiny, but not too big that they are veiny, just strong looking. The definition down into his low hung bottoms, that V shape. *Wowzers.* Pecks that he could definitely move, but not so big they freak you out and look like boobs. I don't want to be with a man who has better boobs than me. That would be rubbish. To top it off he has a few tattoos too. Hot. Hot. Hot. He looks like a model.

> Aww you too. x

Polite. Obviously just being polite. I bet he is thinking that he will send a couple of messages back and forth then remove the match tomorrow.

> So what do you do for a living? Do you have any kids?

> I am a music producer. You're a hairdresser yeah? I have two kids, one of each.

What an awesome job. Another creative, like Yorkie. I adore creative people. They are my kind of people. A dad too. This is great. I'm thinking husband material. I can't stop smiling and chuckling to myself that this conversation is even happening.

> Aww cute! The golden pair. Yeah I am a hairdresser, I love my job. Yours sounds great, do you like it?

> Yeah, of course! It's the best when you enjoy what you do.

Much to my amazement, we continue to chat through texts for a couple of days. He happily texts first or replies if I text first. There is no power struggle or game playing, thank God. I can never work out the rules to the games and I am pretty sure I lose every time. Why do people play them? If two people want to get to know each other, can't we just chat freely and explore the match? Simple as that?

It's Friday night and the girls are with their dad. Kim (one of The Nine) has come round to the cottage to watch trash TV and drink wine with me. We are belly laughing away watching a new programme called 'Naked Attraction'. Whoever thought of this concept, definitely thought outside of the box. There are a few cubicles each with one person in, and one man or woman chooses to take one of these cubicle candidates out on a date. They pick the person based on what they look like naked. It's absolutely hilarious and rather fascinating to see just how different people's bits and bobs look.

My phone is ringing. It's the model man! He has never rung before. It's been roughly ten days of texts (OK, not roughly, but exactly ten days of texting) and I still can't believe the match. I pick up my phone nervously and as I click I realise it's a video call. *Oh, you're fucking shitting me. How? Why? Who does this?* Models, that's who. Bloody models, with their beautiful faces. They are the only people on earth who randomly video call. I have absolutely no makeup on, I'm wearing old PJs, sitting alongside my model-like, fresh-faced best mate. *Oh bollocks. Only me. This shit only happens to me.* I can't believe I didn't realise it was a video call. If I had, I could have run down to my bedroom, changed into cute PJs and put a bit of makeup on, then called back.

Well, I'm doing it now. I have no choice. His stunning face fills my screen. I can't help but let out a high-pitched squeak which resembles 'Hi' and then turn the phone to Kim. *Oh crap! Why did I do that? He is going to wish he was getting to know her now.* I giggle, feeling like a giddy schoolgirl, who's crush has just called her. I turn the screen back to me.

"Why are you FaceTiming me? Who does that? I haven't got any makeup on and I'm in my PJs. And I am fully aware of just how stunning Kim is, but she has a boyfriend, so you, I'm afraid, are stuck with me."

Why on earth did I just blurt that out? I seriously have no filter at all. Oh my god, Kate, calm down. Get a grip. Try and claw back some dignity. I can't seem to even get control over the giggles. I have really not played this moment cool at all.

"I just wanted to see what you looked like and get to know you a little better by chatting to you on video call." The sexy deep voice totally fits the face.

"I'm glad you answered. You look hot. I'm not really a fan of a lot of makeup. I prefer a natural woman. Plus, you are both hot."

"Errrr, please feel free *not* to get flirty with my mate," I laugh. I'm joking but he knows I mean it from my tone. *Jeez, it's like I'm all possessive and I haven't even met him. I can't claim him already.*

We chat for about fifteen minutes, but it's a relief when he's off the phone. Kim and I laugh hard and chat about how nice he seems. I tell Kim all about my nicknames for the men in my life and we decided that he is most definitely a smooth and full-flavoured chocolate bar. Not your everyday bar this one. He is absolutely Bournville. Delicious and in a whole other league.

Another week goes by and texts continue along with phone calls. I'm still so very nervous to meet this man. However, it's time to bite the bullet. I'm going for a night out with some friends in London, so I ask Bournville if he would like a quick drink before I go out with them. We organise a meeting spot near the train station. I've arrived before him so order a glass of rosé and sit outside enjoying the warm evening.

> I'm on my way. Just getting out of the tube.

> OK cool. See you in a minute.

I take a sip of rosé, then, oh wow, this is a slow-motion moment. Bournville walks towards me. He looks exactly like his photos. I need to take a moment here. I just want to acknowledge that this unbelievably hot man has come to hang out with me. *Wow. Actually wow. OK Kate, breathe love, start breathing now. And talk. Oh Kate, you need to answer. Kate, say something!*

"Kate?" he says whilst leaning in to hug me and kiss my cheek.

"Hi, yes. Hi." I say, as I kiss his cheek back. I feel like a teenager when the boy you have a massive crush on comes up and talks to you. I feel numb. I have a massive smile across my face. It must be infectious because he does too. He sits down facing me with one leg in front, bent into him. He's completely chilled out. I, on the other hand, am desperately trying to play it cool, but my body language probably says otherwise.

Bournville doesn't drink alcohol. He used to but doesn't like it anymore. He really takes care of himself now and I adore this about him. I'm not a big drinker. Don't get me wrong, I enjoy alcohol when I'm out with my friends, and evenings with Yorkie nearly broke me, but I'm equally happy to enjoy an evening with a cup of tea or Diet Coke. Bournville introduces me to Oreo milkshakes. You can have them with alcohol or without. We both choose without. I think if I mix wine and an alcoholic milkshake, it might not end well.

Bournville lets me chat away. He is listening and interested, asking questions. He's so easy to talk to, chilled, but not overly talkative himself.

We've been in each other's company for a couple of hours now. We're comfortable and enjoying ourselves when my phone starts pinging away. My friends are on at me to join them. It's nine o'clock. If I hadn't arranged this night out with them all a while ago, I would have stayed. He walks me to the Underground and we kiss. I enjoy it and want to do it more. We say our goodbyes. I look back as I'm walking away from him. So does he. I smile and think just how lucky I am to have matched with such a lovely, decent, absolutely stunning, strikingly, model-like man.

I cannot wait for date two.

Bournville and I call each other regularly, conversations always flowing well. It's so exciting. My belly fills with butterflies when I see his name pop up on my phone. We talk pretty much every night, enjoying a really comfortable chat before settling down to sleep. He has such a wonderfully positive outlook on life. He really looks after himself, mind, body and soul. It's so refreshing. Bournville's attitude towards life inspires me and I can't wait to see him again.

We've organised another date. This time at Bournville's place. He lives on the edge of London so I'm driving there. It takes an hour and a quarter to reach Bournville's flat and I enjoy the drive listening to my tunes, singing happily all the way there.

I have messaged the Chit Chat group with Bournville's address and his picture, plus a photo of me showing what I'm wearing. After what happened in London with Yorkie, I was told in no uncertain terms that I must never go to anybody's house, or on a first date with someone, without telling The Nine who, where, what and when. Jessica is a police officer and is particularly concerned. I love them for keeping me safe. It's so important when you meet people in person having only known them online.

I get out of the car, adjust my dress, check my hair and face in the wing mirror, lock the car and head up to his front door. I knock on the brown varnished door and wait patiently for Bournville to answer. We greet each other and kiss cheeks on the doorstep before he invites me in. Bournville uses his flat for a bit of work so part of the front room is set up as a recording studio. It's rather awesome to say the least.

"It's a great flat. I love the recording area," I say, impressed.

"Thanks. Yeah, I like it. It could do with some plants though really."

I can't say I have met many men that fussed for house plants and good home décor. He is just so cute.

He offers me a drink and we sit on the couch chatting away about what we've been up to since we'd last spoken, which was only yesterday. We're a little flirty with each other. Soft touches on each other's arms, legs, hands. I take in his beautiful face and I notice a birthmark on his eyelid. It makes the lid just slightly darker than the other. I think this mark makes him perfect, adding character to his beautiful face.

Bournville is just so chilled. I've only known him for four weeks, but nothing seems to stress him out. He's kind and patient. I like the fact that he is spiritual too. He's really into his healthy living, mind and body. He said he used to drink and smoke but decided to change his ways and get the most out of life.

I can feel the chemistry building between us as we talk. We get closer on the couch. I want to kiss him but I'm not bold enough to make the first move. I need him to take the lead. I just keep looking at his beautiful face, willing him on. When he smiles at me, he raises his eyebrows and relaxes them again.

His charms are working. I mean, his sexy deep voice works down the phone line, never mind when he's talking with me in the flesh. I feel like the last week and a half has been foreplay just for this night. His smile becomes one that declares "I'm having a naughty thought."

I know it's only date two, and yes, there are rules to this dating lark, but if he makes a move and wants to sleep with me, I would regret driving away more than I would breaking date night rules. If it happens, then it happens. *My god, I hope it happens,* I think to myself. I raise and relax my eyebrows, giving him that knowing look. *Yes, Mister, I am having naughty thoughts too.* I have spent the last eight months hanging out with Yorkie, a man who could only ever be my friend. I haven't had lustful sex for what feels like a lifetime and this beautiful, hot, sexy man is giving me the come to bed eyes. *And I really want to cum on his bed rather than to it. Kate! You dirty woman!* I giggle to myself.

"What're you laughing at?" he asks.

"Well, you are the hottest man I have ever seen. Honestly, you are like a model. And I'm having very naughty thoughts about you, right now." *Bloody hell Kate! Where did this gutsy girl come from? Well done!* He kisses me. I think he liked gutsy Kate.

"You are one damn beautiful, sexy woman and believe me when I say I am having naughty thoughts of my own right now too."

Oh my god. Green light! I am going to keep kissing this man. Kissing and letting our hands explore each other. He stands up and takes me towards his bedroom. I start to undress him, pulling his black t-shirt up and off over his head exposing his god-like physique. I undo his belt and his jean buttons. He takes my dress off, exposing my lacey pale pink French knickers and my funny little stick-on bra. *OMG. You hadn't thought this through Kate.* I couldn't wear a full bra because my dress had a strappy back. He is intrigued and chuckles with me about this remarkable invention. I take it off exposing my breasts, but we are now both distracted, very interested in the sticky panels that keep the bra fixed to my body.

"Stop talking about my bra. You'll make me want to put it back on, along with my dress, and leave. I'm self-conscious enough already," I laugh.

"Why are you so self-conscious? Look at your tiny waist and hot bum!"

"I have far from a hot bum Mister."

He stands back, keeping his fingers entwined with mine and tells me he thinks I'm hot. He has a glimmer in his eyes. He makes me feel amazing. Right at this moment, I no longer feel self-conscious. I pull him in closer and tell him I want him kissing me, touching me. He happily and willingly obliges. He lays me down on his bed, kissing my mouth, my neck, my nipples, gently caressing my body with his hands. He is so sensual. Soft touches, but purposeful. I can feel the passion between us intensify. I want him closer to me. My body is heating up more than ever. He's moving down to my place.

Bournville isn't rushing anything, not one single move. He takes his time making every move, touch and kiss count. I am unbelievably turned on right now. I can't get enough of him. I want him. I cannot wait any longer. I need him. I want to feel him deep inside of me. And then he gives me what I've been waiting for. *Oh God. This is amazing.* I don't want this to end and with the control this man is showing I don't think it will be ending any time soon. He is making sure I am truly satisfied and it's as if he has known my body forever. I climax over and over until I'm laughing because I can't take it anymore, yet he is still going. I beg him to cum with me. Just as he seems like he's about to, he stops. This is new.

"That was bloody amazing! Intense as hell. Wow, oh, just wow!" I say breathlessly laying back onto the bed. "Why didn't you finish?"

"Yeah, it was great," he whispers, laying down next to me. "Don't worry, I did cum. I just didn't release sperm. It's a tantric thing. You not seen that before then?"

"Nope," I reply, my eyes wide with bewilderment. I think about what just happened as we lay together for a little longer. That was the most amazing sex I have ever had since Dairy Milk. I could lay in Bournville's beautiful arms for days, but the journey home awaits me. I need to go home as I have so much to do tomorrow with the school run and then work for twelve hours. I get up and sort my clothes out to put them back on. We say our goodbyes and plan to see each other again soon.

I need to send a quick message to the Chit Chat group on WhatsApp before I start the drive home.

> Bloody hell ladies, that is what I am talking about! I was naughty and slept with him but I don't even feel one little bit of guilt. It was bloody amazing and this stunning man looks fucking delicious naked! He knew his stuff. I haven't had a man know my body like that since Dairy Milk, and bloody hell I loved it! About to drive home now but just letting you know that I'm safe, had an amazing time and I'm all sexed out! Yay for me 😂😂 Xxx

Another new week has arrived. Bournville is influencing my mood in more ways than one. I feel energised into making a fresh start and new goals with my diet and fitness. His attitude to living well and healthy eating is encouraging me. I even enjoy going to the gym now. *OK that's pushing it. I don't like the gym.* I am chuckling to myself as I endure the leg press and think people must find my random outbursts of laughter quite strange. I don't care though. I'm an odd ball and proud of it. And I'm bloody happy! I know we, as individuals, should find happiness within ourselves, that we should validate ourselves, but I have met this beautiful sexy man who wants to hang out with me, get to know me, and tells me I'm beautiful and sexy too. And I enjoy this validation very, very much.

It has taken four weeks for Bournville to convince me to go into the weights section of the gym to use the leg press. This area of the gym scares me. It's bit where all the buff men and women work out, checking themselves out in the mirror. I'm neither buff, nor that confident. I don't understand how the equipment works and I'm too self-conscious to ask people, but Bournville talked me through what I need to do. Ah, this man is wonderful. I can't wait to see him this week.

I usually head up to London to visit him on Thursdays after I finish work and we've progressed to sleepovers. I love cuddling into him. He makes a perfect big spoon. When he is laying on his back, I cuddle right into his chest. We both like the way our bodies fit together. He's as cuddly as me. It's just so nice. *Hmmm, I miss him now that I'm thinking about Thursday to come.*

Thursday has finally arrived. Sometimes, during the drive to Bournville's, I call Anthony or Adira and put the world to rights. On hands-free of course. In fact, I often use this time to catch up with friends and family. I enjoy the drive. I have all my girly pop tunes blasting out of my naff speakers and I'm singing my heart out, smiling all the way, excited to see this very gorgeous man.

I arrive at his apartment, knock on the door, and he greets me with a kiss as he scoops me into his arms. *Oh, I am feeling the feels right now.* He is the perfect height for me. Five feet ten inches with arms that fold around me as if made for me. And lips I could kiss all day long.

'Celebrity Big Brother' is on the television. I find it so cute that he likes these programmes. He enjoys 'The X Factor' too. I don't, but I find it so endearing about him. We snuggle up on the couch together, but it's not long before we're kissing. His lips gently touch mine. We enjoy a long and meaningful kiss.

Nothing about Bournville is rushed. He takes his time over every move and does it with real intention. His hands are softer, different to the builder hands I've been used to in the past. He gently lifts my blue top up and over my head. He removes his top, exposing his tattoos. My hands immediately want to explore his body. His jeans are cut low revealing the little bit of hair on his lower stomach, an invitation tempting me downwards. I unbutton them, accepting the invitation and feel him harden beneath his pants. I don't go under. I tease him a little. I give him the time to want me. He pushes me up off the couch and pulls at my jeans to take them off. They join my top on the floor. My bra and knickers follow. I allow him to see me, all of me, in the low lighting of the room. I feel brave. It's dim light. I'm not mad. No way would I let this model man stare at me in full lighting.

He stands up to join me and we kiss. His hands caress my arms, waist, bum and now my place. His fingers play away, while we enjoy the kiss. We make our way to the bedroom. Bournville lays me down and goes straight to my place to kiss me, this time using his fingers too. I climax and he continues. This time he moves his fingers inside of me but higher, deeper, further inside of me. *Erm, fuck this is truly feeling good. Oh my god! His* fingers are pressing up and twisting back and forth. *Oh fuck. What is he doing? This feels amazing, unbelievable. Shit, I think he should stop. This is too much! Or is it?*

I murmur, "OK, stop, stop. No, don't stop. Oh fuck! What are you doing?"

He carries on as I squirm beneath him. "Oh my god, oh my god," I cry out impulsively. This is intense. I'm climaxing over and over and now. I'm laughing. No, I'm crying. *What the fuck? Did I just wet myself? What? Oh fuck.* He is still going and sure enough I cum again. Stopping his hand, he grins, pleased with himself. He says, "I think we need a towel."

He gets off the bed as I lay there writhing in some kind of euphoric state, not fully understanding what has just happened. I'm in pure ecstasy. He comes back, gently kisses my belly, my breasts, my neck and then my lips. Then he moves his weight on top of me and slips himself inside. He feels amazing. I feel every bit of him, well-endowed and all mine. I climax over and over again until he finishes.

"What the fuck? That was absolutely amazing," I say, shaking with adrenaline.

"You enjoyed that, yeah?"

"Oh, you beautiful man. I bloody loved it!" *Bring on the morning when we get to do it again.* I roll onto my side, facing Bournville. He pulls me into him. I lay my head on his chest, my legs entwined with his. I softly run my fingers over his chest and stomach. His arm is wrapped around me and we peacefully fall to sleep.

The next morning, after I have driven home and the girls have been fed, clothed, screamed at:

"Just get in the car!"

"We are going to be late"

"No you can't have your hair plaited!"

"What part of we are going to be late, did you not understand?"

And dropped off at school with *"I love you. Have a great day"*, I decide I must call Kim.

"Oh my god, I need to ask you something," I say, the moment she answers the phone.

"Oh, OK. You alright?"

"Erm, well I don't know. I don't know how to say it."

Kim chuckles. "Spit it out woman."

"OK. Oh fuck. OK. Bournville was playing with me. Well. He. Erm." I'm stuttering and stumbling over finding the right words.

"Come on, just say it. It's only me. You can talk to me about anything. Tell me!"

"OK. I know. I'm trying." I'm giggling now. "So, he was playing, put his fingers right inside and started twisting them and well, something happened, but I'm not sure what."

"Did it feel like you pissed yourself?" she asks excitedly.

"Yes!" I exclaim.

"It's fucking amazing, isn't it?" She bursts into laughter. We both do, and then chat away about it for the next ten minutes before work. I bloody love this girl. We can always chat about these things.

Things have been going really well with Bournville. We've been meeting for a couple of months. He's a really decent man. He takes time to listen to what I have to say. He wants to know what I'm up to and always shows an interest in my day. Plus, he's excited when he talks about Christmas. This wins him endless points.

As we move into December, it becomes harder for us to see each other as much. It's an incredibly busy month for hairdressers and I have to work nearly every day. "Just hold out until January," I tell him over the phone. "I have the first two weeks off so we can hang out more then."

Even though he wants to see me, Bournville is quite chilled about it, understanding that my hours have gone crazy. We chat on the phone, video call, and text a lot. When I am at work though I can't always answer. Occasionally I've called him back a few hours later, after I've left a client's house, and he's seemed a bit off with me.

Today is one of those times. He questions why I didn't just answer the phone to tell him I couldn't talk right then.

"Because that would be inappropriate," I tell him.

"But if your phone is ringing you could just pick up and say you're with a client, then you could call me back later," he suggests.

Hmmmm, come to think of it. He has been like this from the start. He questions where I have been if I don't reply immediately. He also talks a lot about the exes who have cheated on him. *Damn.* I hadn't realised until now that he is actually quite insecure, despite appearances. I decide to make a conscious effort to make him feel more secure. Though we aren't in an official relationship, calling each other boyfriend or girlfriend, we are seeing only each other. Long distance is hard on relationships, so I am going to give him a bit more reassurance.

We finally have a night together for what seems like ages. It's not long 'til Christmas and things are hectic, so we make the most of it. We decide to go to bed to watch telly tucked up together. As he is getting undressed to join me, I notice his socks. Christmas socks! *Jeez, I like him even more now. I need to kiss him, right now.* I love our growing relationship, although I know I'm not ready to say 'I love you' yet. It takes time for my walls to come down. Tonight though, I think I am getting very close to it.

It's Christmas day and we've had the best day. It's been full on and completely crazy with our girls and I have loved every single bit of it. When I say 'we' I mean me and Dairy Milk. This year it has been Dairy Milk's turn to host. We take turns to hold Christmas dinner as neither of us want to take it in turns to not have the girls, so we share and spend holidays together. We both think that our children won't be young forever and neither of us want to miss out.

Bournville FaceTimes me so we can wish each other a happy Christmas. I answer in the front room and Dairy Milk leans over to say hi. I laugh and jokingly push him away slightly, then leave the living room to have a few minutes alone to chat. As we chat away happily, Bournville mentions that he finds it strange that Dairy Milk and I have this arrangement.

"I get why you think that, but it really isn't. We've worked incredibly hard to get to the point that we are friends, great friends!"

Dairy Milk is actually one of my best friends. I need Bournville to know and to understand that I am proud of the things I have managed to achieve with Dairy Milk and my girls. We both are. I explain we are all happy with the way things are. Bournville assures me he hasn't got a problem with it and I feel more comfortable. I know that there are people who would have an issue with two exes being friends, but anyone who thinks like that would not be the right person for me.

9.06am: It's now three days after Christmas. My thirty-third birthday. I wake to find lots of wonderful messages on my phone, all wishing me a happy birthday. Now my mum is calling.

"Hello Mum." I answer the phone to hear Mum joyfully singing Happy Birthday. I can't help but laugh as I lay back in bed and let her sing the song through, note perfect as ever. She does this every year, for every one of us and I love her so much for it. We have a short chat and I promise I will be over for two o'clock to see her.

"Perfect. Love you darling," she says, and we end the call.

I open my messages and there it is.

> Happy Birthday Kate xxx

I stare at the message. Wonka. I am a little shocked he has remembered, but I adore that he has. He's still hiding away from the world of Kate though. I don't even want to know why.

No birthday text from Bournville yet though. Hmm. He must still be sleeping.

I've got up now and my babies have made me breakfast and given me their little presents. An hour later, I check my phone and see even more messages from my friends and family. I am really feeling the love. Still nothing from Bournville. Maybe he is working. I'm not his official girlfriend so I'm not expecting hearts and flowers, but a message? Yeah, I am expecting a message. More to the point, a first thing in the morning birthday text. Or a phone call.

I spend the rest of the day with my daughters. We visit Mum then go to our local pub for dinner before my friends join us for some evening drinks. I check my phone. Still nothing. I'm a little pissed off now. I'm not messaging first. He should know it's my birthday and if not, Facebook would tell him. I upload some pictures of my birthday to Facebook and Instagram and there it is. A notification. Bournville has written a message on my timeline. *Happy Birthday xx*

Is he joking? Nine minutes past eight at night and I get a 'Happy Birthday' on my Facebook timeline. Not even a text? Yeah, it's safe to say I am massively pissed off. I refuse to message back. I'm actually really hurt. My birthday is not a time to play it cool. Plus, I didn't think this man played games, so it just means he forgot. He clearly doesn't think I am worth a phone call. Or maybe he doesn't think it's his place to call me? I have no idea. I don't want to give him any more of my thoughts today. This evening I am surrounded by people who want to be here with me. I down my drink and ask, "Who wants another?" deliberately pushing my way past the hot guy standing at the bar.

Dating? Nah, I'm over and out. For now, at least.

The next morning, I lay awake in bed with a dry mouth and a pounding head. I hadn't even taken off last night's underwear. Urgh, I need something to drink. I am regretting the eight or more vodka and cokes. I scramble up the stairs into the absolutely freezing kitchen. The sharp cold is refreshing on my skin. I leave the lights off and make some orange squash, gulp it down, make another and head back downstairs to my bedroom and my cosy warm blanket. I reflect on my birthday and Bournville's lack of interest. I realise I feel a little lost in the dating world. Well, completely lost.

The rules have changed so much since before I was married. Back then, you met someone on a night out, at work or through friends. Nowadays, it seems that most couples meet through online dating sites, the apps. Every 'single' person I know is dating online. It is very efficient. And it is fun. What I don't understand though, is how to move from dating, seeing someone, into the official relationship zone. And that has nothing to do with online dating. I realise I am happy in the seeing someone stage. So, maybe it's not that I don't know how to move forward with someone, but more that I'm not ready to?

I know my walls are built high. Letting them down, letting someone in, means I become vulnerable. If they walk away after my walls have come down then I have to live with someone else leaving my life, and that is tough. The loss of my brother, then my dad moving away not soon after really did affect me badly. I sigh to myself as I reflect on those sad years.

And what if I'm not happy? What happens if I take the responsibility of being the one to leave? I truly don't know if I would have the strength to do that again. I have been the one to leave once. My girls had their hearts broken because I was no longer in love with their dad. To bring someone into their lives, have them love him, have my brothers, my parents, my friends all accept someone new into the fold. Jeez, the thought of having to split again is a lot for me to deal with.

I think about all my what ifs. If I am being completely honest with myself it's not the rules that I don't understand. It's me that I don't understand. I realise I need to work on me. Yes, it's one thing to be self-aware, quite another if you don't do anything about your own bullshit.

I know I have been overthinking my birthday and Bournville's seeming lack of interest, but there are some things I think I am right to question. I do really like him, and he is such a positive influence in my life. I feel inspired when I am around him. If I let my walls down and let him in, well, we will need to make changes. He hasn't come down to visit me here even though we've been dating for four months, almost five now. It is a little frustrating. Although I don't mind the drive, I would like him to see where I live, meet my friends one day. If not, then we can't move into the next stage. He will need to make more effort, and never forget my birthday ever again, that's for sure.

Another thing I worry about is his insecurity. The fact that I count Yorkie and Dairy Milk as my best friends and that I don't want to give them up probably isn't helping. He doesn't complain about it though, and if he asks any questions about them, he listens and understands why I want to keep them in my life. I think he is starting to see that you can be friends with exes once you realise the friendship means more to you than the sexual relationship ever did. Why should we never see people again if you have both come to accept that you don't work as a couple? How can you share every minute with someone then just cut them out of your life as if they were dead? I don't like that and unless they are some kind of nasty bastard, I want to stay in touch, holding onto good times, rather than bad feeling.

Yes Kate, you have found a nice one here. You just need to figure out what happened on your birthday. Maybe I'm just way more into this than he is.

"Aww Kate!" I chastise myself out loud. "You're hungover and massively over thinking. Get a grip. Bournville wouldn't have given this a second thought, probably not even a first one."

It's time to get my act together. I throw off the covers and shriek as I jump out of bed and the goose bumps hit.

It's a new day and I'm out and about with my girls. I have taken the youngest two to a play centre whilst my eldest is at her friend's house. Bournville is calling me.

"Hi," he says. Then immediately, out of the blue, states, "You don't plan on moving to London do you."

"Well, no," I say, surprised. "I don't see myself living in London. I love visiting and spending time there, but living there isn't something I want to do. What made you ask that?"

"I've been thinking over the last week."

Well, that makes two of us!

"We haven't been able to meet up and it has made me think. I don't want to move out of the city. I'm not sure where we can go with this. I know you don't mind the long distance, but I want to live with someone one day. If neither of us will move, then what is our future? Maybe it's time to walk away before we invest too much?"

Wow. He has been thinking about this.

"I am close to falling in love with you," he continues. "Moving further into this knowing we won't get what we want would be foolish."

He has made up his mind. I know he is making statements that he doesn't expect a response to. I knew things had been strange and distant since my birthday. We say our goodbyes and wish each other well. It's all very matter of fact, a rushed conversation for something that should have been so serious and intimate.

I'm numb. I want to cry, but I can't cry here at the play centre. I have to hold it together. *Shit.* I'm absolutely gutted. I was gearing myself up to bring my walls down. Now I'm glad I didn't. *Oh jeez.* My heart is stinging. My littlest runs up to me and asks for a drink. I hold back the tears and put on my mum mask. I try and shake off the hurt and disappointment of the cutting, short conversation, and head to the little café to get what my baby needs, accepting, or trying to accept, that he is right.

I am happy to never live with anyone again. I like my life, my home. I want the man in my life to complement that, yes, but I don't need them to support that. God, maybe I am too stubborn and independent for my own good? I am not fighting for a man who doesn't think we can be fought for. That I do know.

A toddler's shriek makes me look up and I see a couple of kids fighting over a toy rabbit. The girl is trying to make friends but doesn't want to share her toy with the boy. "Keep it for yourself little girl," I mutter. "Make the little shit work for it."

I take a deep breath and force myself to hold it together until I get home, until I get the kids to bed.

I am now once again tucked up in my big old bed alone. I'm torturing myself, re-reading every text we have sent, over and over. I look through every photo and try to come to terms with the latest disappointment and loss. I will miss him so very much. *Fuck! This is really bloody shit.* I can't change it though. He is right. Bournville just never seemed to falter. He knew what he was, what he wanted. It turns out I don't know who I am just yet, nor where I'm going.

As intense and incredibly satisfying as Bournville is, you only need a square or two of this solid bar to fix the sugar craving. It's just unfortunate I wasn't allowed more time to consume the whole bar. He taught me so much and held such a positive outlook on life that really was so refreshing to be around. A healthier yet still satisfying treat. I will always look back fondly on the time I had with him.

Bad News

It's just an average weekday afternoon pick up from school. For now anyway. Me and the girls are hanging out at Dairy Milk's flat whilst we wait for him to get back from work so I can get back to mine. I enjoy sitting in his spacious new build flat surrounded by his things. It feels familiar. The big black sofa (that matches my pink one), his motor racing pictures hung on the walls. He loves it here too, looking out of his lounge window onto the village shops below, people watching.

I am sitting on his sofa enjoying a cup of tea when he gets home. I ask if he wants one too, but he says he thinks he'd better have some water. Never, in all the years I have known him, has Dairy Milk asked for water. My face must say it all. I'm wide-eyed and shocked at his request.

"I do drink water sometimes, I'll have you know!" he says, half-joking.

"Sometimes, being the operative word!" I laugh.

He flops down onto a chair at the dining table and I join him. Something's wrong.

"Something weird is happening," he says. "It's a bit embarrassing."

"OK. Tell me. I can try and help," I encourage him.

He hesitates. "I've been passing a little bit of blood when I go for a pee." He looks grim.

"Well, we both know that's not right. Have you been to the doctor?" I ask. "How long has it been going on?"

"A few days or so," he says ruefully. "I keep meaning to call the doc but just haven't got round to it."

"What do you mean you haven't been to the doctor?" I feel like a mother telling off a naughty child. "Promise me you will get yourself to the doctors tomorrow. If you don't, I will use the wife card and book it myself. Estranged or not!"

The next evening, Dairy Milk calls to let me know the doctor isn't too worried. They believe it's most likely to be a urine infection. He has antibiotics and has been told to go back if the bleeding continues after the week is through.

"That's great!" I say. "See how easy that was to deal with? Antibiotics and lots of water. Now, that was worth a visit to the doctor. You will be feeling better in no time."

A month later Dairy Milk and I are chatting at his flat over a cup of tea when he tells me the urine infection keeps coming back.

"What do you mean? How many times have you had it? Have you seen the doctor again?" I exclaim.

"Calm down Kate. It's just a urine infection. It comes and goes. I'm drinking more water though and flushing it through when it does come back."

"But have you gone back to the doctor?"

He says no. He says he will make an appointment if it continues.

"Stop being such a complete idiot and go back tomorrow," I tell him.

He tries to laugh it off. "Believe it or not, Kate, I don't really feel great ringing up the doctors first thing in the morning from work on a building site to talk about peeing blood!"

I am so mad at him. If he won't do it, I'll just do it for him. We agree that I will call the surgery first thing in the morning and get him an appointment after work.

The doctor thinks I might have a blockage in the urethra. She is sending me for blood tests and a scan. Don't start stressing. She said it is extremely unlikely to be anything sinister at my age.

Oh fucking hell! Ok. Well, keep me informed and let me know dates and things. I am sure my mum can have the girls and I can join you.

> You don't need to but thanks
> sweetheart. I will let you know. x

The appointment for the scan comes through quickly and two weeks later, Dairy Milk receives the results. Bloods are all clear and it's such a relief to know that there is nothing bad. The CT did show that there is indeed a blockage at the top of the urethra though and we await the date for the small operation to remove it.

A month later, myself and Rhiannon, Dairy Milk's ex-girlfriend, accompany him to the hospital to give him moral support. We laugh and joke about him having his two exes with him. Rhiannon and Dairy Milk only recently split up, but I still have my fingers crossed that they will get back together. They totally click with each other. I have never seen two people laughing the way they do together. They understand every single joke between them. All their jokes are totally lost on me, but I laugh along anyway. I chuckle just thinking about the fact that I have absolutely no idea what they are talking about half of the time. I really wish they would figure things out and just get back together. Rhiannon is so good with my girls too. And they adore her. It's such a waste, but that's life I guess. They obviously have their own reasons and it's not for me to get involved.

We sit in the bland grey waiting room, chairs lining the walls, reception area in the centre. There are a few other patients waiting. We chat to a few of them and it seems that they have had this procedure done before and it's really nothing to worry about. Their tales reassure us and when Dairy Milk is called into the consultant, Rhiannon and I chat away, relieved that everything will be sorted by bedtime.

We're hungry and ask the nurse where we can get food whilst Dairy Milk has his operation later on. As she's telling us, Dairy Milk emerges from the consultation room and joins us to wait a while longer.

"It's alright for you two going off in search of grub. Me? Nothing. You best make sure I have something for after all this."

A short while later the doctor calls him through and we hug him and send him on his merry way through the double doors. We are nervous for Dairy Milk, but we don't want him to know that. After all, we have been told over and over again that we have nothing to worry about.

"I just hope they don't make a mistake and mess his downstairs up," I say cheekily to Rhiannon as we leave the hospital in search of food. "You might need it if you get back together, eh?"

"I think that ship has sailed, but you never know," she replies softly.

Rhiannon and I go back to the hospital for the time we were told Dairy Milk's operation would be finished, but he is still in theatre. We both try hard not to make any assumptions and fight the nerves away, desperate not to let them in. An hour later we are shown through to the side room to see him. I busy myself so that Rhiannon and Dairy Milk can have a moment together. I feel more like his mum these days than an ex-wife, but I don't mind. I want to be here.

Dairy Milk is droopy eyed and sleepy. I hug him and ask if he's OK or needs anything, though I doubted he would want food. As I pour him some water, the doctor arrives and asks who we both are.

"Rhiannon is the ex-girlfriend and I'm the ex-wife," I joke. We both laugh but the look on his face stops us in our tracks. He isn't in the mood for jokes.

"We've removed the blockage," says the doctor, "But I can't be sure it isn't cancerous. We took as much as possible away and will do some tests."

I feel the blood drain from my face. My body weakens and I reach for Dairy Milk's hand. I hold it as tightly as I can and the doctor continues to tell us about what to expect next, but the information is lost on me. I just want to wake up from this incredibly horrendous dream. But how do I wake up from real life? I need a pause button, stop, rewind. Let's just rewind to laughing about dinner. Or how about five months ago when the doctor thought this was a urine infection, when my gut was saying something different? *What the actual fuck is happening?*

My mind re-joins the room and I hear the doctor tell us that we should have the results very soon, that he is just so sorry, and that at just 35-years-old Dairy Milk is incredibly young to be going through something like this. It's generally an older man's disease.

The doctor leaves us alone with our thoughts and I perch on the edge of Dairy Milk's bed, his hand still in mine. He's in shock. For a second, he looks just like my brother John. Pale-faced with freckly arms. Tears well in my eyes and he's Dairy Milk again. I don't know what to say, or how to show support. All I can do is be here for him, whatever it takes to get him better. *Oh Christ. His mum. I should tell his mum and dad.* I leave Dairy Milk and Rhiannon to themselves for a moment and stand in the corridor leaning against the wall. I need to compose myself before I call his parents.

They pick up after a few rings. "The original operation was completed, but they believe the blockage is cancerous. We won't know for sure until the biopsy returns next week."

His mum cries out in shock at the horrific news. She hands the phone to Dairy Milk's dad and I explain what I know to him. I hear the disbelief and concern in his voice before he passes the phone back to Dairy Milk's mum. She's calmed down and tells me not to worry, that he will be OK.

"He's young and we don't know for sure," she says.

I can tell she is trying to be strong. We say our goodbyes and before I go back to Dairy Milk, I quickly call my mum to let her know what's happening. It's not long before the nurse in charge says gently that it is time for Rhiannon and I to leave so that Dairy Milk can settle in for the night. *So much for this all being over by bedtime.* We say our goodbyes and I tell him that I will be back first thing in the morning to take him home.

After we leave Dairy Milk's room, Rhiannon and I give each other an almighty hug, trying to stop the tears from flowing. What a night. I feel completely numb, exhausted, scared. Dairy Milk is my best friend, the father of my children. I want so desperately to fix this, but I can't.

The next morning, I wake with the same gut-wrenching feeling of the night before. Tears fall from my sore, blood-red eyes, as I realise it wasn't all a nightmare. I try hard to compose myself and put on my mum mask. I wake the girls from their restful sleep and comfy beds and get them ready for school. They are blissfully unaware of anything other than the fact their dad had an operation and is coming home today. I drop them off at school and drive over to the hospital.

Dairy Milk is sitting up in bed, chatting to a nurse when I arrive. When she leaves, he tells me not to worry too much. "We don't know for sure what it is until we get the results."

"The doctor told us what he thinks it is though, didn't he." I remind him.

He stares wide-eyed and pale. "I was still pretty out of it when he came in to speak to us. I thought he was saying that he won't know until the biopsy is returned, but I'm young so it probably isn't anything to worry about."

"No, Sweet. He told us that they have taken a few biopsies to confirm if the blockage, tumours, was cancerous. We won't know until the results come back, but you need to be prepared. He does believe they are cancerous. He was shocked because of your age."

I'm the bearer of bad news again, repeating the conversation with him that I had had with his parents.

"Well, that is shit, isn't it?" He remarks drily, trying to laugh a little to lighten the mood.

I know this is his way of coping with such completely shitty news. I stay with him a while longer to keep him company. His mum and dad are on their way up to the hospital and are fetching him the bits and bobs he'd forgotten to bring with him. They will take him home then and I will go over to his flat in the evening to check that he's OK.

That evening we try to talk in his bedroom whilst the kids play in the front room.

"We need to talk about it with the girls. I don't want them overhearing whispers from secret conversations. They aren't silly and they have a right to know. I'm not suggesting we say anything just yet, but if the results are confirmed then we must. And you need to tell Freya too."

Freya is Dairy Milk's daughter from a relationship he had before he met me. Oh, the tangled lives people lead. This was another reason I had felt so bad leaving him, taking three more daughters away from him.

"How on earth are we going to do this?" Dairy Milk sighs. "I don't even want to know myself, let alone tell the girls. But yes, I know you're right. Our three are especially nosy little Herberts and would definitely overhear something."

He's trying to keep the mood light again. I am in awe of him and the way he can do this. Maybe he is getting good at using masks too. We chat about it a short while longer before deciding we will explain it all to the girls, and Freya, once we have the results of the biopsy.

A week in limbo feels like a year. I wish every single day away in the hope that I will hear they made a mistake. Results day finally arrives and we drive through pouring rain to the hospital to meet the consultant. The news isn't good. The tumours are cancerous. We're stunned.

At the moment they are contained within the bladder, so they haven't spread, but the treatment is potentially lifechanging. The consultant explains the safest option is to remove the bladder completely, but there is another option that's possible because of Dairy Milk's age. It's a bit like chemotherapy. He explains that if Dairy Milk chooses this option, he will need to attend a course of treatment for six weeks, then have another biopsy and a scan at the end. The only catch is that if the tumours are still there, or if they return within two years, the doctors will insist on removing the bladder.

Dairy Milk agrees to try the six weeks of treatment. The thought of losing his bladder is terrifying. We leave the hospital and get a cup of tea in a café on the way home. We need the time to piece together different parts of the conversation with the doctor and laugh about how rubbish our memories are.

"We should record the consultation next time," I say.

"Knock yourself out dear, but I won't. I retain what I need. The key facts about what they will do. The rest I am happy to let pass over my head. It's depressing otherwise."

I nod. "I know what you mean, I get that." I realise I've agreed with him on something and chuckle. "It's not often I agree with you either."

"It's 'cos I have the big C. I shall use its power to get you to do what I say because the rest of its power is fucking bollocks, I can tell ya!"

"Yeah, I know. It's proper shit. Make the most of it though. I will be the boss again soon enough when you are better. Actually, scrap that. Cancer or no cancer, I am still totally the boss."

"Nothing new there then," he laughs.

We finish our tea, taking the decision to allow ourselves a little time to absorb the cancer diagnosis before telling the girls about it at the end of the week.

Friday comes all too quickly. Dairy Milk has explained about his illness to his eldest daughter and her mum. We are telling the girls after school today but have decided to tell them only what they need to know. No what ifs and maybes. I've made the school aware so that they are prepared that the girls might want to talk to someone if they are upset.

We take the girls to Dairy Milk's flat and we sit together around the coffee table. I explain as simply as possible what the doctor told us and tell them gently. "We don't want you to be scared. Your dad is getting the best treatment and the doctors are really looking after him."

The girls sob and it breaks our hearts all over again. As we console them, Dairy Milk tries to reassure them. "The doctors know what they are doing, girls. Honestly. They do have to give me some medicine, right into my bladder, but that will make sure that anything left over from the tumours will be gone too. Nothing to worry about."

"That's right," I say. "And we can all help by looking after Dad when he is home from the hospital each week after each treatment."

We take control of our tears, changing the subject to dinner, and I cheer the girls up with a promise of a special treat for pudding.

Six long weeks pass and Dairy Milk has had his second biopsy. Not a day has gone by that we haven't been worried to our cores that the cancer will still show up and today we are at the hospital for the results.

The consultant joyfully tells us that the results are good. The tumours are gone. He says we can't be complacent though. Dairy Milk is still at high risk of them returning and he must continue to be checked every six months for the next few years. He reminds us that if the tumours do return, whether that's in six months or six years, he would have no choice but to recommend removing the bladder.

We leave the hospital feeling relieved, with a little worry nagging at the back of our minds. But we need to be positive. We tentatively go back to our lives with a fresh outlook on life.

I return to the house and put the kettle on. With the drama behind us I realise how quiet my phone is. Before the water boils, I find myself downloading Tinder again. Life is worth living and we need to make the most of it.

Green and Black's:
What's Wrong with Me?

So back to Tinder I do go, ee ay, ee ay, oh… Swiping, swiping. No, no, and no. Argh, a trillion no's! OK maybe a few yeses. I'm trying to not be overly picky, but I like what I like. As does everyone. I get a couple of matches, but after messaging back and forth a few times it's clear we don't have much in common. Un-match. Next.

Oh, what's this? I've matched. This is exciting. He's really good looking! I'd hoped he would match with me. Hang on, it's gone! Where did the match go? Oh my god! Did he instantly un-match me? Wow. Harsh! Jeez at least play the game first. Chat, then ghost. I laugh to myself, knowing that's what so many online daters do, me included. It's a nicer way. More polite.

Hmm, maybe I should pick some new pictures? No, no, no. My pictures are up to date and I just have to accept that I'm not that guy's type. It's harsh, but accidental matches happen to us all. He changed his mind. Ah well, Kate.

Nope, no denying it, that was just mortifying! He saw me and 'unmatched'. I keep on swiping to restore my self-esteem with a nice match.

It's not long before I match with another handsome man. *Whoop whoop to me. This is awesome.* I had thought I might be punching above my weight with this match. I'm giggling to myself with excitement. Then a horrid thought fills my mind. *I hope he didn't accidentally swipe me too? Oh my god, please not again!*

Nope. He sends me a message to say hello and we get chatting away. *Yay!*

So many boxes are being ticked. Age forty-two, older, tick. Two sons under seven. Similar age to my younger ones. Another tick. Personal trainer and loves food. Really cares about the ingredients and where they are sourced. Big ticks right now. I share this passion. If this yummy man ends up in my phone book there is only one name that will be good enough for him. Green and Black's. It's not a type of bar I'd normally pick up, but as I'm trying to grow and mature then I must learn to appreciate this grown-up chocolate bar. I mean, it's ethically guilt-free and sweet at the same time.

This man definitely works out too. *Mmmm, hot as! Just look at those arms. Kate, you need to meet this one.* I have a few rules now.

1. I have to meet them within the first two weeks, or I delete. Falling in love with my phone will never be allowed to happen again.
2. At least three (ideally four) dates, and they should be spread over a few weeks, before anyone gets naked. Although I do think it's important to know if you are compatible in bed. I don't want to rush into bed just because there is major chemistry. But I don't want to end up friend-zoning by waiting too long either. And I definitely don't want to fall for someone and then after the wait find that the sex is terrible again. That was bloody rubbish. *Oh jeez, this is such a minefield!*

I'm truly enjoying this process though. A whole week of texting and getting to know one another, and now a date is set for Friday. The two-week deadline has been met. *Whoop whoop. Mini wave to us.*

This man is worth impressing and seeing as we're off to the theatre to watch a play I'm making a real effort. I've done my hair in a curly up-do. I'm even wearing a deep red lipstick, classic style. This is a new one for me. I don't have very full lips and I'm nervous to draw attention to that. I'm a lip balm girl normally. But why not go for the lippy? It's a date night at the theatre after all.

As I arrive at the theatre, I check my make up in my little compact mirror. *Shit! Thank God I looked! It's on my teeth! Red lipstick on my goddamn teeth! I'm bloody useless at this stuff!* I wipe it off my teeth discreetly and touch up on my lips once more. *Damn, now I am feeling self-conscious.*

My phone buzzes and the distraction from my anxious thoughts is welcome. He has texted.

> Kate, I'm outside the tube station. I can't see you. x

> Oops, sorry. Didn't realise you were meeting me there. I walked round to the theatre. xx

> OK I'll walk round now x

Oh my god. I always hate this bit. Butterflies are building and my belly flips over and over. I'm glad I had the glass of rosé on the train with the crisps.

I can see him. He catches my eye, as he walks up to me. "Kate? Oh wow, you look absolutely gorgeous. Even better than your pictures!"

Shit, I hope not too different from my pictures! Maybe he was just being polite. He is so gorgeous. Yummy. I thank him and return his compliment. He leans in to hug me and kiss my cheek and I smell his cool sharp cologne. I do like a man who smells good.

We go into the theatre and settle into our seats. This is a good start. We have great seats. At the interval I buy a bottle of red wine to say thank you. Back in our seats, he takes my hand in his, his arm and shoulder are up close and skimming mine. I like this moment. I feel really comfortable with him. Everything about this man screams gentleman. His whole demeanour is kind, strong, dignified. Yep, I absolutely and most definitely like this man.

After the show we go to the bar around the corner from the theatre. I need to get the ten after midnight train home so I can't stay for long and we're both a little tipsy anyway, so we agree to have just the one. I'm having so much fun though and would have stayed longer if I weren't getting the last train home.

Oh my. He really surprises me when we leave the bar. He is riding the Tube with me so he can walk me to the train. *How nice is this man? A true gent.* Then at the station he literally sweeps me off my feet. As we chat away about the show, he scoops me into his arms and dances with me. "I just have to dance with you. Right in this moment."

I laugh. "But there is no music?"

"So?"

Oh jeez, this is actually the most romantic moment of my entire life! So many people care so much what others may think of them, including me normally. This man is so confident. I lose myself in the moment. Green and Black's is the most wonderful man. I just feel so lucky to have matched with him and so happy to be sharing this moment with him. I hope we will share many more. What a truly romantic first date, with a real gentleman.

As I settle in my seat on the train home, I realise that I haven't stopped smiling. What an enjoyable evening.

Over the next few weeks, we go for dates at bars and restaurants. We're taking things slowly and I love getting to know him. But tonight, I'm going to his place. He wants to cook dinner for us. I can't wait. As I stand at his door, I think about this wonderful, beautiful, intelligent, kind, romantic man. And then the door opens. Jeez, he's wearing ripped loose jeans and a tightish t-shirt. His feet are bare and he smells, as always, of fresh washing and gorgeous cologne. *Fuck me, he is hot!*

Wow, his home is perfect too! It's clean and decorated well. It's homely. I feel comfortable here and can really see me and this man spending many an hour here.

Green and Black's invites me through to the kitchen after giving me a little tour of his three-bed, two-storey, new build property. A real family home. He has his boys quite a bit and I can see he absolutely dotes on them. There are pictures everywhere and it's so nice to see.

Dinner smells amazing. "What are we having?" I ask.

"I thought I would make a vegetable curry. You like spicy hot food, yeah? I'm sure you said you do."

"Oh, yes. Absolutely. You get extra points for remembering and putting thought into dinner Mister."

He takes two glasses and pours the bottle of wine I brought with me. We had already had the conversation that I would more than likely be staying so I could have a few drinks and not worry about driving back. He is just so thoughtful. He has brought me things for the morning that he wouldn't normally have in: some English breakfast tea and cow's milk. "Aw, you are so cute," I say and give him a kiss.

Then he surprises me again by handing me an organic Easter egg. "What's this for? It's not Easter for another couple of weeks," I say.

"I saw it and thought of you. You might not want to date me in a few weeks, so while we are dating, well, I wanted you to have it."

Oh wow, I actually cannot cope. This man is the sweetest man I have ever met. Never have I met a man so thoughtful. I am never going to want this to end.

"That is so kind and thoughtful. Don't be so pessimistic though!" We laugh about his cuteness and kiss against the side in the kitchen whilst the curry bubbles away.

Dinner was fantastic. This man can cook. We have a delicious dessert too, then finish the bottle of wine before going up to bed. We both freshen up in his en-suite and I feel like we've been together for a really long time. We're so comfortable in each other's company. I didn't bring PJs, only underwear, so this man needs to get his sexy on before I'm too uncomfortable to get undressed. I think I might have to take the lead a little here, because he is just climbing into bed. *Fuck.* I don't normally need to take the lead. I'm not too sure I know how to if he hasn't even given me the come to bed eyes.

OK, well, I don't have PJs, so it's underwear or nothing. Here goes. The lights are still on, so I remove my dress and climb straight into bed as quickly as I have ever moved in my life. *Brave moment Kate, well done,* I think to myself with a little grin on my face. OK, I'm in the bed, quilt over me, feeling better already. He turns his bedside lamp off, then rolls over to face me. He leans in to kiss me, thank God. With the kiss, I am starting to relax again. He is very boob happy and focuses all his attention on my breasts with his hands. We are both a bit awkward and I'm puzzled as to why. We had great chemistry in the kitchen. Before I can really get out of my head and relax into things, it's over and we are cuddling together to go to sleep.

It wasn't awful, but jeez, was that it? I tell myself we were both nervous. I'm sure that in the morning, we will both be much better. I hope so. If not, I will need to up my game and bring some moves to the bed myself, but I don't think I have too many. I'm so used to the man taking the lead. I may have to Google some moves. But for now, I'm all cuddled into his embrace. And actually, it is really nice.

I awake in the morning, not to *that* morning stir and sexy fondling, but to a cup of tea and a bowl of fresh cut fruit. Strawberries, melon, grapes, banana, you name it. What a wonderfully new way to wake up to the man I'm dating. He kisses me lightly. "I hope you slept well," he says.

"Are you joking? Your bed is so comfy! I slept great and now you wake me up to this? You are spoiling me. Thank you so much."

"I knew you were leaving early to get home for work and didn't want you to rush out without breakfast and tea."

Wowzers. This one is most definitely husband material. Such a gentleman!

So that I can see Green and Black's more regularly, I start finishing up work a little earlier one evening a week. He can drive, but he doesn't have a car yet. He says he's planning on getting one though as it will be handy for picking his sons up. When he does have a car, he will come and stay at mine occasionally too. It makes me so happy that he will come down to mine. I've been raving to The Nine and Adira, in fact anyone who will listen, about how amazing this man is. I honestly cannot believe my luck. We have the best nights together, whether we go out for dinner, or spend nights in, cooking together. Always flirting, kissing. And when we are out, he always takes my hand. So romantic.

There's just one problem. I miss orgasms. I am so sexually frustrated. *Urgh, I am so disappointed with myself right now, but bloody hell, am I really wrong to feel this way?* I am really trying in the bedroom, but he just isn't into it like me. I know the chemistry is there and that we are definitely attracted to each other, but it's just not happening in bed. So, I have decided that tonight, when we go to bed, I am going to take my time. I have my sexy underwear on and am going to explore his extremely hot body.

I start by kissing his mouth, his neck, his chest, his stomach. I run my tongue lightly on his skin and lightly bite him. I take the lead and show him how I like things done. I keep on heading down south and remove his tightly fitted black boxers. I use my hand first. Warming him up and making sure he is fully hard. I take him in my mouth. He is clearly enjoying himself. I work my magic but want to hold back to make sure I still get my fun too. Teasing him a little, showing him that I enjoy him, that I want him. Then before I know it, he cums. In. My. Mouth. Without warning. *Oh my god! What about me? My god, the boy needs to make me cum!*

After we clean up a little and lay back in bed, I start wishing that he will at least start using his fingers on me, but no. Even that is apparently too much effort. Now the boy is cuddled into me and falling asleep. *Are you kidding me? What the...?* I sigh, quietly to myself and try to sleep through my sexual frustration. He, on the other hand, falls straight to sleep and is breathing heavily in my ear.

The next morning, I awake to one of his beautiful breakfasts and tea. All I can think of is Lily Allen's song 'Not Fair'. I can't help but chuckle.

"What's so funny, my beautiful?"

Well, what can I say here? You're selfishly shit in bed, but your breakfast is amazing? I'll leave breakfast and take the orgasm please? No, no, I can't say that! Look at his little face, so cute and wanting to make me happy. I would crush his ego! And his heart!

Instead, I say, "Ah, nothing. You are just so cute, that's all. Such a sweetheart." Then I lean forward and kiss him because he really truly is.

On the way home that morning I put the Lily Allen song on the stereo and cannot stop laughing when I listen to it. The song is interrupted with a call from my brother. I can't stop myself blurting out to Anthony all the bedroom problems.

"I think the problem is that he doesn't explore my body. His fingers try, I guess, but they don't know where they are going, and his mouth does not venture past my breasts. He definitely couldn't pick my vagina out of a line up. *Urghhhhhhhh!* I am so frustrated. My rabbit is being used far more than it should be at this point of time in our relationship. The man's gotta go down!"

"Jeez Kate! I'm your brother. Do I need to know this?" We both burst out laughing.

"Well, yes, you do. You called me, so get over it and tell me what to do!"

"You're going to have to bite the bullet here. Just ask him. Be straight."

I have a long and honest think about it all. I don't want to walk away from someone who is romantic, thoughtful, kind, gorgeous, a great dad, a true family man, ambitious, intelligent, emotionally stable. *Fuck no. No, no and definitely no.* I am not walking away. I'm sure he will be up for more bedroom fun if I talk to him. Who doesn't like a little bit of spicing up in the bedroom? I will act in a mature, respectful way and talk to him about this delicate issue. At some point. Maybe not face to face. God, I feel like a teenager right now.

Green and Black's is away with work. The last time he was away he brought me back a liqueur in a little love heart bottle. Just so scrummy. This time though, I'm slightly confused as I have just received a picture of his lunch. It's a dead baby cow.

> Erm, OK then. Was that meant for me?

> Hahaha, I wanted to see if you would have something to say. Vegetarians like to preach and you do like a good debate. I wondered if you'd take the bait LOL xx

> Well, yeah I have a lot to say but we can have that debate when you're back. xx

I do really enjoy our debates. Even if initially we both agree, we like to take opposing sides to really talk matters through. That makes it way more fun. But veal is most certainly not my food of choice. Unfortunately, jokes are lost on me when they involve dead baby animals on a plate. It's his only misjudged moment so far though, so I decide to let it go. I mean, if I want to start self-destructing then I have plenty other things to work with.

I'm not silly. I know we aren't a perfect match. We don't belly laugh together and we don't watch the same things on TV. Plus our work hours are totally incompatible. He works the early shifts at the gym and is always home by five o'clock. I work long days and I feel bad that we have to head out later than I think he would like to, especially as I can only have one early finish a week. When I head up on the second evening of the week, I feel terrible that he is waiting up later for me. He says he doesn't mind though.

What he does mind is that I like to pay half when we are out on a date. I've explained over and over that it's just the way I am. I don't like people paying for me. I love to treat others but feel so uncomfortable when someone treats me. *Note to self, must work on that.* One day when I'm a little more settled in I might let him treat me.

OK, I'm going to use this time while he is away to try and bring up our bedtime fun issues, plus I am desperately trying to move on from the lunch plate disaster. I decide to have a little flirt with him first. I steer the conversation towards the hotel room, the shower, him in the shower, telling him just how hot it would be to be with him in the shower. Then I just can't help myself sending a direct text about our south situation.

> So, I have noticed that you don't go downstairs. With me.

I don't understand what you mean?

Oh damn, maybe not so straight to the point. Be clear Kate.

> Well, I go down on you, happily. I enjoy it, but you don't go down on me.

What are you talking about, Kate. I'm lost 😆 x

Are you kidding me? Is he playing dumb? Green and Black's why are you making me break out the adult words?

> Oral sex! You don't participate. Why?

Oh, well. I've never even thought of it. I've never done it. I wouldn't even know where to start.

Oh my fucking god. My eyes are so big I think they might pop out of my head. What do I say to that? If he has made it to forty-two without participating, then I am pretty sure he isn't going to start now. *Oh fuck!* I am used to men who love this. This is obviously why he has absolutely no idea where my clitoris is. A life with no clitoral orgasms?

Oh wow. Surely I can get past this? Come on Kate, it's just sex. Maybe we can work on other things. Scrabble and gardening maybe?

It was so good to be in a growing serious adult relationship, with someone who shared the same morals as me. We could have a real in-depth conversation about things, and it wasn't just all about the sex. *Oh, who the fuck am I kidding? No amount of good food or romantic gestures can suppress my need for an orgasm! He doesn't even get me there through sex. I might as well date Lily if it's going to be an orgasmless relationship. Over and out.*

Green and Black's really was a gentlemanly and ethical treat. One that you should marry, but unfortunately, just not indulgent enough.

Fruit and Nut: I'll Be The Best

"So Green and Black's? What was that about? Still sticking to the posh bars?" Neil is asking me about my latest chocolate fads.

It's just after quarter past six and Dairy Milk will be at my cottage any minute with the girls. I've been held up and I needed to dash into the village shop for a few essentials.

"Well, no. That was a short-lived phase, but as you keep clocking the amount and type of chocolate I purchase here, I'm having to think outside the box now," I joke as I place my milk, bread, apples and of course chocolate onto the counter. "Anyway, how on earth can you remember what chocolate preferences I have? Do I need to rally up more locals to push the sales up?"

I smirk and then I think, *Sod it*, and run back to the chocolate shelf for two more bars and place them on the counter with the rest of my shopping. "I may as well stock up for my mum stash at home. And as you are so interested, this is my favourite bar, the best I have ever tasted by a long stretch. Fruit and Nut. Judge me all you like for my chocolate obsession, but I need the dairy and the sugar with all the fruit and the nuts added in. Yes, it's a sharing bar, and no, I doubt very much I'll be sharing it with anyone."

Neil chuckles. "I just think that it's sweet you have these different preferences, that you like to try new bars. Sometimes you seem to take a while in choosing, really thinking about things. I like to guess which one you might choose next."

"Creepy and sweet. Bless you, Neil. Yep, that is it. I will rally up the villagers to get you more business because you definitely have too much time on your hands." I grab my things together as he pretends to be offended.

"See you next time, but these bars need to last me, or I will be huge and Weight Watchers will take back my Gold Member card for being reckless. That isn't a thing, by the way. They love me. I'm a lifer there. Mainly because I over-indulge on chocolate and have to keep returning to meetings. Anyway, have a good evening."

Having talked about my weight, I'm horribly conscious that Neil might be checking my figure out as I back out of the shop and I momentarily regret buying the sharing bar. Momentarily.

Halfway through my chocolate bar, a cup of tea resting on the arm of the sofa, I'm back on Tinder. Swipe left, left, left, left. No, no, no, no.

Adira told me to get back out there, date loads of men to find a good one. The only problem with that is that I feel like I'm cheating on all these guys. Not that I am, but I feel weird when I'm on a date if my phone pings with a message from someone else.

I have matched with a new guy who's not my usual type. He seems quite a pretty boy, and he looks different in every picture on his profile. But I like him in all of them. I normally like skinny guys, slim guys, but he seems bigger built. It's time to find out some information. Nothing is on his profile, other than his age, which is the same as me, thirty-three. I need to start question and answer time. This can be fun... or it can be extremely dull and feel like you are interviewing someone for the position of boyfriend, finding out if the individual suits the role of long-term love or whether a different role may be more suitable, like occasional flirty text guy, two date max man, or fuck buddy.

Oh. He has just messaged me. This is good. I much prefer it if they message first.

> Well, hello Kate, how are you doing?

> Hi ya, I'm good thank you... Glad we matched x

> I'm very glad we matched too. You look very much like my type, you have a lovely smile... What are you up to today? x

I'm just working today. What do you do?

Oh and where do you live?

I run a building firm, lovely in the summer, not so great in the winter! How about you?

I live in Margate but I'm working in Deal ATM.

I live in a village just outside of Ashford.

I bet it's bloody freezing

I'm a hairdresser and I truly love my job.

Have you got any kiddies?

Oh that's cool. That's how it should be. Good for you.

It's the wind it cuts right through you but never mind I'm nearly done for the day.

I have two little monsters. I like to be hands on with my boys.

Haha I only have one more than you. A house full of crazy little ladies. I love it. Two boys, cute! How long you been single?

Hahahaha! Yeah but I know how much of a difference 1 makes. Going from 1 to 2 was hard enough lol!!...

Ahh that's lovely though. My boys are little legends even though they do get away with murder!! 😆

Only about 3 months, I'm pretty new to all this malarkey, how about you? x

Hahaha yeah it is crazy but I'm used to it all now. Although very strange having a nearly teen. I can just imagine my little cottage then. Three, full on teenage girls is gonna be testing. Think it'll be a lot harder than little ones 😆

Aaaahhhhh the world of online dating... jeez your gonna come across some very odd ones 😆

Yeah I can imagine!

Are you one of the odd ones??

So how does it work with you coming out to play?

Hahaha yeah I'm definitely one of the odd ones 😁

Well we have to find out a few things about each other first.

See this is where it differs from the old days because back then you asked for their number and then met up for a date and found out all about them then! These days people want to know your life story before they even think about meeting you.

Where's the excitement of the first date if I tell you everything now?

Do you not like a bit of excitement? Do you not like a bit of mystery? x

So in summary here is what I know about you…

You are a short, very attractive female hairdresser, with a lovely smile, who has three little girls, is a bit odd and lives near Ashford!

How am I doing? 😁

Wow, this guy likes to text! I think to myself.

Yep that's me!

You are sooo right but finding out about people is good or you just end up meeting so many people that maybe, if you had text a bit more, well, you wouldn't have met them.

You little newbie you, changing all the rules...

So you are a dad of two boys. Newish to single life, work in the building trade. You like to think outside of the box. In fact, I'm guessing you don't like boxes at all 😄 x

Hahaha!... well look at little miss antisocial here, worried she might get taken out for a date and not enjoy herself!

Lol...I'm a bit different. I see it as an experience good or bad, what have you got to lose?

😄 you are very very right. I certainly do not fit into any 'box' and me and rules don't really get along lol!

I like you very much already!

I realise a smile is filling my face. I really do like this guy's manner.

See. What did I tell you?

We already both know
we will have a great time!

I can feel the chemistry
through the phone.

Lol OK Mr, when is this date then?

Now we are talking!!

I give him my number and suggest we arrange something via text.

Jeez so much for getting to know each other
first. The magical digits have been revealed!!

Lol I don't think I have ever
given my number out so quickly!

But I bet you have a big smile on your
face right now though, don't you?

Yep! Xxx

This is gonna be fun, I promise xx

We end up chatting for nearly two weeks before we are eventually able to set a date. He is the funniest man I've spoken to yet. He totally gets my sense of humour. I am smiling all the time at the moment. I love waking up to 'hello you' messages. I cannot wait to meet this guy.

The only thing that concerns me is that he has only been out of a fifteen-year relationship for three months. It doesn't bode well for commitment. It's possible I have met him at the wrong time for this to become more than either a couple of dates or fuck buddy. *Urgh… right.* I won't know until I meet him and that is happening tomorrow night. So, this evening I'm going to make the most of going out in London with Adira to dance the night away.

Oh man! I don't know why I drink. A few, well, five double vodkas and I have a headache and a dry mouth. Water, I need water. Time? Just turned half nine. *Nice.* It's strange waking up on a Sunday and not having the girls. They're staying for the whole weekend with their dad. *Oooh, I'm going to make a cup of tea and marmite crumpets.* I like my crumpets over done so they are more crunchy than soft. I enjoy them with a big glass of water then climb back into bed for a couple more hours. I feel like a teenage version of myself today. It's bliss.

Morning you. x

Looking forward to seeing you later. The pub is a casual one so no arriving in your night out attire with four inch heels on cos you might seem over dressed and I know you women worry about these things 😂

Hello you. x

Thanks for the heads up. I'm actually a little hungover so I'm happy to wear a casual outfit and flats. PJs and slippers work, right?! Hahahaha

Thanks for making the effort babe, means a lot hahahaha!...

> Hahaha, you're welcome babe! x

We meet in Deal. A nice little pub, roughly half-way between our houses. I'm excited, but I'm pretty sure this guy isn't boyfriend material. Not when he is so newly single. I have properly dressed down. There is just no point in trying to impress this man too much as I doubt it'll be more than a couple of dates at the most.

I arrive in the car park ten minutes late. That's pretty good for me to be honest. I'm always late. I can see him sitting in his blue van. He's on his phone. He looks up as I'm walking past and gets out to greet me. *Oh, he smells so good.* He actually smells like nice washing powder and cologne. He is back living at his mum's house so I'm guessing she might have a lot to do with that.

We walk into the bar and get a couple of drinks then find a small table, with comfy seats, sit down and get chatting. The conversation flows really easily. I know I'm a chatty person, but this guy doesn't stop talking either. We have so much to talk about.

He is really open about his life, just as I am. I learn so much about him. He lives with his mum and his brother who's ten years younger than him. He doesn't know his biological father but doesn't really want to. He doesn't have any respect for a man who left his mum at a young age, leaving her raising him alone. He would like to know where he comes from though, what his heritage is, for his boys as much as for himself. He does know his father's name and thought once that he might have found him using Facebook but didn't want to message him.

Him and his ex may have only been broken up for three months, but they have broken up before. They have also got back together many times. *Ding ding ding. Alarm bells are ringing!*

We are both driving so we have a couple of soft drinks while we continue our evening. The time has just flown by. I really enjoy his company. He's a real man's man. He's opinionated, which I love because it means I can have debates with him. Before we know it, the barman tells us they are closing shortly. We hadn't realised the time. Outside the pub, we hug goodbye then we kiss. *Wow! This boy can kiss.* Just the right amount of lips, tongue and gentleness, but an embrace that builds in strength. I want to do that again and we do. *Oh gosh, I could kiss him for hours. Wow.* I don't want to leave, but I have to. We say goodbye and head to our cars alone.

Wow! What a great night. Thank you. I could have kissed all night, but not on a first date xxx

Well, I don't like first date rules.

If you had wanted to break them I would have been following you home and showing you a very good time indeed. Just so as you know.

I had such a great evening, truly. I really enjoyed getting to know you.

As it wouldn't be appropriate to come over to your mum's house, would you like to come to mine next time? That way we can have more than one alcoholic drink and there won't be a curfew to leave.

Are you inviting me to your home, for wine and no curfew? Erm, sorry it's all a bit quick for me.

Hahahaha only joking. Yes, definitely. It'll be fun.

Oh you bloody panicked me then!!! Glad to read it. Tuesday?

That was a bit keen, wasn't it?! Damn, sorry. It's just that kiss. That kiss has made me want so many more kisses.

Oh believe me, there will be so many more kisses.

Tuesday works for me. I'll have to head over after football though so won't get to you until 9pm

That is perfect cos I'm working until 8.30 on Tuesday.

Great, Tuesday it is. Looking forward to it.

OK babe, must sleep. Work first thing. Had a great night. xx

Yeah me too. Night babe x

On the drive home I start thinking about what I could call this guy. I haven't saved him into my phonebook so it's just digits at the moment. I hadn't given him a name as I wasn't too sure what to think with him being so newly single. But after that date, the laughter, the chat, the flirting, the bloody amazing kissing... *Oh God, the kissing. Oh, and that he is even better looking in person* ... I have to go all out and name him Fruit and Nut. Let's just hope he lives up to the name because this is great chocolate taste with the nuts and fruit combined. What is there not to like?

I never date at my home. It's my refuge. I don't want men who I am getting to know coming into my home until I know they are who I think they are. Yorkie stayed once, but I had known him a year by then and we were just friends. But this is different. Fruit and Nut is different.

Non-stop messaging and I love it. *Damn.* I am liking it all a bit too much. I ask myself if I can I keep this as just fun because he is newly single. This might be a problem. I mean, I did go and fall in love with my phone when Wonka was on the scene. How will I not fall in love with this dude?

OK. Well, just think about it all later, Kate, because this manly builder and footballer is coming over in a few hours. Keep your head focused on work, rather than worrying if this man might break your heart one day. Right now, you need to be finishing your lady's colour so you can run home and get ready.

Fruit and Nut is running half an hour late, which is great because I am running fifteen minutes behind too. Time for a quick bath with my favourite body wash and moisturisers. I'm not wearing sexy pants tonight though, just nice ones. I don't want it to look like I am expecting sex, but at least if it does get down to pants-level, I haven't got my supermarket specials on.

I'm not even nervous tonight. I just can't wait to have him here. He arrives and I open the door and show him through into the lounge, closing the door behind him. I apologise for my cottage being so tiny. I don't know why. I do really love my tiny home. It's just right for me and my girls, a haven, perfect for this time in my life. I adore the fire too. I could stare at it for hours, losing myself in the flames. It's mesmerising.

He asks if it's OK to have a quick shower because he has come straight from football. *Yeah, it is! I just wish I was taking it with you! Mmmmmmm, he is yummy,* I think to myself. I show him where the bathroom is and laugh while I explain how to use my extraordinarily naff shower that has absolutely no water pressure. I leave him with a fresh towel, warm from the airing cupboard.

I head downstairs and get him a fruit cider from the fridge. I pour myself a glass of red wine and wait for him in the lounge. I smile to myself. I love the fact he just arrived all sweaty, wanting to have a shower. It feels so familiar. I love how relaxed he makes me feel and can't wait to get to know him better.

Ten minutes later Fruit and Nut is downstairs in my lounge. He has changed into grey trackie bottoms and a white t-shirt. He seems so chilled and relaxed. We watch YouTube on the television, allowing the music videos to play through. He questions my taste, all pop and nineties, and we laugh. We chat away for a couple of hours about life events, funny growing up stories, tales about parenthood. The conversation flows just like it did on our first date. *Ah, this guy!*

As we relax more, we begin to open up about some of the things that had really let us down in life. We both have suffered the gutting feeling of not being able to live our dreams. A few years ago, he had played semi-professional football and was on course for becoming professional, but it all fell through and his dreams were shattered.

I feel so bad for him. The same had happened to me, but with a singing career.

"I used to be part of a teeny bopper band. It was fun, but the industry was really superficial. I had to be no bigger than a size six to be accepted. It was such a struggle for me."

I explain to him that it wasn't all about the voice back then. Because I had polycystic ovaries I struggled to keep weight off and it meant I was a size fourteen to sixteen.

"For the industry, that was too big. I was always dieting and never getting anywhere. All I wanted to do was sing but the weight thing got me down so much I quit the band. I wanted to be happy again. A year later I'd joined a slimming club and lost three and a half stone. But I was happy. I had done it for me, not for the band, or for an expected image."

I show him pictures of bigger Kate and he can't believe it was me. He's pleased for me that I was able to make myself happy again. The next thing I know we are kissing. That amazing kiss that he does so damn well. He kisses my neck. *Oh man! That is my spot. Yep, I'm a happy woman now.* He moves back to my mouth and his hands move down to my jeans. He undoes the button and pulls them down. I finish taking them off.

"Shall we go downstairs to my bedroom?"

He laughs. "Oh, should I go into a basement with a near stranger? Should I be scared?"

"It'll be fine, I won't keep you prisoner!"

"You'll want to when I've had my way with you."

We start kissing again at the bottom of my bedroom stairs. He pulls me in tighter, one hand placed around my neck, lost in my curly hair. Pulling at each other's clothes we slowly get naked apart from my sexy-ish, navy French knickers, which he leaves on. He lays me back on to my bed. Kissing my breasts, lightly brushing his lips across my hard nipples. Teasing, sensual. Moving down, he kisses my belly, his hand is between my legs, pushing and rubbing lightly on top of my knickers. Turning me on, yet still not taking them off. He starts kissing me there, making me want him so badly, desperate for him to take my knickers off, willing him to. After a few more seconds, he does. He kisses my place, using his fingers to make me climax. *Wow. That was intense.*

Even though I have climaxed he goes for it again and again. *OMG, OMG, OMG! This man is amazing at this.* He turns me over and kisses my bum cheek. Moving up, he kisses my hip, the curve in my waist, my back, my neck, all the while his fingers are still working away. He kisses my neck and bites it lightly moving up towards my ear. He removes his fingers and replaces them with what I have so badly wanted. *Fuck. This is so good.* He makes me climax over and over again, then flips me onto my back and uses his fingers, this time deeper inside of me and pressing up on to my G spot.

I still myself, knowing what he is waiting to do. "Oh my god, you know the trick. How do you *know* this trick?"

"Doesn't everyone?" He says it softly, with that cocky look in his eyes, knowing full well that not everyone knows this platinum trick. A trick which I absolutely believe everyone should learn because it is out of this world.

We continue to have amazing sex, absolutely amazing sex.

Afterwards we lay in my bed, talking softly about what has just happened between us. We're touching each other gently with our hands, legs entwined, facing each other.

He says, "I told you I would be good. I bet I'm in the top two."

To his shock, I reply, "Third. The other two in this little competition had all the moves, but they also had the emotion. When you combine the two, it's absolutely mind blowing my dear."

He tells me to stop talking because he's ready to go again. *What? How is he ready to go again? It has only been fifteen minutes since our last hour-long session. Wowzers. Yep, I can see, he is definitely ready to go again. Jackpot!*

We spend the next couple of months texting or calling every day, and meeting on Thursday nights. Either Fruit and Nut drives to me or we get a hotel room near his. The sex never misses the spot and I'm pleased we are seeing each other regularly. As we move towards the summer, I ask him where he thinks this is all going.

"We're having fun aren't we? Do we need commitment yet? Why not see how it's going by the end of July? See if we want more then?"

I agree. After all, with him being so newly single after such a long relationship, I didn't think we would last as long as we have, so I'm happy to see how things progress by the summer. I told myself at the start to just enjoy this for what it was. Fun. I had never been able to do this before, so this was a first for me. It's time for me to find myself and enjoy being free. He sends me naughty texts throughout the day and I send them back. Flirting all the time. It's great. It's fun and it makes me feel alive.

Fruit and Nut is coming over later, after I have been out for an evening with the girls. I have just realised that he has never seen me dressed up for a night out. How is that even possible? In fact, we haven't been out for dinner or weekend drinks yet. That's weird, isn't it? We only see each other on Thursdays after work and football. Disheartened, it suddenly dawns on that I'm in a fuck buddy situation.

Right Kate, this evening you are going to go all out. Sexy underwear beneath your new black slip, just above knee-length dress. That way, when he arrives at the cottage, you'll be looking good. This is perfect. A night out with the ladies, ending with this very gorgeous man arriving at your home. Whoop whoop, mini wave to me! I make myself chuckle at least.

I really enjoy getting ready for an evening out. I like to have a pre-drinks drink while I'm getting ready. I have learnt over the years that I am such an unbelievable light weight that I can really only have one. I have music on and enjoy taking time doing my makeup, not that I'm a makeup girl. I understand basic makeup, as in the nineties style of basic. I have absolutely no idea about highlighting and contouring and have only heard of them through my eldest daughter.

Just as I'm heading out of the door to the taxi, I receive a text from Fruit and Nut.

> Babe, what time you going to be home?

> I'm just thinking about timings, as I'm meeting up with the lads first.

> About 11? Good? You don't need to rush over. Just when you can.

OK cool. xx

Eeeeeeek. I can't wait for him to see me with this non-casual look.

My friends and I, just four of us, are having dinner and wine at a local bar where everyone knows everyone. A text comes in.

Babe, I don't think I'm gonna make it. The lads want me to stay out and you're out with the girls. They are on my case to have a few drinks with them. We might as well stay where we are tonight and I will try and come over Tuesday instead.

> Yeah makes sense. I understand.

I do not bloody understand at all. Not one little bit. In fact, I am mighty pissed off. I was so excited about seeing him. I really wanted to end my evening with him and he wants to choose beer over having a fun night with me.

Oh, for fuck's sake. This is going to ruin my night, if I let it. Come on Kate. You shouldn't be his booty call anyway! This is just a fuck buddy situation. He owes you nothing. You owe him nothing. You knew it would be hard with him just having become single, so accept it or stop contact with him.

But I don't want to stop contact. I really like him.

And there we have it, ladies and gents. Kate, you have bloody well gone and confirmed you like him. Feelings are occurring. Shit!

Don't be mad babe, I will make it up to you. I promise. xx

Don't be mad? I'm fucking fuming! I feel really let down. I've told the ladies and they agree. He made a shit move, but they remind me that this whole thing was only supposed to be about sex. I understand that, but the trouble is that I'm starting to wish it wasn't.

> I'm not mad. Have a good night.

I get back to my cottage at half eleven. As I take my shoes off there's a knock at the door. *Who could that be? Shit, did I leave something in the taxi?* I open the door and there he is. Fruit and Nut. My heart leaps and I'm beaming. I'm crap. I can't play it cool. I'm just ridiculously happy.

"What are you doing here?"

"Well, you were being a little brat, weren't you?"

I smile even more, if that's even possible and he smiles back. "I told you it was fine in the texts."

"It was clear it wasn't! I know you well enough to know when you're pissed off."

He kisses me and we have another incredible night together. This time I really wish I could just keep him captive in the basement. *Oh crap. I am really falling for this guy.*

We continue with our weekly Thursday nights together until July hits. I know it's time to re-visit the where are we heading conversation, but I'm nervous. I know I need to speak up though as I feel like I'm in limbo.

> Morning you. xx

> It's mid-July. We have been talking and meeting up for a while now. I know you said we can revisit this conversation, so here I am. Revisiting.

Hours. Hours and no reply. *Is he fucking kidding me?* Oh, this is doing my head in. He is the only thing I think about. *If he doesn't reply in the next hour, I'm going to double text him.* This is me. I totally overthink things. And I have no shame in a double text situation.

> Babe, killing me. Can you reply please.

Smooth Kate, really fucking smooth!

> Sorry babe, I'm at work.

> I was going to call you once I have finished, have a proper chat.

Shit. That doesn't sound good at all.

> The thing is, I just don't think I can give you what you need or want, I'm happy right where we are. Having fun. I just haven't been on my own for long enough and with you living an hour away I just don't think it will work out long term. I'm sorry babe. x

Yep, that wasn't the outcome I wanted. *Kate, you knew from the beginning that this was just sex, fuck buddy territory.* I'm rubbish at all this. I went and got attached to amazing sex and the fun banter and the birth mark on his stomach that I like to kiss because it's just so damn cute. I was hoping he might have become attached enough to want to carry it on too, but no.

> Ah, OK babe. I'm gutted but I understand. I didn't think this would turn into more than fun, but I had really hoped it would. I totally understand. You have only been out of a 15 year relationship for a few months. Honestly, I get it. x

> I really am sorry babe. I will miss you, for sure!

Honestly, I wish you all the happiness in the world. You deserve it. You really are such a great guy. I will miss you too xxx

You too babe, I hope you find what you're looking for. xx

My friend Bambi is here. I'm explaining all about Fruit and Nut and the situation I've got into. I go to WhatsApp and look up the messages to show her and his picture is gone. *What the fuck? Why would he block me? I only got the text ending things ten minutes ago?*

I send him a text message instead of WhatsApp.

That's a bit extreme isn't it?

Is it though Kate? I know this plays to your insecurities, but is it actually extreme? You have both decided it was done, that it didn't have legs to go anywhere. Let him go. It's best all round to let him walk away.

Bit extreme to block me, don't you think?

Why? Why do you feel the need to keep it open? Close the fucking door Kate! In fact, he closed the door and now you're banging at it. Now you aren't WhatsApping him, you're hunting him down on texts. What is wrong with you? This isn't playing hard to get, nor is it cool. This is you showing him the crazy lady that you are. Why don't you just send him a picture of you with all the cats or go one step further and get some bunnies to boil. Fucking hell. Let him go!

> Sorry babe. I'm not very good with breaking up and tbh, if I have your number on my phone then I will want to text you and I will definitely text if I have a few drinks. Do you want to keep it open then?

> I'm just thinking we might like to say hi at a later date, further down the line. You might be feeling differently and as neither of us have anyone else in the picture I didn't think keeping numbers would be a problem until then. x

> OK then babe. If you're sure. We can leave it open. x

Head is saying shut the door. Heart is freaking out.

I need to be honest with myself and the issues I know I have. One minute I want a relationship, the next I don't. When I am in one, I build barriers, then when I start to let those barriers down, the man lets me down. And then when they have let me down, I can't just say ta-ta! I need to let them go, close doors. Be done with it.

In all honesty though, he is fucking amazing in bed and perhaps in a month or so, I may be really happy that I still have his number.

It's an emotional battle I need to learn to fight, or I am never going to win.

Tell Me It's Not True

I've been trying to convince Dairy Milk to see the consultant in London. I've been worried about what might happen if the cancer does come back within two years. We need to be prepared for the possibility he may have to have his bladder removed. And we need to know what this might mean in the long term. He has finally agreed, and today we are travelling to Guy's Hospital to meet the main man himself. The top consultant.

As we sit in the waiting room, I reassure Dairy Milk. "It will be OK. We just need to know what the future may hold."

"I am never having my bladder removed Kate. I'm only here for you. This is to put your mind at ease. Not mine."

"I just don't want you to die, my dear," I say with a jokey tone to my voice to keep the mood light.

"Sweetheart, I won't be dying any time soon. Don't worry. They removed it all. It's OK. I'm OK."

We're called through for our appointment and we shake hands with the consultant. He's pleased to meet with us and has been speaking to Dairy Milk's doctors in Kent. When he explains what treatments and operations are available if the cancer is to return, we're stunned.

The first option is to remove the bladder and prostate leaving him with a catheter for the rest of his life.

The second option prevents the need for a catheter. Surgeons will remove the bladder and prostate, as well as part of his bowel too, then use his bowel to build a new bladder plumbed into the kidney and urethra.

The third option, if the cancer has spread further, is the same as option two but instead of connecting his newly made bladder to his kidney and urethra, it will be connected to a tube which will exit his body via the belly button with a valve to release the urine from it.

We sit still, wide eyed, the colour drained from our faces. The consultant asks some questions I don't hear. I'm shocked with the hard reality of the situation. My hearing kicks back in when Dairy Milk speaks about his prostate being removed in all three options. The consultant looks Dairy Milk straight in the eyes and says, "We cannot guarantee that the cancer would not be in the prostate. I could leave it there, but if there are any cancerous cells it could result in your death."

I look at Dairy Milk as I say sternly, "He'll have it removed if the cancer comes back. He has four daughters. This isn't just down to him alone."

Dairy Milk reluctantly agrees. He is totally deflated. He's tried to be upbeat and positive until now, but the reality of the situation has hit home today. The consultant tells us he would like to do his own biopsy, recall the original ones and conduct a thorough check up. He thinks it will help us to think more positively. An appointment will be sent in the post.

As we leave the hospital Dairy Milk says, "I won't be having any of that done Kate. The cancer is gone. They got rid of it. I will take care of myself and it won't come back. OK?"

I hug him. Both of us are trying so hard to hold back tears. "It had better fucking not!"

We return home, shell shocked, but empowered to keep him healthy and to stay strong for our girls.

I have just had a text come through from Guys, telling me I need to go up on Friday.

Friday? As in this Friday?

Yeah.

What is it for?

Just the pre-op stuff for the biopsy I think. Nothing to worry about. They just need to see me to plan it all.

You sure?

Yeah, don't stress!

I am working but I can move people.

No don't worry about all that, you have moved so many appointments already. Honestly stop stressing. This whole thing is just a precaution.

I hate all of this.

Funnily enough, I don't like it all very much either.

Oh it's all about you, isn't it?

Yeah, you know I need all the attention right now, you dick! 😂

Friday comes around quickly. I'm meeting some friends for lunch in between clients. In normal circumstances I'd be watching other mums do their thing, baby watching, laughing with my friends, but today, I'm distant. I've asked Dairy Milk to call me straight after his appointment. He told me not to worry, but I can't help it. I just want it all to be over. I wish there could be no more talk of cancer, but there will be. He will be monitored closely for the rest of his life.

I hardly touch my lunch and I nurse my Diet Coke, trying not to look at my phone every ten seconds. Then it rings. It's Dairy Milk. I take the call outside.

"It's not good Kate. Fuck, I wish you were here right now," his voice cracked. I could hear him starting to crumble.

"What? What the fuck did they say? Shit. Tell me."

"When they recalled the original biopsy they found it was worse than they thought. They were wrong Kate. The Kent lot were fucking wrong. It was already growing out of the bladder wall. It wasn't all contained inside the bladder at all. It's been left to grow for another six months! They want to operate in the next two weeks. If they leave it, I'll be dead in a year."

I hear his voice break and I know he is crying. I can't hold back the tears.

"Fucking hell. I should be there. I knew I should be there. Please just get home. I will meet you off the train, just get home."

I'm numb. Tears fall down my cheeks and then the shaking kicks in. How is this happening? I don't know what to do. I don't know how to help. How do I fix this? Oh God, the girls. How do we tell the girls? I compose myself enough and say goodbye to my friends, apologising that I need to leave earlier than planned.

I sit in my car sobbing. I know I will need to be strong for Dairy Milk. I drive to the station to wait for his train and call our friends and family to explain what is happening. Everyone wants to help and give support, but like me, nobody has any idea how we can.

After speaking to the consultant and gaining more clarity on the situation we asked if the operation could be pushed back by a few days so that we could tell the girls and take them away for a theme park adventure. A little holiday with their dad. The doctor understood it was an important trip to take and agreed to hold back. The severity of this situation had been made perfectly clear to us both.

Dairy Milk told Freya and her mother first. Today we are telling our girls. It is by far the hardest thing we have ever had to do. I struggle to find the words, even though we have it all planned out. My mind is blurry as words flow. I tell them we all need to be strong and look after him. I'm failing entirely. Tears fall as I try to be strong while he takes care of me, placing his hand on my back in a familiar way, reminding me of how close we once were and how close we still are. The girls cry.

"Will Dad die?"

How do I answer that? I can't lie. I had promised I wouldn't lie, but I also promised I would be gentle. I don't even know the answer to this question.

I start to answer but Dairy Milk interrupts. "The doctors are going to operate to take the cancer away. If they can take it all away, I won't die."

Then he says excitedly, "Listen, we are all going to go away for a week. All six of us. We're taking Freya too. We have told the school and we leave next week."

Dairy Milk is trying to lighten the mood. I find the strength to pull myself together and we tell them what we have planned. A week of theme park fun staying in different bed and breakfasts along the way. It will be an adventure we will make the most of because Dad will need to rest to fully recover after the operation.

Our family and even our closest friends had randomly put money into our accounts for our holiday, wanting to make sure the girls have the best time. I hate handouts as it makes me feel inadequate and uncomfortable, but they all told me to shut up and that this wasn't for me anyway. Who was I to deny my kids a good time? They are each entitled to give their god kids, nieces (honorary or otherwise) holiday treats.

We leave Kent for our family trip on a bright morning, all four girls piled in the back of the seven-seater hire car. We're feeling positive and want to have a great time.

First stop is Alton Towers. We have a brilliant first day. As it's term-time the park is really quiet so queues are minimal. We go on ride after ride and love our time together. I film us all on my phone, dating apps set aside for now. My heart is full as I hear my crazy family laugh and joke. We run from ride to ride, laughing and calling at each other in excitement.

"We should come again Mum, shouldn't we?" my eldest cries. Then I see her face drop as she remembers why we're here. It has a ripple effect and the mood sinks a little, but we all agree that once their dad is through the operation we should make a plan for another holiday. We compose ourselves and continue enjoying the theme park. We are here for fun, all together as a family.

After two days at Alton Towers, we're off to Blackpool. We arrive at our accommodation just after ten and settle in for the night. It's a tightly packed space. The two older girls are in the lounge on the sofa bed and the little ones are on a bunk bed in the same room as me and Dairy Milk. We're sharing a double bed. We sit up for a little while as all four children sleep soundly, completely exhausted.

"How you feeling?" I ask him.

"Yeah, I'm fine. The funny thing is, I don't feel ill. I don't look ill. Yet all this shit is going on inside my body."

"It's mad, isn't it. I just thank God every day that we went to see the doctor at Guys."

He drifts off to sleep and I watch him sleeping beautifully next to me. I love this man. A man I am no longer in love with, but a man who is my best friend. I am so glad he made babies with me. I adore our little humans and I really need him to be OK.

What a fabulous couple of days we have had in Blackpool. The Tower, The Ballroom, The Dungeons, The Sea Life Centre, Madame Tussauds. Not forgetting The Pleasure Beach. We've done it all and loved every minute of it. We've eaten our weight in ice creams, doughnuts and sweets too.

"We will be obese by the end of this trip," I call out to them, as they run off to the beach and I tuck into a bag of candy floss.

"Speak for yourself!" Dairy Milk shouts back.

I find myself a spot on the wide steps leading down to the beach and Dairy Milk joins me. We sit here quietly, peacefully, watching the girls play on the sand. I take some photos of them and then I see him. He's staring down at the girls, lost in his thoughts and enjoying the last of the day's sun. I take a picture and I know now that I will cherish this photo for the rest of my life.

Far too soon, it's time to leave. We call the girls back and walk to the car. We clamber in and settle down with blankets, tablets, colouring books and, of course, food. Not to feed hunger, but to ensure a happier, less stressed-out journey as we make our way to our next B&B near Thorpe Park back down south.

After two days of yet more rollercoasters and carousels, it's time to head back to Kent.

We wake up early, pack up the room all six of us squidged into and head across the hall for breakfast. Dairy Milk sits and waits for his full English. He pours himself a tea and I watch as he stirs in his sugar and vigorously knocks his teaspoon on the edge of the mug.

Oh my god. This is what he does, every time, like he is breaking down cement or something. It's a cup of tea and a sachet of sugar. Why does he do that? Oh man, I know what's coming next. He is going to slurp the tea. Wait for it. Yep, there it is. Slurping. I laugh.

"What's so funny?" the girls and Dairy Milk ask.

"You and your noisy tea habits. Why do you do that?" I ask with a chuckle as the kids laugh and agree with me.

These small moments make me content. I will soon be home to the peace of my tiny home (without rattling teacups) and my heart is happy that we had the chance to have the family trip away as friends.

We have been given the date for the operation. There are seven days to countdown.

Dairy Milk has decided he wants to get some friends together at a pub and hang out with them for the evening. I'm nervous though as I don't want him to get too drunk. He needs to be in full health for the next stage of his treatment.

"If you have a drink then please only have lager? No shots. Please," I beg, knowing he takes his time with a long drink and won't get too drunk. Thankfully, he agrees and I relax.

I talk to Lily. She asks me if I would sleep with Dairy Milk. "He should have sex one last time. You're both single."

"Erm, Lily, I'm his ex-wife," I exclaim. "We're friends. It would be weird now. A year ago then, yeah, maybe, but too much has happened. Plus, I'm hanging out with Fruit and Nut! I don't want to be sleeping with my ex-husband!"

"I know, but I just thought, well, maybe you would."

"That ship has sailed. He wouldn't want to do it with me now anyway. We had goodbye sex long ago. I'm sure if he wants to have sex with someone he will. I'm hoping he'll get back with Rhiannon. She's single again and I know they still have feelings for each other."

It's time I were leaving soon. I turn to Rick, one of Dairy Milk's best friends.

"Rick, I'm taking the girls home. Can you look out for him this evening? Please don't let him move onto shots. I need him to be physically strong for the operation so he can have more nights out in the future. And I want him to walk his daughters down the aisle one day, so please keep an eye on him. And let me know if they get it on," I say nodding over at Dairy Milk and Rhiannon chatting away.

"Yeah, OK. I will. Don't stress. I will let you know the goss' tomorrow," he says laughing.

I say my goodbyes and take the girls back to the cottage. The next morning, I receive a text from Rick. Sure enough Dairy Milk and Rhiannon got it on and I'm thankful.

It's the day of the operation. Dairy Milk is quiet, clearly nervous. When he does talk, it's to crack a joke to try to lighten the mood. Laughter is the only thing helping us face this morning and I am petrified it will stop. How will I help him without trying to see the positives, with only worry and fear?

We make our way to the ward. After some initial observations, Dairy Milk changes into a white and blue hospital gown and long red socks. He has kept his dark grey dressing gown with him and is wearing it while we wait. He makes little jokes about how silly he looks. We laugh, our nerves rising. It's still early, only half past eight. The doctor arrives and explains how long the operation is likely to take. They advise me not to sit in the hospital all day saying it would be no good for anyone. They will call me as soon as he is out of theatre and when he is in recovery.

I look at Dairy Milk on the hospital bed and I bend to kiss his head. "I will see you the moment you're awake. I promise."

I watch the porters wheel his bed down the corridor and try to hold it together. Defeated, I can't stop the tears as they roll down my cheeks the moment the doors close behind him.

I have been walking blindly listening to music for the last two hours. I've no idea where I've been. I'm lost in my thoughts about Dairy Milk. Oh, the times we've had together. I remember just how much I loved him once. I used to hate the fact that we were two separate humans, wishing we could become one person. I just wanted to snuggle into him so tightly.

I remember the times when we were trying for our babies and how I would lay upside down, my legs resting up on the wall so I could keep hold of everything he had given to me, wishing for it to turn into a baby. And it worked. Three times. He was an amazing birthing partner. It's the only time he wouldn't make silly jokes. He was just sensible, supportive, calm, loving, encouraging. Yes, I never had a bad word to say about him then.

Oh, how time changed us. In the end we became far more separate humans than we had ever been before. Time was not our friend.

Time. Yes. What is the time? It's just turned one o'clock. The doctors had told us that all being well they will use the second option for surgery, making part of his bowel into a bladder and connecting it to the kidneys and urethra. We are praying so hard for this. No catheter or valve. They expect he will be out by six tonight. If they open him up and it becomes clear they can't use the bowel, that they need to go for the option with the catheter, he will be out a lot sooner. If the cancer has spread and they have to go for the third option with the valve, then it will be more like seven o'clock. *Oh I just wish the time was passing faster.*

I'm staying at Yorkie's apartment whilst I'm in London. I want to be close to the hospital just in case Dairy Milk needs me. He messages me.

> How you doing, shit for brains? Shall we meet for late lunch. I've arranged to get out of work. Don't think you should be on your own.

> Yeah. I'll head over. I've just been walking for a couple hours. Don't really know what else I should do.

> Well, continue you're walking and come over to Piccadilly. I can be done in an hour.

I meet with Yorkie. He is being kind and sweet, trying to keep the mood light. "Fuck me. Depressed much? Come on, shit house, let's get you some food."

I'm so glad to have him with me. I was so focused on being here for Dairy Milk, I didn't think about myself. That I would need someone. I'm so glad Yorkie had thought of me. After eating we walk for a while, just chatting about anything and everything before I say I need to get back to Dairy Milk, so I am there for when he wakes.

I arrive at the hospital just after five and settle down in the waiting room. I text everyone to let them know I'm here and there's nothing to report just yet. My brain is working overtime. As it's turned five, I'm certain they can't have gone for the first option with the catheter. I hope and pray he will be out at six o'clock, the anticipated time for the best surgical option. No catheter, no valve.

I mindlessly watch Netflix on my iPad, waiting for the doctors, looking up to the clock every five minutes. *Oh God, it's six thirty. Where is he?* I decide to ask around. Nothing. All they can tell me is that they haven't heard a thing and that Dairy Milk is still in theatre.

My heart is thumping away. Anxiety rises with every breath I take. He didn't want the belly button valve. *Oh my god, it's spread. I don't know what to do. I need to fix this. I need this not to be true.*

I calm myself and go back to the waiting room. An hour later I am still sitting in the empty waiting room. I've been here alone for the last two and a half hours. I realise I haven't thought this through. I'm on my own. Dairy Milk will be unconscious when they come to speak to me, his estranged wife, but his next of kin. I am not strong enough for this. I just don't know how to be. I stare at the ten empty chairs around me and imagine them filled with our loved ones. I need extra strength here.

As I sit, I pray, like I had been doing intermittently all day. I'm begging we don't lose him. I don't want the girls to live with loss like I did. I can't have them lose their dad. I pray to every god and saint I can think of. I beg for him to be OK. We can live with the valve in the belly button, but we can't live without Dairy Milk. I realise I can't live without Dairy Milk. He is my family, my best friend. I need him to be OK. I beg and plead, hoping desperately that my prayers will be answered.

It's eight thirty. I feel as though I could be sick. I cannot make sense of how good news can follow nearly twelve hours of waiting and still no sign. Rhiannon has been messaging all day and is calling me now. We are both out of our minds with worry and she wishes she could be at the hospital too. I tell her I will call her as soon as I know anything.

Oh my god, I don't want to be on my own to receive the news. Hold it together Kate. I love him unconditionally and I will be strong for him. I can do this. No, I can't do this! I shake my head and look down at my hands, clenched in my lap. I feel like my eight-year-old self about to be told my biggest brother has died. I feel like my world is about to end all over again and I won't be able to stop it. My girls will no longer have their dad and the truth is, I am a rubbish parent without him. They need their dad. I need the doctors to come and tell me now. I can't wait any longer.

Each minute ticks by slower than the last. I watch the clock, focusing on the sound of the ticking.

It's almost nine thirty when the anaesthetist arrives in the doorway. *At last.* He walks towards me and sits on the empty chair nearest to me.

"Oh my god, please tell me he is OK!" I cry.

"Yes, yes, he is OK. He's just coming around from the anaesthetic and you'll be able to see him really soon. The surgeon will come in and explain everything to you shortly, but I just wanted to tell you that he is OK and that he is coming round."

Oh, thank God he is OK. Then I realise I still have absolutely no idea what that means. Before I know it, the surgeon walks in. I look at him expectantly, eyes wide.

"We have been able to give him a new bladder as was the preferred option."

"He wanted that!" I interrupt, crying with joy. "That was what he wanted. And you removed it all? You really did that? Thank you so much, I can't express to you just how grateful I am. It took so long I didn't know what to think."

I can't stop crying tears of joy, of relief, of all the pent-up anxiety and emotion.

The surgeon allows me time to calm down a little then explains to me that it had taken longer because they were able to use a larger section of the bowel which meant more stitches were needed. They were also able to save seventy per cent of the nerves surrounding the prostate, twice as many as they had originally expected to save. They were ecstatic at how well the surgery went.

I hug him and thank him again before he leaves.

I walk towards Dairy Milk. The surgeon had warned me that he would look a bit battered and bruised and will still be disoriented from the anaesthetic. He is exactly that. In fact, he seems to be totally pissed up to the eyeballs.

"There you are! You are so beautiful," he calls out when he sees me. "You really are just so beautiful."

"You're not too bad yourself." I kiss him on his forehead.

"I have an idea. You will love it. I think we should get married," he exclaims.

"We've tried that once haven't we? It was a great idea the first-time round, but it didn't work. I don't think we should do that again, should we?" Kindly. Jokingly.

"Yeah, why not? We can do it again. It was great fun," he laughs, then whispers very loudly, "Shhhhhh! Don't tell anyone but I'm completely off my face. This stuff is great!"

Dairy Milk's face fills with a big grin. "Kate, I got the one I wanted. I got the right one!"

"I know. It's amazing. I am so happy you're OK. And they took it all this time. The cancer is gone." I can't stop the flood of tears. I wipe them away on the sleeve of my cardigan. I used up all my tissues when I was with the surgeon.

"Don't cry. It's good. I got the one I wanted. Did they tell you?" he says again, high as a kite. "Don't cry. You're so beautiful. Do you know that?"

I hold his hand and say, "Ah, I love you so much. Always."

"I love you too. Shall we get married?" he asks again, smiling with this fantastic idea.

Again, I tell him, "We tried that one didn't we. We just said that."

"Ah yeah. Didn't work, did it?" he says, remembering.

"No, it didn't. Friends does though."

"Yeah, that works. I didn't have the belly button one. I got the one I wanted," he repeats.

I quietly shush him and he drifts off to sleep for a while. I send messages to everyone to let them know all is well, then go to talk to the nurse.

"He's a right character, isn't he?" she says. "Really sweet. Hasn't stopped making jokes since he came round."

We chat for a short while in this miraculous place, whilst Dairy Milk sleeps off his anaesthetic and starts his road to recovery. I need to let him rest so decide it's time to leave the hospital and make my way to Yorkie's place. I have his keys and let myself in. I'm exhausted. It's time for bed. I brush my teeth, have a wee, put on my PJs and climb into Yorkie's bed trying not to wake him, but he gives me a huge, sleepy hug. Just what I need. I fall asleep, my mind filled with thoughts of just how lucky Dairy Milk has been and that I am so happy to have a friend right now. Yorkie really is one of my best mates.

I spend the next few days at the hospital. I arrive early in the morning and leave as night falls. Dairy Milk sleeps for most of the day and I watch Netflix on the iPad.

Dairy Milk's strength and humour through this hellish time has astounded me. He has shown such courage and he amazes me every day with how far he pushes himself to recover. I wish he would be a little easier on himself though. He is eating to keep his strength up but is sick after nearly every meal. The doctors are concerned that his bowel hasn't yet woken up too. Every check-up they ask if he has passed wind, but no. Dairy Milk makes light of it though. The jokes are killing me. We're scared he might take off from the bed after a day and a half of nothing.

As I watch a movie on Netflix, I hear Dairy Milk murmur my name. "Kate. Kate?"

"Yes? You OK?"

"No. I need you to look at this drain." He waves me over to the bed.

"Oh God, do I have to?" I pretend to shudder. He says he isn't sure if it is actually working.

"What do you think?" he asks.

"How do I know? I'm not a nurse, you div! I'll call one for you."

I get the nurse to check and sure enough it needs changing. He's all sorted just in time for dinner. Afterwards Dairy Milk asks me to check something else.

"Again?" I roll my eyes at him. "I don't like this part of the job. I'm not into gory stuff!"

"Man up woman! I need you to look at my balls," he demands.

"What the fuck..? My days of checking out your balls are well over!" I laugh.

"Kate, honestly, they are on fire," he exclaims as he lifts back the blankets for me to investigate.

"Oh fuck! They're like apples. They're bloody massive." I can't stop laughing, partly shocked, partly embarrassed.

"Kate, stop laughing and help," he replies, laughing himself.

"You stop laughing then," I chuckle and walk away to get the nurse, trying to hold it together. *Don't laugh Kate. This isn't the time to be laughing. Bloody hell, though. Those balls. They were like elephant balls.*

We see the nurse and she says that some of the cleaning solution they used when they changed his dressing must have got on them. She tells him to have a shower and use some talc. They will be swollen and uncomfortable for a good week. We slowly make our way to the shower. He has only been out of bed a handful of times since the operation two days ago.

"You finally got me naked again, eh?" he jokes.

"Yes my dear, just how I picture our naked shower reunion… me washing your ever-swelling melon balls. Oh, and I get to talc them too. This is so damn hot right now."

"I'm a real catch," he says with a stupid voice and we laugh. It's the least awkward way to manage this situation.

"You sure are," I say genuinely.

I dry him and help him into a gown and back to his bed.

It's three days since the operation and the girls are coming to see their dad for the first time. My mum brings them up on the train and we've decided they can stay with him for an hour before I take them out and go on the London Eye. They need to see their dad, but we can't expect them to sit there quietly all day and I need a break from the hospital for a little while too. Mum is happy to sit with Dairy Milk in case he needs anything.

The girls arrive and tentatively approach their dad. It's quite a lot for them to see their dad looking weak, tired and skinnier than ever. He's normally boisterous, playful, busy. It's strange how now the cancer has been removed, he looks more like he has cancer than he did before. They chat with him about what they have been up to at home and tell him how much they love him and have missed him. It's beautiful. I'm so proud of their strength.

After a quick trip to the London Eye we stay a little while longer before I head back home with the girls and Mum. I don't need to stay in London now, taking over Yorkie's place. I have been with Dairy Milk for four days. Now that he can sit up in the chair for a while each day, and is eating and drinking, it's time for me to leave and be with our girls. He was sad to see us go but knows I need to get home to work and support us all.

Like me, Dairy Milk is self-employed. We're so lucky that my brothers and dad are making up the shortfall in his income whilst he can't work. His parents and my mum are helping with food shopping and childcare too. Not only that, but some of our friends got details of our family account and quietly put money in it, all contributing. I feel extremely uncomfortable with this, but I can't stop them. I feel for all those people who might not be so lucky to have family to help. It's very humbling.

My phone startles me awake in the middle of the night. Dairy Milk is calling me. *Shit. I knew I should have stayed in London.* I answer the call, my voice all croaky.

"Kate, Kate, something has gone wrong Kate. I'm in agony, I think it must have burst! I think it must have gone wrong! I can't move. The nurses are calling the surgeon." He is crying down the phone.

"What on earth do you mean?" I reply, panicked. "I'm sure it hasn't. It can't have. Oh fuck, I wish I hadn't come home."

"Tell the girls I love them, more than they could ever comprehend," he says desperately. "Tell them I tried, I really tried to get better. I love you Kate. Thank you for marrying me, having children with me and being my best friend. I'm so sorry. I really am so sorry," he sobs down the phone. I can't stop crying either.

"I love you too. You'll be OK. I'll get my mum to watch the girls. I will call the nurses now and then drive up."

I hang up and call the hospital. I eventually get through and a nurse kindly and calmly reports that the doctors are with him now. Nothing has gone wrong. In fact, it's good news. His bowel has woken up. Unfortunately, it's incredibly painful and they are putting him back on the morphine.

Oh, thank God. I call him back to let him know I won't drive up after all, but he doesn't answer. I keep trying for an hour and when he eventually answers we laugh lightly, calming ourselves down after the shock.

The next day, I receive a text.

> Well, that was very messy and embarrassing. Shit myself Kate. I physically shit myself. I cleaned it up the best I could by myself to help the nurses but I was absolutely mortified. Hope your day is less messy than mine. LOL!!!

After another week in hospital, Dairy Milk is declared well enough to make the journey home. I pack up his possessions, gathering them together in his small suitcase. We say our goodbyes and give the staff boxes of chocolates and a thank you card. They wish him well and we make our way, slowly and steadily to the train.

As I order a coffee at the station, I look over to Dairy Milk. He's sitting on a bench, exhausted from the short walk between Guys Hospital and the platform at London Bridge Station. He's thin and gaunt, his body pushed beyond its limits. I have never been happier to see him sitting on a bench lost in thought though. What a beautiful man. I am honoured to call him my family, father to my daughters and most importantly, my friend.

Around and Around We Go, and Here We Go Again

The heat hits my body as I step off the plane. It's humid and bright. I love it. I have landed with Adira in Dubai after a seven-hour flight. We're here to see her sisters, Sadie and Emily. It's twenty years since we were last all together. Sadie lives in Sydney and Emily here in Dubai.

They are my trio of honorary sisters. After John passed away, life was incredibly hard to navigate. They took me in. Their parents helped to look after me. And thank God they did. My younger years would have been incredibly different without their support. This holiday visit in Dubai makes my ten-year-old self so happy. I missed them all so much when we moved away after John died, and it crushed my already broken heart.

But now is not the time to ponder over the sad times. Now is the time to celebrate and enjoy the chance to spend time with my honorary nephews, one of which, was born just six weeks ago.

Adira and I reach Emily's beautiful, four-bedroom home late in the evening. We have a cup of tea, but we are all keen to get a good night's sleep, especially as we want to be up with the boys first thing in the morning. Adira and Sadie are in the double bed and I'm in a bed made up on the floor. Emily is in the other room, and we laugh about it being the same as when we were growing up. She is the oldest so had her own room. Adira and Sadie always shared, and I was always on a made-up bed.

As we settle down in bed it inevitably becomes the time for chatting. Again, just like when we were kids. It's the perfect time to put the world to rights.

"We lost you for a while Kate," Adira tells me quietly.

"I know."

"We didn't have a number for you after the second move and obviously no social media or email then. We were worried, but there was nothing we could do."

"I got lost in life, I think. I could never get back to you. I was too little to get the bus. Do you remember my old house?"

"I don't remember it before John died," Adira says.

Sadie agrees. "I think before then it was just a regular home, so you don't remember much about it."

"Before the chaos and sadness filled its walls," adds Adira.

I shake my head at the memories running through my mind. "Bloody hell the stuff... so much stuff, everywhere."

"And kittens," Adira and Sadie say together, laughing.

"And kitten shit!" I giggle back at them. Then, solemnly, "It was a dark time for me. I find it hard to access the memories because I've buried them so deeply. Family life as I knew it vanished overnight. Everyone was lost in grief. Thank God for you all. I loved that your mum even had a toothbrush and bath sponge for me. And when you used to stay at your dad's house, I always joined you. Like I had visiting rights with him too."

"You did," Adira says. "Anytime Granny and Grandpa were taking us out for the day, we just presumed that meant you too, and you always came along!"

We carry on chatting, piecing together missing memories. Our conversation comes back round to the present day. Children, work and, of course, men. I tell them all about the men I've named after chocolate bars. I tell them about Fruit and Nut. We've continued to text message each other intermittently since he ended things, but we haven't seen each other since.

"That is you all over," says Adira.

"How do you mean?"

"Well, you never really let go of anyone do you? When we lost touch as teenagers, I never doubted you'd get back in touch. Sure, you disappear from time to time, but it's like you save all your relationships in a secret stash in the cupboard ready to dip into when you need them."

"Except that box isn't full of the likes of us anymore. It's full of Fruit and Nut and other delights," adds Sadie.

"Sweet temptations," says Adira, laughing.

I laugh too, but I fall asleep trying to think of men I've truly let go out of my life, and how many I still have stashed away ready to fill a lonely moment.

As it always was, and will always be, everyone in this family has woken up before me. I can hear voices downstairs as I begin to stir. I check my phone. Fruit and Nut's name fills the screen. *Hmm, that's funny. We were talking about you last night,* I think to myself, pleased he has texted.

Hello you. Sorry I went quiet.

Hello you. How are you?

Not great. I've hurt my foot. It's in one of those boot things and I can't play footy for a good few weeks. Killing me. You?

Oh shit, really? How?

I'm actually in Dubai with Adira and her sisters.

Sadie flew in from Sydney.

Some little fucker tackled me, now I'm off work and can't play football.

Oh wow, that's cool babe. Bet you're having a great time.

Well, I will let you get back to them. Text me when you're home babe. x

OK cool. I will. Miss you. xx

Me too xx

I can't stop thinking about Fruit and Nut now. I want to get naked with him so badly. He may not be 'the one' but bloody hell, I'm glad he was 'one'.

> I'm sunbathing. I have lost the plot. It's 48 degrees.

I share a picture of me sunbathing, the pool in the background. It's any excuse to text him really. I'm unashamedly raiding the stash.

Well hello missy. You're mad but mmmmm 😺 😺

I think I should be there, with my face in-between those legs.

We would definitely be arrested if I was there with you. xx

Fffffuuuuuccccccckkkkk!

> Mmmmm! We should meet up when I'm home

Yeah. We should make it happen. But you will need to come here cos of my foot. I can't drive.

> OK babe, we can sort it all out when I'm home. xx

> Glad you're back xx

Me too xx

See, bet you're happy you undeleted me now 😵

I don't know about that, think you might be trouble 😆 xx

Enjoy the rest of your holiday xx

Fruit and Nut's foot is still in the protective boot, so I'm going over to his house. His mum and brother are out so he has the place to himself. It's the first time I've been here. We had never reached the meeting friends, let alone the family, stage.

When I arrive, we go straight to his bedroom. I feel like a teenager again, going to a boyfriend's house for the first time and hiding away in the bedroom. He has a small wardrobe, a corner unit with his TV, computer and gaming consoles placed on top, and a small double bed. We sit awkwardly side by side on the edge of his bed for all of two minutes before we are kissing and pulling at each other's clothes.

I just can't get enough of Fruit and Nut. I want him naked, skin to skin contact all the time. He's like a drug. An addiction. The more I have of him, the more I want. The orgasms I have are so intense. He knows exactly every move you could ever imagine.

Afterwards, we spend a couple of hours in his bedroom, like the naughty teenagers we imagine we are, no cares in the world. We decide we should go for a drink and as we make our way through the house to the front door, I see pictures on the wall. I see a picture of his ex, his boy's mum. *Wow, she's absolutely gorgeous. Stunning in fact.* I feel like a fat, frumpy little woman when I look at her picture. *Why would he leave her? Bloody hell! Slim, tall, with long brunette hair.* I spot a picture of them together and they look so happy.

I suddenly feel incredibly uncomfortable. I want to get out of here. I feel as though we are cheating and being sneaky. I don't know why. They broke up seven months ago so I shouldn't feel bad, but just over half a year since ending a fifteen-year relationship is not actually very long at all. I feel icky about it. *Yep, take this slow Kate, enjoy the time you have with him. This could all just be a rebound situation. I must keep it light, even though I cannot deny I am attached. Just be attached physically. This is all too new for him for it to be anything more.*

We go out for a quiet drink in the local pub and chat away about nothing in particular. We're just happy to be out together again, catching up.

On the way back to his house, he says, "Let's make a detour. I know a quiet secluded place. I want to do naughty things with you before you go home."

"Mmmmmm, it sounds like a very bad idea, but go on then. I want lots of naughty things to happen before I leave too."

We pull up in a narrow, dead-end road, with a path leading to the woods. It's pitch black and I laugh about whether we should be scared. Even though I hate horror movies and don't watch them, I know that this is how they start. He laughs and tells me not to be so daft.

"Take off your tights and leave them in the car," he says huskily.

"Oooh, OK," I say breathing hard, excited. I take them off then put my ankle boots back on.

"I don't want to go into the woods without something on my feet," I say. "You never know what might be out there."

We laugh like the giddy teens we're pretending to be. We get out of the car and he starts kissing me again. It's one of those Fruit and Nut, legs weakening, body trembling, absolutely amazing kisses. Hand on my neck, the other around my waist, then he brings the other arm down around my waist, pushing against me. I can feel him hard beneath his jeans. He lifts me onto the bonnet of my little car. One hand moves up my thigh to my underwear and moves my knickers to the side as he slips his fingers underneath. He leans me back towards the windscreen. He kisses my neck, my chest and my breasts over my top, down past my belly and then lifts my skirt up. He goes down to my place, removes my knickers and puts them in his pocket. *Wowzers.* He works his magic with his mouth and his tongue, all the while still using his fingers on my G spot. I climax so damn hard over and over until I can't take any more. *Fuck! He is amazing at this.* He flips me over on the bonnet and enters me, moving in rhythm until we both climax.

"What we just did was so damn naughty!" I tell him as he breathes heavily into my neck.

"I know and that's why we both loved it."

We're as naughty as each other. I have absolutely found my match. I can be myself around him. I'm no longer shy or concerned about being naked. When I'm with him, I have confidence. I'm fun. This whole mini relationship we have, that we are rekindling, is just so much fun. *Oh God Kate! Remember, that is exactly what it is. FUN! Not a mini relationship.*

It's Saturday and Adira is visiting from London so we use this time to do her hair. I tell her all about going to Fruit and Nut's house and the picture of his ex on the wall, how gorgeous she is.

"What's her name? Let's find her on Facebook."

"I'm not even friends with him on Facebook" I say, suddenly realising that's a bit odd.

"It's not odd. I never friend any guy I'm dating on Facebook either. I'd let it just play out." Adira looks Fruit and Nut up, looks at his pictures, and his profile. She finds his mum through a comment she has left, then looks through his mum's friends and looks for his ex.

Genius! I would never have known how to do that little bit of stalking!

We both chuckle away until we see it. It's right there on the phone screen. Her profile. Her profile picture. Her and Fruit and Nut, cuddled in together, with drinks at a pub. *Shit.* My heart sinks. I start shaking.

"Fuck! What an arsehole, Adira! What a fucking arsehole! He's still with her. There's no way on this earth that you keep your profile as a couple once you break up. No shitting way."

I'm so pissed off and hurt, feeling like a complete idiot. Why would he do this? I'm ranting away to Adira. I need to delete and block the bastard and never speak to him again.

"Calm down for a minute. Yes, you could absolutely block, delete, never speak to him again. Or you can wait and talk to him first. Find out what's going on. It might all be her. His profile doesn't say he's in a relationship, neither of them do. I know you well enough to know that you won't be able to forget him or move on unless you talk to him. You're just reacting to the shock. Find out what's going on, then act when you have the knowledge."

I half smile, fireworks going off in my head. "OK. You're so wise Adira. But this is just so shit! Like you say though, at the end of the day, I know the questions I have in my head won't leave until I get the answers."

> Hello you

I feel sick, sending him a nice message.

> How's your day going? You still good for Tuesday after football? xx

I'm not 100% sure at the moment babe as we have an away match.

My day's the same old, fixing a roof today. You ok? x

> Yeah all good here

Not good at all you cheating piece of shit. Maybe not in fact cheating Kate. Calm down.

> OK well let me know when you do because I really do want to see you babe. Miss you x

Aww missing me after two days?

I think you're missing my bedroom skills 😂

Damn he really is good in bed. That and the laughter. I really hope that he is not this awful guy I have now created in my head.

> Well, they do definitely make you extremely appealing.

> Let's make Tuesday happen, I know we can xx

> OK leave it with me. I will see what I can do. x

I definitely need to see him face to face to have this conversation. I need to look him in the eyes to really be able to read him and see if he is completely bullshitting me or not.

The weekend and Monday pass. I'm barely texting him. I have become completely obsessed at the thought that he has lied to me and I'm fuming.

We ended up arranging to meet on Thursday. We meet near the football pitch where he's been playing football. I park up next to him, climb out of my car and get into his van so that we can decide what we want to do. We get chatting about football, but I can't stand it anymore.

"I saw your ex-wife's profile picture on Facebook," I blurt out.

He's a little shocked. I sound like a complete stalker.

"It's not my profile!" he exclaims. "We took down the status in a relationship from our accounts, and to be honest with you Kate, after fifteen years, this has been really tough on us both. If she wants to leave her profile picture as it was before we broke up, then I'm not going to hurt her any more by telling her to change it. It's a bloody social media profile, not a marriage certificate!"

Shit. Shit! Shit! I feel awful. In fact, I feel really foolish. He has just broken up his entire family. When I did that, I kept anyone I was dating completely under wraps so I didn't hurt Dairy Milk's feelings any more than I already had. *Jeez, he's right. You can't ask your ex to change profile pictures. And we aren't teenagers, even though we're pretending to be half the time.*

"Let's drop this. I can't believe you didn't just ask me out-right when you saw it, rather than waiting all week."

We go for a quick drink then I drive home. After sex in the van. It wouldn't be us if we weren't tearing each other's clothes off.

It's the weekend and Dairy Milk has stopped in for a cuppa.

"Do you remember when you changed your profile picture after we broke up?" I ask him, then tell him about the Fruit and Nut situation.

"You're not being stupid at all. I was completely heartbroken when we split and I changed my profile picture within a week. There's no way I wouldn't have changed it after half a year. No way! Maybe she is hoping they will get back together like they've done before?"

"Hmmmm. That could well be the case," I agree.

The picture situation is really weighing on my mind. I talk with Fruit and Nut about it again and ask him if this is why he doesn't add me on Facebook. He says it's because it's still awkward between him and her and that I'm just going to have to believe that nothing is happening and to stop being a little stalker.

Once again, he has reassured me as much as he can.

And once again, I feel foolish.

Another week has passed and I can't shake the feeling that something just doesn't add up. Every single one of The Nine believe he is a cheat. But how? Why? He lives back at home with his mum. He calls me every night and when he stays at his ex's house, he sleeps on the sofa, like I do when I stay at Dairy Milk's. He's even called me from there and he always texts late at night. Some other girlfriends say they have known women who have done this with profile pictures as a way to keep other women away from their exes.

I call Fruit and Nut and tell him I'm sorry, but I just feel weird about it.

"Let's just go for a drink tonight and nothing else. We need to talk about everything and clear the air," he says.

I agree. It's eating away at me and if we don't sort it out then this will all fall flat on its face and I don't want that to happen.

We meet up at a beautiful old country pub. I really enjoy our little tour of random old pubs. We get a drink and sit down. He isn't his normal self and I'm starting to think he's going to tell me that he is, in fact, back with her and that he wants to end this, whatever this is.

Oh God, I don't want him to. My heart is banging in my chest. *OK, just hear him out, get the answers you need. This is your only opportunity. This time you are going to sit here quietly and let him tell you everything.*

Fruit and Nut spends the next two and half hours telling me everything about the last fifteen years. When he first cheated, why he cheated, why he left, why he went back, why he never wanted them to break up and so desperately wanted to make the family work. He explained how, by the end, the relationship between them was no longer a physical one and only friendship remained. He wants to make that friendship strong, like the relationship I have with Dairy Milk, and he wants me to accept that it will take time. He cannot and will not rock the boat because it's taking all he has to keep it afloat.

"You've probably told me far more than you should. Your past is terrible," I say a little sadly.

"I like you that much, that I just wanted to tell you everything. So that you know me for who I am. Yes, I have a past, but that was because I was in a relationship that was no longer working. And yes, I was a coward by staying with her, but I didn't want to lose my family. Now that I have left though, I know I will never go back. I've made the leap and it took a hell of a long time to gain the courage to do that. It broke a lot of hearts and now it is done we can all move on. But slowly." No laughing, just heartfelt honesty. I absolutely believe him. I am letting this all go.

We leave the pub, kiss softly, and reassuringly make plans for the week ahead.

As I drive home, I process what he has told me. His past is his past. We all have one. It has absolutely nothing to do with me. What we have now is great, so I am happy to continue down this road with him and look forward to what we could have in time.

Fruit and Nut and I now make sure we see each other twice a week. Tuesdays just for a drink, ending with sex in the van or the car because we just can't help ourselves, and Thursdays all night at hotels or my house. It's all still so much fun, even though we've been doing this for six months now. Fruit and Nut always tells me he isn't a cuddly guy, yet in the middle of the night he always cuddles me. I feel him pull me closer if I've rolled away and I do the same to him. If he has been rained off work, he comes over to mine after I drop the kids at school, if I have no work on myself, and we spend the day watching boxsets in bed. Bliss. I adore the little birthmark he has on his stomach and kiss it regularly.

It's Thursday and we're staying at a hotel we've stayed at before. It's arranged like little apartments. *Very cute.* I meet him in the car park and we drive into town to pick up a pizza. It feels like we are a proper couple now and I feel comfortable in these situations. I still have my walls up, although I'm fighting to let them down. That's a good thing, but I know I still need to be careful. We are not in a secure enough space for me to bring them down really.

Back at the apartment, we eat our pizza and Fruit and Nut talks about his family. Family is everything to him. I really hope he and his ex can stay friends. It will mean the world to him.

We finish our pizza and he sits down on the edge of the bed next to the table where I'm still seated. He reaches his hand out, inviting me towards him. I stand between his legs. Fruit and Nut stands up, kisses me softly. He kisses my forehead. I'm still. I feel lost in him at this moment in time. Only Dairy Milk has ever kissed me there.

A forehead kiss to me is a sweet kiss, an unconditional, loving kiss. I know things are changing between us. I think about my wall. Am I ready to bring it down yet? I don't know, but I do have such strong feelings for him and for him to kiss me like that, well, I feel the bricks are definitely starting to crumble. *Ah, who am I kidding? The bricks are definitely crumbling. In fact, tumbling down around me, more and more every day.*

He pulls at my top to reveal my bra. He kisses my neck and my body weakens. His lips move down to my breasts and he removes my bra, kissing my hardened nipples, then down to my belly, my mum tum with stretch marks. He stops and kisses them. Now I'm completely weak. Fully lost in his soft lingering kisses and the touch of his hands. This feels different. We're different. The way he holds me close, kissing me throughout. Satisfying me all the time. We both climax and he holds me close, my head on his chest, my arm resting on his stomach. He kisses my forehead again. I fully realise that

I'm falling for him big time and I'm helpless to stop. My heart is unlocked and beating hard.

We remain happy in our bubble of kissing, amazing sex, and boxsets for another month. Then out of the blue some shit happens, some drama, which he won't even try to tell me about fully. During a night out with the boys he is arrested for being in a fight and he ends our relationship. That's it. Full stop. I can't understand why. I am lost in confusion and shock. I beg him to reconsider, but he won't. All I receive is a text.

> Babe, I'm just a mess right now. This was only meant to be fun. We have made it into something that I'm no way ready for. I like you, and more than I should. But my life is a fucking mess. I'm living back at my mum's. Broken up my family. I need to think about what I want to do with my life, with my career and I can't focus on anything. I'm hiding away with you, which is great, but not where I need my head to be at. I'm sorry but I need to walk away.

> I'm gutted. Totally and utterly. I think this would have been a great time for us to grow together. I want to be in a relationship with you. Figure things out with you. Fall in love with you. My walls are just starting to come down. I want you to know that I will really miss you and that I'm falling for you, big time. Xxx

Two weeks pass and I've tried to stay busy. Right now I'm curled up in bed with the flu and can't help but miss him. I try to understand that he just isn't coming back. I have sent the occasional message but had no reply. I just need to accept it for what it was only ever meant to be. Fun. *Funny how fun feels so shit though, eh?*

I know I'm not ready to get back out there, but I feel stupid not bouncing back and getting on with my life. Fruit and Nut isn't interested. I could wait for him for the rest of my life, but what good will that do. I upload new pictures onto Tinder, then get stupidly upset about the whole thing after I match with a man. I end up participating in a meaningless, boring conversation with him, un-match and text Fruit and Nut.

> I miss you so much. I want you back really badly. xxx

Desperate, I know, but it is the truth.

> I just don't know what to do because I don't want to lose you, but at the same time my life has gone to shit. I think maybe we should just meet up and talk, see what we can decide to do. I'm trying to make a plan, figure out where my life is going. I don't want to stay living at my mum's house forever and the job I'm doing. I just don't want either. I'm still where I was two weeks ago babe but I do know I miss you too.

Oh, yes! A reply! And he wants to see me. Kate, is this the right thing to do? Ultimately, he is still in the exact same place. Is this what you want? A man who is lost and unsure about what he wants, who when times get tough, throws you away? Yes, he makes you laugh, and the banter is on top form. Yes, he is a father who adores his boys and has a great relationship with his ex. A man who is a provider. A man's man. A man who can tell you no, and to shut up when you need to hear that. A gorgeous, sexy, beautiful man, who is amazing in bed and holds you in a way that you have longed for, for such a long time. Yes! Yes! And yes some more! I absolutely want this man.

I calm myself down and respond to his text message. Casual.

> It is late. I'm tucked up in bed with a headache and fever. I really need sleep.

I quickly screen shot our conversation, so happy to be able to tell Lily that he wants to see me again, then snuggle down to sleep.

The next morning I wake to a shock.

> I thought it was a bit strange, after telling me you needed to sleep as you are ill, you remained online. Especially after us not speaking for a while and after the break we have just had. So, I did a little checking up of my own. I checked my Tinder, as neither of us spoke about deleting it. I was hoping to see that you would have. But what I found were the new pictures uploaded. That's fucking nice! You tell me you feel things for me, that you want to make this more, that you miss me. Clearly not. You have not only remained on Tinder but uploaded new pictures. Don't speak to me again! I didn't think you were just some Tinder girl. I actually fucking liked you and believed what you had said. Hope you find what you're looking for. My head didn't think you would wait but my heart had hoped you would.

Shit. Shit! Shit! I feel bloody awful. I try to explain that I didn't think he was coming back and that I fucked up. That I only matched with one guy, had a shit three-text conversation, and just wanted him back. He deletes me and blocks me off WhatsApp. I move to text, out of desperation for him to understand. I try to reason with him and tell him that the only reason he could see my profile was because he was still on Tinder himself.

> I thought things between us were over and I was trying to save face by getting back out there. I didn't want to be back out. You were the one who put me back on the market and I didn't think you were coming back to me.

A long three days pass before he messages me again. He wants to talk. *Shit!* I want to see him so bad, but I know he is still angry and hurt that I didn't wait, not even for a month. *Oh, Kate. What a mess.* I don't even know why I didn't wait. Well, I do really. I didn't think he would come back.

We have decided to meet face to face at a pub halfway between our houses. I pull up next to his van in the pub car park and he gets in my car. "I thought we were going to a pub," I say.

He is so angry. I know I'm in the shit. I have never seen him like this. He tells me to drive around the corner so we can talk.

"It's not a conversation to have in the pub," he says.

Fuck, fuck, fuck.

"Look, I have fucked this right up and I can't justify why I played such a shit hand and went on Tinder. I didn't even want to be on there. It's not a place I like at all really."

I try to explain and he tells me his side of events, why he needed a break to sort his head out. He says he didn't think I was one of those Tinder girls.

Shit. Am I?

"What do you mean?" I ask.

"Kate, I thought you really liked me, I believed you. You spout all this bullshit about how much you like me, how you are falling for me. I was feeling the same and yet two weeks pass and you are ready to get back to dating? Like I mean nothing? Your words and your actions don't match. Yes, I was the one to end things, but because I was in a bad place, not because I didn't like you. Going on Tinder uploading new pictures to freshen up your account was a shit move, yes! It showed me that you just like the attention that you can get."

I have really hurt him. "I'm so sorry. I like you so much, but I've kept my walls up because of your circumstances. I never know where I am, whether you want in with me fully or not. You have one foot in the room and one foot out."

After an hour of straight talking in the car, he softens. He's returned to the man I know and adore. We decide to give things between us a chance.

This time we will both be in the room with both feet in, but we'll leave doors open to allow us to get used to this new relationship of sorts. There are still no boyfriend or girlfriend titles, but we're on our way to them.

God, I like him so damn much. The truth is, I'm in love with him, but I can't tell him that. He isn't ready to say it back. We kiss, one of those amazing kisses he does so well. I'm still so nervous he will leave again, because he has left so many times. But when he does come back, we grow in strength. I hope that time will sort us out and allow us to trust one another enough to make this last.

December has arrived and I ask him to meet my friends on my birthday. It's a Thursday so I know he doesn't have the boys. It turns out his brother's birthday is the day before mine, on the twenty-seventh, but he thinks it shouldn't be a problem coming over the next day for my birthday. *Result!* I'm so excited. I tell the ladies and they are happy to finally be meeting Fruit and Nut. I'm nervous, but I think he will get on with them. He's so chatty. I think he will do well entering the lionesses' lair.

We don't see each other over Christmas, but we don't mind as we both believe the kids and their needs should come first, as well as our other family commitments. We talk every day on the phone saying we can't wait to see each other.

The excitement doesn't last long. His brother ends up celebrating his birthday on the twenty-eighth so Fruit and Nut cancels seeing me. To say I am totally gutted is an understatement, but in true Kate form, I don't tell him.

> Happy birthday though babe, I hope you have a great night with the ladies, and we will see each other soon.

> Yeah no worries, it can't be helped. You can make it up to me when I see you.

I need to stand up for myself. He has let me down and I've swept it under the carpet. I'm embarrassed by my reaction and the fact that my friends will all have something to say about it this evening.

A text from Yorkie pings.

> Happy birthday shit stain. Have a good day.
> Come up in the new year, we can drink too much
> wine and retro game. I'm missing your face.

> You are such a poo face! Yeah I
> definitely will. I'm missing you too.
> You love me really!

> Of course I love you, you haemorrhoid!

And then... Wonka. He remembered again.

> Happy Birthday Kate. I hope you are
> being spoilt. One day I hope I will be
> the one to spoil you. Until that day. Xxx

And then Lily. *God!* She can't wait to see my new man. The shame of telling them all he won't be coming.

My phone is ringing and it's my mum, right on queue with my birthday call. "Happy birthday to you, happy birthday to you, happy birthday darling Kate, happy birthday to you! Love you darling!"

"Aww, I love you Mum."

I feel better having spoken with Mum and head out with Lily, Bambi and Kim.

"Fruit and Nut won't be joining us," I tell them, counting the seconds as I wait for their reaction.

"I don't trust him anyway," says Lily.

It's hard for me to hear and I find myself sticking up for him. Excuse after excuse.

"You're not friends on Facebook or Instagram, you haven't met any friends after months and months of dating."

I stumble a little, saying, "But then again we actually don't have much time. Our relationship was only meant to be a bit of fun due to him being not long out of a relationship. And I totally understand the lack of social media and not going public. We don't even really know what we are yet, so he doesn't want friends and family knowing either. Plus, he doesn't want to hurt his baby mum. It's just how I was after I split my marriage, remember?"

They are extremely sceptical about it and I'm truly hurt. I find myself struggling. I try to shrug off their opinions. They don't understand. None of them have broken up a family and tried to keep it friendly. It's bloody hard and I commend him for trying as hard as he is to make all areas work.

The more the girls' comments play in my head, the more I can't escape them. What they have been saying makes a lot of sense. I realise Fruit and Nut just isn't ready. But I am. I love seeing him Tuesdays and Thursdays, it really works for me. But emotionally, I am two years ahead of him. I've moved on from my marriage. I need to take the next step, not to live together or anything, but to confirm our relationship. He's just not there yet.

We talk about it and he agrees. One day in the future when he is in the right head space then we can check in and see. We walk away from each other. Again. Heartbroken. Again. Crying. Again. How could this ever work long term anyway?

Three weeks later he is back.

We talk it all out over the phone. We agree that I am ahead of him in the healing process after separating from Dairy Milk. He feels that in one more year he will be where I am, all his issues should be ironed out for him. He thinks if we really want this, we can continue as we are, and we will get there in our own time. He agrees to meet my friends.

This is everything I want to hear.

Fruit and Nut tells me all about the last few weeks. A girl had contacted his ex and told her that two years ago they'd fooled around. His ex has stopped him popping to her house after work and only lets him see the boys at the weekends at his mum's now. He has been making it work the best he can, and they have little sleepovers in the lounge, but he can't stand not just popping in, being friendly. This is everything he didn't want and now he feels more lost than ever.

It's a rainy day so he can't work. I invite him to mine so we can talk properly. This is the first time we have seen each other in three weeks. The moment he walks into the cottage we are kissing and pulling off our clothes, desperately wanting each other. It's that kind of lust you just can't fight and it becomes an addiction. I need his touch and crave it when he isn't about. I really am addicted to him, his body, his touch, the smell of his skin, the taste of his lips, the feel of his tongue and the way he can make me climax over and over.

Can I do this for another year? Yeah, I believe I can. But then I also believe that I can do most things then end up crying to Lily because I am the impulsive one, running before I can walk. She is always there to pick me back up and help me to my feet, then I go and do it all over again. *Thank God for Lily.*

Please Tell Me I Peed on It Wrong

I'm enjoying pizza and wine with my not-so-gay best mate, Yorkie. We're having a retro gaming night and I'm staying over at his place in London. That's OK with Fruit and Nut though. He knows we're just mates so he has no problem with it.

However, Yorkie has a problem with Fruit and Nut. Like Lily, he thinks he isn't being honest with me. I receive a text from Fruit and Nut.

> Hope you're having a good night. Can I just ask you not to message me for a couple of hours. I'm heading round kid's mum's house as she wants to talk to me. I just badly want to clear the air as not seeing the boys is killing me. Hope you understand. I'll call you later. x

"Shit, that doesn't sound good does it?" I say.

Yorkie tells me I should consider they might want to get back together. He's a good friend and is looking out for me, but it's not what I want to hear.

"Shit, no. You're wrong. They haven't been together in over a year. No, I think they are just clearing the air. He's just been so unhappy with all the fighting."

I put my phone away, doing as Fruit and Nut asked. I won't text him. I'll wait to see what he has to say later.

Next morning, Yorkie and I are chatting away over breakfast. I mention I'm about a week late for my period. "Oh my god," he says. "You're totally preggers!"

"Stop trying to freak me out. There's no way I can be." I hadn't been worried about it as I have a coil and my ovaries are crap.

"I'm more concerned with the fact that Fruit and Nut didn't call or even message me last night."

"Yep, you are preggers and he is back with his ex. I'm afraid that kinda shit would only happen to you."

He's teasing me, joking, but there's an air of truth to it. My heart is in my chest. Fruit and Nut told me to bring my walls down, that he couldn't understand why they were still built so high after nearly a year of knowing me. He told me it was safe to start bringing them down. If I am pregnant then they really will need to come down. Could it be I'm pregnant with his baby?

It's late morning and I leave to catch my train home. I have totally stressed myself out, overthinking. I need to put my mind at ease. I'm on the phone chatting to Kim about the whole situation and decide to buy a pregnancy test at the station. I assure myself that it will be negative.

"Let's face it, I have a coil and I've been late before, so no need to panic," I say to Kim. "And doing the test will clear my mind and I'll come on."

I walk to the platform and jump on my train all the while chatting to Kim. The train begins its journey.

"I'm going to find the toilet. I need to get this stupid test done so I can stop worrying," I tell Kim.

We carry on chatting while I pee. I smile. I love that we are this close. Kim is reassuring me that I'm late because I'm just stressed and overthinking the Fruit and Nut shit. I pull up my pants and jeans, wrap the test in a bit of tissue, wash my hands and return to my seat. I check the test.

"Oh my fucking god. Oh my fucking God," I repeat. I can't breathe. "Kim. I can't breathe. I'm pregnant! I'm bloody pregnant!"

"You can't be Kate. You fucking can't be!" She's stunned too.

"I know, but I am. I shitting well am!" *Fuck, fuck, fuck!* I tell Kim I have to go and that I'll call her later. I'm panicking and need to talk to Lily. She will calm me down and talk me through this.

She answers her phone cheerfully and I tell her what's happened. "I can't possibly have a baby with a man who has too much shit going on with his current family situation. A man who doesn't want a baby. A man I'm not entirely sure even wants me!" I cry.

She tries her best to calm me down. "We will be OK," she says. "I'm totally here for you. Do the second test when you get home to make sure."

When I get home, I run up the narrow creaky staircase to my bathroom. I pee on the stick and wait for the longest two minutes of my entire life. I can't bear to look at it. All I want to see is a single little line. One happy little line all by itself then I can just laugh about the dodgy first test. Put the experience down to another freakish moment in my life.

Two minutes finally pass. I pick up the second test from its resting place on the side of my bath. Two lines. Two lousy lines. Pregnant. Definitely pregnant.

Half an hour later my phone vibrates in my pocket. Fruit and Nut is calling. I'm still in my bathroom. I'm numb, sitting on the bathroom floor, leaning with my back up against the wall. I think I've gone into shock. *Oh God! I don't want to talk to him right now.* I know I have to answer though. I need to know what happened last night.

I tap the green button and allow Fruit and Nut to dive straight in. He's upset and frustrated. He's obviously unhappy, as he tells me the inevitable. "We spent a few hours talking everything through. She told me how much she has missed me, missed being a family with me. She wants to see if we can make it work again after the break that we've had. Babe, I'm sorry. I'm lost."

"Wow! A break? Really? I was a break?" I'm completely numb. The day is going from awful to goddamn depressing.

"Babe, please. I need to see if we can work now. We have kids together. I told you I was lost at the moment. I don't want to lose you. That's the last thing I want. If this was based simply on two adults being together, then I would absolutely be with you. But it's the family. My boys."

He continues trying to justify everything. I quietly listen. She had stopped him seeing the boys other than at his weekends and he just can't handle that. She's punishing him, angry about what he's done to her. She can't be friendly with him unless they get back together and wants to see if they can make it work. She misses him and needs to give it one more chance. If it doesn't work this time, then they must go their separate ways and just move on.

When he's finished, I am furious. "I thought you had already moved on, but I guess not, eh? Wow, what a fool I am. I was so foolish, so pig headed to want to keep you when so much doubt surrounded you."

Tears fall down my cheeks. My mind is full of a thousand questions and millions of thoughts that I just can't share with him. *Well Kate, you've made this bed and now you have to lay your pregnant self down in it.*

All I say is, "Please don't delete or block me." It sounds pitiful and I am angry with myself for asking so I justify my request. "I totally get that you need to leave me in the past, but I may need to talk to you."

He agrees. Not a care in the world and completely unaware of our growing baby inside me.

I spend the rest of the evening looking through pictures of him, re-reading messages from weeks before. I speak to Lily a few times. I lay in bed crying, panicking, trying to think about anything but this sad situation. I can't. I keep returning to my phone, torturing myself with past messages. I try to make sense of the day.

Before I decide to try to get some sleep, I look at my phone again hoping that he may have messaged me. His WhatsApp picture has disappeared. He has deleted me. I am blocked. I feel completely defeated. I know I have to respect this man's wishes and allow him to walk away. I can't fight for him any longer. Fighting for us would mean the ultimate sacrifice for him. He would lose his family. It's time for me to accept he is with another woman. My heart is breaking. I had thought I was strong enough for the two of us to make our relationship flourish. Turns out I was wrong. This whole situation is fucking my head right up.

I spend three days burying my head in the sand. Lily calls me and texts me every day. She tells me she will help me every step of the way and will come to all the scans. "I don't need help with the scans Lil! I need help with the night feeds and the screaming baby."

We both laugh mirthlessly and I think to myself that it's the first time I've laughed since I saw the two lines appear. I realise I need to start trying to get my head around all this and take some action.

I'm in the bath, enjoying the head space away from my girls and, more importantly, away from my phone. I find myself apologising to the baby. I absolutely do not want a baby. The thought of being on my own raising this child is completely unreal. How can I bring a baby into this world when it wouldn't know its father and its mother is already a single mum raising three children on a mobile hairdresser's salary? *Oh fuck. I won't be able to work.* The career I love so much will be put on hold. The girls will have to go without the little they actually already have. All because my stupid coil failed. I know that the sensible thing to do would be to terminate this pregnancy. I just can't do that though.

"I'm so sorry," I say out loud. "I'm going to be completely rubbish at this. You don't have a Dairy Milk to be the fun one. I'm the strict one. You've gone and found the strict one to be your only one. I promise I will do my very best though. I can't bring myself to evict you when you must so clearly want to be here. You made it past a coil after all. If you can do that, you must be a strong little thing indeed. We will find a way together."

I tell Lily on the phone later that I know I shouldn't keep this baby.

"You absolutely shouldn't," she says. "It will change everything in your life. But we both know you will, so you need to sort yourself out. You can either spend the next month trying to convince yourself to terminate, or you can just accept that this baby is coming. I bet you've already started talking to it."

"Oh, Lily!" I exclaim. "Yes, I have." We laugh together, this time more joyously. She knows me too well.

Four days have passed and I finally feel ready to accept the change of events of my life.

My first point of action is to tell my mum. Mum has always said it takes a village to raise a child and in this case I really do need the village on hand. My heart beats fast as I wait for her to answer the phone and I am so relieved by her reaction. She is supportive and reassuring. She tells me how she will help me every step of the way. I should have known. She has been my rock through raising my girls. She completely and utterly adores her granddaughters and they adore her right back. I know that a new addition would be fully accepted and loved. I actually think she seems quite happy about it all.

My second call is to the doctors. I explain I have had two positive pregnancy test results even though I have a coil.

"Can you please pop in and see the nurse to give a urine sample? Just so we can test it here. We'll get you booked in for a scan too," she says, concerned that I could be pregnant despite having the coil fitted.

Later that afternoon I pop in with my sample. I see the nurse who fitted the coil originally and she's shocked, wondering why it may have failed. "Perhaps it moved," she suggests.

"I have no idea," I respond sarcastically, all the while cursing the fact that three years ago, when I asked to have my tubes tied, she had convinced me the coil would be better. She'd advised me that I didn't know where life would take me. I was young and newly single. *Well, thanks for that.* I think to myself. *I didn't expect to wind up a single mum to a poor little baby whose dad has fucked off and has no idea that it even exists. Oh, I'm screwed!*

I leave the surgery and go to Dairy Milk's flat to collect the girls. I can't help but tell him everything. "I still need the doctors to confirm, then I need to have a scan to make sure it's even viable due to the coil."

His face is completely blank for a moment, then he hugs me. A huge protective hug. He kisses the top of my head and tells me he will help too. "Oh God, I just cannot believe this is happening. I just wish that I could hide away and not think about it all," I say into his chest.

He rubs my back as he pulls away from the embrace and says, "Stop overthinking Kate. It will all be OK."

I try to lighten the mood with a joke. "I just might not sleep for a few years!" I smile, but he knows behind that smile I'm completely overwhelmed by everything.

I get a call from the doctors the next day. The scan is booked for two days' time but the urine test that was carried out has come back negative. *What. The. Fuck!*

"Oh my god. Really? Are you sure?"

The nurse explains it could have been a chemical pregnancy, but we can't be sure of anything until I have the scan.

The next morning, I come on my period.

I sit on my sofa, snuggled in with a blanket and a cup of tea, and allow my mind to wander. I think about the last week's experience and allow myself to fully acknowledge how I am feeling. I am relieved. I did not want my family to grow any bigger and I would have been on my own raising the baby. But in my heart? Well, my heart had made space for another and the loss of what could have been has left a hole. As I wipe away the tears from my cheeks, I know in my mind that it's for the best though.

Not A Big Butch Lesbian

It's February. The snow has arrived with an Arctic blast and the pipes in my cottage have frozen. In fact, the cottage is so cold I woke to an icy washing up bowl. We have no water, and it is just too cold to stay there. My open fire just won't manage to warm us up on its own and I still don't know how to use these poxy storage heaters. *Kate, you really should learn how they work for next winter.*

Dairy Milk is single again and is happy for me and the girls to stay until it warms up. I'm so grateful. We have worked hard to be friends and since his operation we have been closer than ever. I adore that I have made friends with each of his girlfriends and that he still joins family weekends with my side of the family. The journey to friendship may have been difficult, but I'm so glad we made it happen and got to this point in our lives.

The situation we find ourselves in when my house freezes is surreal though. Just Dairy Milk, myself and the girls. Parenting together with no partners or other family and friends around is a little weird. But then again, it's really quite nice to hang out like this, without the pressure of a marriage.

The sofa is my bed for the week and is actually quite comfy. We bought it together when we were married. Two matching sofas in pink and black. I have the pink one and he took the black one. I guess that's why it feels like home away from home.

I love having the heating too. I'm so grateful to him for letting us stay. Every day when he returns from work he exclaims, "It's like a bloody sauna in here, Kate! What is wrong with you? Enjoying the joys of modern heating?"

"I bloody love it my dear. Instant heat. Nothing like my cottage with my fire, hot water bottles and blankets!"

"Yeah, but you love it," he says with a wink and a smile on his face.

The niceties last two days. Now we moan about each other's stuff and explain more efficient ways to do the most ridiculous of things, like the washing, cooking, cleaning. *I mean, the man doesn't clean out the fridge! He's*

killing me! I popped in and out helping when he was recovering from the operation, but we haven't spent this much time together since he moved out.

I stir from my sleep as I hear Dairy Milk make his way to the bathroom. I check my phone to see the time and find a Snapchat from Wonka. *Wonka Bar, Fuck! Eeeeeeee!* My heart leaps, a smile spreads across my face, heart pounding. I sometimes randomly message him, as he does me. Normally on special occasions. I excitedly open it. *Oh. My. God. It's a video one!* This is the first time he has sent a video.

Oh my fucking god. He is a man! This is really him. Not a catfish. Not a spotty teenage boy pretending to be a flamboyant, excitingly fun man. Not a butch lesbian! My heart pounds and adrenaline streams through my body. He's walking around a set that he's working on, chatting away to me, hoping the girls are well and that he is looking forward to his birthday next month. He looks just like his perfect, extraordinary self.

Oh wow. We have a reached a whole new level. Years of intermittent texts and photos, but always a nagging doubt about who he was. This is just amazing. *Damn, there's no one else here to see it. There's no one around to witness that he's real. Damn, I can't wake my eldest up. She would love to see this proof.* I can't save it as it's a Snap and will disappear when I close the screen. I can only replay it once then he will be gone forever.

Dairy Milk! Dairy Milk is awake. He can witness. Before I know it, I'm opening the bathroom door and rushing in. He's having a wee, but I don't care.

"Kate, what the fuck are you doing in here? I'm having a wee!" He isn't really bothered that I'm in here though.

I show him the video and exclaim, "That's him! It's Wonka Bar!"

"Who the fuck? What are you talking about? It's the middle of the night and you're showing me a video of a random man, with wild hair and a massive beard! He looks like Dr Eggman from Sonic!" He laughs at his own joke.

"Amazing, isn't he?" The biggest smile fills my face. "I needed someone to witness that he was real. Everyone I know thought I was mad, but look, he is real."

"You are truly mad Kate! I'm happy you're happy that I have witnessed this for you. But, of course, only you would think it's appropriate to walk in on her ex-husband having a wee in the middle of the night to show him a video of a love interest. Only you. Now, get out so I can finish up and get back to my bed!"

I can't stop laughing. Dairy Milk is right. I am truly bonkers. I don't care. Right now, tonight, I found out that my Wonka Bar is a real man. Yes, a real man out in the world, somewhere. *Oh, the pang in my heart. Ouch! He is truly real. But not mine. Still not wanting to meet and not even because he is a spotty teenager or butch lesbian. Why then? Why not meet me? Married? He has repeatedly said he isn't.* I think about all the reasons why we have never met. I guess I may never know. *Or maybe this is the beginning of getting to know him better and finally meeting him?*

I try to go back to sleep but keep replaying the video in my mind, trying to memorise his face. The more I try, the more difficult it becomes. His face keeps changing into people from my past. People I'd rather forget. And yet somehow, they keep coming back.

My Past has Found Me

Who is texting me? 7.02am? Who texts that early on a Saturday? I'm not a morning person. I'm still half asleep. *It's bloody freezing too. When is Spring going to arrive? It's April!!* I need to turn my heated blanket back on. *Not as bad as when I put it on in June,* I think to myself.

Holy fuck. My heart is still. I hold my breath. It's my past. It's from Him. *Holy Christ!*

OK, open it. Shit! What would he want to text me for? Why would he want to talk to me about anything? Oh, God. Oh my god! OK. Open it.

It's a blank text? *What…?* I wonder why he would send a blank message. *To get in my head? To see if he still warrants a response? Why, why, why?*

Oh! My heart beats harder. *I bloody know why! This is nice, this is. After all these years? Texting me to see if I'm on my own? Ugh! This man infuriates me! How dare he presume that I would be up for speaking to him again? How dare he! There's no way I will reply to him. Just wait until I tell The Nine at the barbecue later. They won't believe it!*

This cheeky, disrespectful bastard of a man left me to deal with everyone and the small-town shit. All the backlash. He disappeared from my life right when I needed him. This man left me in the street, outside his house in the pouring rain at two in the morning with no phone. He didn't even call me a taxi.

Kate, this guy has disrespected you in the worst possible way, over and over and over again. And each time it takes you so long to get over him. I plead with myself to delete his message and put him right back in the past, where he belongs. *Oh man, why can't I do it?*

The barbecue is at Penelope's parents' house, a beautiful cottage in the middle of nowhere, secluded, surrounded by fields. I merrily drink the night away and rant to The Nine about the message. We are all seated around the fire pit, blankets over our knees and hoodies on. It turned into a warm spring day, but it's getting chilly again now.

"I've known this guy since I was seventeen. You know what I'm like around him. I mean, let's be honest, he is just so handsome and just gets better with age. But he's never committed to me. We've only ever used each other to end the relationships we wanted out of. We've never loved each other."

"It's just lust, Kate." Bambi interrupts. "You know that."

"Do you really want to let him back in?" Jessica asks.

Lottie joins in. "I always liked him, never had a problem with him, but you both hurt a lot of people, Kate."

"Just lust? I wouldn't completely agree with that. Don't misunderstand me," I continue with my drunken ranting, "I know how confusing this is, but I think we could love each other. I don't think we'd ever let ourselves find out though. Oh, this man, this man! He has always been under my skin."

None of The Nine think I should reply to his message, even though they want to understand why he would message at all. They say it's more important I should leave it in the past because I'm weak when it comes to him and that we've hurt each other.

"This is not moving forward with your life, Kate. This is just heading right on backwards," says Jessica.

They all know there is unfinished business though. *Am I strong enough for round one hundred and ninety-nine? I need to send him a text. Why did he get in touch?*

> You have got some nerve, messaging me first thing in the morning. We both know what that was for. What were you hoping it would lead to? Well, I'm telling you now, I'm worth more than you have ever been able to offer me! How dare you?!

> OMG Kate, I'm sorry! I would never have messaged you if you hadn't messaged me first.

> What do you mean? I didn't message you!

> Yeah, you did.

> There is no way on this earth I would have messaged you and if I did, I would have remembered it!!

> OK look, I'm sorry. I will leave you alone, but you did message first.

He sends me a picture message. It's a screenshot of the messages I had sent him. A hello text, then one saying I wished I hadn't sent a text. *Oh my. The shame... Shiiiiiiit! When did I send them? How do I not remember?*

I look at the date of the messages on the screenshot. Last Friday. *Oh fuck!* My heart sinks. I was at a wedding. *My god.* I was completely smashed, more drunk than I have been for absolute years. *Oh jeez!* I must have deleted it and completely forgot. *Oh shit, how embarrassing!*

> Right, I'm so unbelievably sorry. I literally was so drunk at a wedding last week. I obviously messaged you then deleted and have no memory. I'm so sorry again.

> No Kate, I'm sorry. I wasn't thinking. Well I was. You have had me thinking about you all week but I shouldn't have messaged you. Sorry again.

He sends a second message quickly after.

> How are you though? You good?

Don't reply, Kate. Don't do it. Step away from your phone. Go and make a nice cup of tea. How about a bath? A walk? Anything. Just do something else. Whatever you do, do not reply!

Yeah I'm good.

Nooooooo! What is wrong with you? You ridiculous woman! Never has there been a woman so weak to this man's charms. You have never stopped being a lust-struck teenager with this dude.

You?

Oh! You have royally gone and fucked it now! Great! Well done, Kate. This guy has well and truly been let back in.

We end up chatting all morning, taking a trip down Nostalgia Lane. Now I can't stop thinking about him. He's so funny! I've missed chatting to him. It was like getting back in touch with an old friend you haven't seen for years. *Well, he is, I guess. But what are you thinking, Kate?* I'm frustrated with myself. I can't believe I just welcomed him right back in, gave him that magical power over me again without him even asking for it. *Why? How? What on earth for?* I realise I want to see him, talk to him. I need this to be my closure. *I can do this.* All I have to do is remember who he is, what he has done, how I have felt through the years when he's let me down. I need to be stronger than ever. I need to get answers once and for all, keep my mind and heart clear, be strong enough to let this boy walk right back out of my life.

I decide I need to relax to think properly about it all. A bath should do it. I throw the kids' toys out of the tub and run the hot water. I watch as the steam rises and the scent of my bubble bath entices me in. The hot water quickly pulls me to my senses and I relax as my body adjusts to the temperature.

OK. Come on, Kate. Get your head out of the clouds. Think of the bad stuff!

We met at college through friends and before I knew it, I was hoping he would turn up at the club I went to on a Friday or Saturday. He was pretty much the only reason I got dressed up. We were both underage, but back then, everyone could sneak in. One weekend his mighty fine self walked straight towards me on the dancefloor, and we got chatting, up close, shouting in each other's ears to be heard over the club music. A little dancing and boom! Suddenly we were kissing right in front of my friends. *Finally. After flirting*

your arse off all night! We exchanged numbers at last. It was perfect. All normal and carefree guy-hitting-on-a-crushing-girl stuff. Until I found out he already had a girlfriend.

After that, he cheated on various girlfriends with me for years. We would meet up like mates, go out drinking, and end up in bed together. We were both complete lightweights, drinking jugs of Blue Lagoon cocktails, ending up absolutely smashed. Once we were trying to stumble home to his place at one in the morning and on the way decided to have sex in the built-up bushes of the roundabout. It didn't happen though. We just stumbled out of the bushes after a lot of kissing, and he puked over a wall.

Nice. I'm laughing so hard right now. *Stop it, Kate! Focus on reasons to be mad and get closure, not fall in love with him,* I tell myself.

One of his friends told him that he liked me and he said he didn't give a shit. He was happy to let his friend 'have' me. He absolutely did not fight for me. *Thanks!* We had been hanging out for three years and he was happy to completely walk away, even though I had been pretty sure he was going to break up with the girlfriend of the hour and I was next on the list. After so long just messing about, I did think he would have more to say than 'I don't give a shit!' *Nice. Bloody nice.*

He even introduced me to his girlfriend on a night out once. He said I was a mate's girlfriend. *Now that was fucking awkward!* She was so lovely. Me and The Nine were told to play nice and we did. Probably a first back then. The poor girl. That was worse than him cheating on her. Instead, he made his current girlfriend hang out with the girl he had been sleeping with. *Fuck. What a bitch I was.*

Though he was with someone else, I sent flirty texts to him when I was married to Dairy Milk too. It was near the end of our marriage and he left me to deal with the backlash of it all, like I was a man-stealing vixen, dead inside and only after another woman's man. He allowed me to take the blame for everything. Nobody knew I had my own issues and felt lost, confused about life, had gut wrenching guilt that I wasn't happy with my relationship and didn't know how to leave. He didn't stick up for me at all. *Not once did he have your back. Nope, in the end, he threw you under the bus.*

He often said he wanted me when his relationships looked to be over. One time he got back into a previous relationship and didn't even have a conversation with me about why. He just ignored me. *That's never a good thing.* I turned into a complete crazy woman after a night out and paid £50 for a taxi to take me to his house to get the answers I thought I so desperately needed.

He was so pissed off. I refused to leave, and his girlfriend arrived to find me sitting on the kerb. She freaked out completely, screaming, shouting at me, calling me every name under the sun, and he didn't stick up for me. Once again, he just let me take the blame. My phone battery died and he wouldn't call me a cab. I was stuck there until two in the morning, in the rain, until eventually they agreed to call me a taxi home. It was shameful. Embarrassing. Infuriating. An awful, hurtful night.

Ultimately, he is not the only person to blame for all of this. He is the mirror to all my own shameful acts, reflecting my own guilt for every situation I chose to walk into. For some reason I blame him for not saving me from the situations I got myself into.

Open your eyes to the mug, and sometimes the complete bitch, that you were, Kate. You are as much to blame for each and every act. You should remember all these things to help you walk away. You were both cowardly, ignorant, mean and damn cruel. You both can't make up your minds about what you want, who you want. Ask yourself why you never ended up together?

The water's cold. Shivering, I find the hot water tap with my toes and turn it on, topping up the heat. *Damn!* I'm not sure I do want to see him again actually. I don't know why I feel I need this closure though. *Urgh! No, no, I do.* I realise I do want the answers to so many questions. It might be the only opportunity I ever get. For once we aren't hurting anyone. We are both single. I want to know his thoughts, understand where he was coming from. If we never see each other again then so be it, but I want to give myself the opportunity to share an evening with him. Guilt-free.

I stumble out of the bath, tripping over a barbie doll who is as naked as I am, and who's hair definitely needs some work. As I put on my dressing gown the one thing I'm certain of is that I absolutely cannot keep his name in my phone. No-one can know that I am this shockingly weak. I need a name. *Which chocolate treat would you be mister? Hmmmm, Ferrero Rocher? Yes. Yes, that's it!*

I don't need to think too hard about this. He is the special occasion treat. The party chocolate with the beautiful wrapper, making its way around the room. I wonder if this could be a chocolate for the cupboard. *God, I have absolutely no idea, but all the same he is a temptation I've never been able to refuse.*

We continue talking for a couple of weeks. We have easily fallen into being flirty again. Talking about the past and everything we have missed about each other and our bodies. He's coming round to my cottage. We have built this night up to be very special indeed. We've agreed one night together. Closure.

> Your mind and body are all mine tonight.

Wowzers!

> I can't wait. It has been a long time coming to get you all to myself.

> I know the feeling, roll on 7pm.

My log fire is burning. The front room is cosy. I've lit some candles, the lighting is low. The night called for a casual but sexy look. I'm wearing a figure-hugging black and grey jumper dress with thick tights. My hair is curly. It's taken me an hour and a half to sort myself out to look this casual.

It's weird. I'm excited and nervous all at the same time. I'm so nervous I'm shaking. I haven't seen him in years and I have never actually spent an entire night with him. I'm giddy. I could do with some wine now, but I don't want a glass until he arrives in case it goes straight to my head. I bought a bottle of rosé which I know he drinks too.

I hear the door knock. *Oh my god.* He's here. I'm so nervous, I can't even bring myself to hug him when I let him in. I was trying to project confidence. Instead, I'm seventeen years old, insecure and totally infatuated with this boy in front of me.

Ferrero Rocher is wearing dark blue jeans, a white t-shirt and trainers. He looks good, confident, at ease. He is so chilled out in my home, like he's been here a million times before. He's brought two bottles of rosé and I remind him that I'm a total lightweight, telling him I already have a bottle for us to share.

"I know exactly who you are Kate, so you can stop pretending you're some sort of sophisticated wine drinker. We both know how fun we are together on wine. Or Blue Lagoon," he adds, teasing.

Fuck! I forgot this boy knows me.

We pour some glasses of wine and settle down on my sofa. I pull a woollen throw onto my lap. We switch the television on to play some music videos, but it doesn't work. He jumps up and starts tinkering around to get it working. I absolutely adore a man who can fix things. Ferrero Rocher is a mechanic and can pretty much fix anything. It turns me on. As much as I try to be independent, I miss having a man around the house for things like this.

Once the television is working, and the music is on, he decides he isn't too fussed for them. "I like the videos," I say.

He raises his eyebrows. "I know you do, but they are so anti-social. We're here to spend just one night together and I've planned to make the most of it."

Fuck! I'm never going to want him to leave at this rate. What have I done? This is closure Kate. You wanted the closure. You explained to Ferrero Rocher that this night was all going to happen for closure. Stick with the plan! Think of a bad thing he has done. The rain! He left you in the rain, on your own, early hours, no phone. Just remember that. Every time he gets all gorgeous, just think about the rain. We need to talk things through!

Two hours pass. We've been putting all the years we have known each other in order. We talk about all the nights out at our local club, the way we each hoped that the other would be there, so we could spend the night flirting, dancing, kissing. "Or sneaking out without telling our friends we had gone, so we could go home together," I laugh out.

We reminisce about the roundabout night, the walks home from the club, kissing and feeling each other up all the way home.

"Remember when I had my tongue pierced and out of the blue you texted me and asked if I wanted to go out for drinks that evening. I didn't want to turn down the opportunity to hang out with you, so I said yes. I took some painkillers and later that evening we went out on the town. I was nineteen and had just moved back to town and rented that small, one bedroom, basement flat."

I continue, "We went out until the early hours then headed back to mine. Randomly, we slept on the floor with blankets and my duvet, I didn't have any lounge furniture yet!"

We're both laughing.

"Why didn't we just sleep in the bed?" he says.

"God knows! Probably because we were young and just didn't care. Do you realise we've never spent a night in my bed together. Not once."

He is surprised. "Well, tonight is a night of firsts, as well as closure then."

We're flirting but I'm still holding back. I need my answers. I need to talk.

We talk about cheating and the times we used each other to end relationships we were in. Usually him more than me. I was just too willing. Infidelity was an easy excuse for ending a relationship. But it was cowardly behaviour that made people believe there was always more feeling between Ferrero Rocher and I than there really was.

Once, one of his exes was out at the club and he used me to wind her up. I was Dairy Milk's girlfriend at the time and had bumped into Ferrero Rocher on a night out.

"Do you remember how I pulled you over to dance with me," he says. "Then when I saw she was looking over I pulled you closer, put my hand over your mouth without her seeing and made out I was kissing you?"

"Yes, I bloody do! You totally took me by surprise and then our friends came running onto the dancefloor, shouting at us, pulling us apart. We tried to explain it was pretend, but they weren't buying it at first. Once everyone believed us, it was bloody funny."

As we chat, we remember that on the first night he took me back to his house, we didn't actually sleep with each other. "I knew you were so drunk that it wouldn't have been right," says Ferrero Rocher.

"I woke up in the morning, not too sure where I was. I looked up from your duvet and saw you looking at me. I was mortified then pulled the duvet back over my head to hide. You pulled it back down and said good morning to me. Then we made up for what we missed out on the night before."

Rain! Rain! My head is screaming at me.

I lightly cough and clear my throat, to wake myself from the infatuation I have with him. I break eye contact before I can get lost in those beautiful brown eyes forever. I clear my head for a moment by drinking some more wine. *Probably not the best thing to drink right now, but hey.*

I pause a moment, then ask him why he thinks we never actually got together.

"I think it was a timing issue. We have never been single at the same time. Never emotionally available at the same time."

"But we've never left a relationship to be with each other. That must mean quite a bit," I say. "I find it strange…"

He stops me, "I did like you, Kate. I thought we would get together, but it just never happened."

Rain, Kate. Rain! This is closing something, not starting something new.

I can't stop myself. Although I'm apprehensive, the words flow. "I hoped you felt that way, but I can't read you. I've never been able to."

I am aware of just how comfortable I am around him now. Completely at ease, as he is with me. It's as if we have finally remembered who we are. Just Kate and Ferrero Rocher. Catching up and talking about our past, tales of fun, laughter, intrigue.

Closely followed with sadness, betrayal, deceit. Nice? Maybe not. Now it's easy to think about the rain. See Kate? Rain. It works.

I lean back against my space on the sofa and he touches my thigh. Shivers run up my body. I know I shouldn't do this. If the next stage of tonight happens, I could lose this battle for closure. *This wasn't a good idea, Kate. Closure was never going to happen with the night you both had planned. You are going to get lost in this. Nope, I can't help it. I want him. I want to kiss him, feel his lips against mine. I always have.*

I have completely lost the fight with myself. I lean over and kiss him. Before I know it, I'm on his lap pulling his top off. He smells so good, the same as he always did. I am intoxicated. Everything is happening so fast. I can no longer think about anything other than getting him naked.

He stops. He lifts me off his lap and pushes me up off the sofa. He stands in front of me, kissing me softly on my lips, then my neck. I lean into him. He pulls away again and quietly says, "The bed Kate. This time we are heading for your bed."

Yep. I am now lost to this completely.

We head downstairs to my bedroom. We lay on the bed, kissing. Every move slows down. This has all become very sensual. Buried feelings of long ago resurface. The kissing is long and meaningful as his hands move around exploring my body. We are both completely naked now. He is on top of me, holding me, kissing my neck then back to my mouth. Tender, kind, loving…

Oh my god. It is so intense. All the history and yet here we are, Kate and Ferrero Rocher. Oh my god. I actually can't cope with this. I have completely failed in my mission.

"The rain!" I blurt out.

Silence.

"You left me outside in the rain at two A M!"

Oh. My. Fucking. God. Shut up! Why would you come out with that? No one does this shit! Oh fail. Epic, epic fail.

I can't help but start to laugh quietly. I feel the tears run down my cheeks, though. I wipe them away.

He starts to explain that whole night. I stop him. I don't want to hear it. I just kiss him and we continue to have the most meaningful sex I think we will ever have. Closure.

Ferrero Rocher has a fancy wrapper and looks so damn good I need to devour it. There's only true chocolate on the outside though. The inside is wafer, hazelnut creamy filling and nuts. I do enjoy the inside, very much, but I can't fully get my head around it. I never quite get enough time to experience the treat before it's gone. I need time to consume a full box, legitimately, before I can truly say whether it is just for a special occasion, if it's simply too indulgent, or if it can be the good old evening favourite that I'm searching for.

The Player and The Fool

> I know you don't owe me anything but I wanted you to know I'm single.

Fuckity, fuck! Fruit and Nut. My heart is pounding. I just want to take him into my arms and keep him all for myself.

> I have missed you more than you can imagine.

I can't play this cool. I don't even remotely want to. I've never missed someone more than him. My heart stills, preparing for his response. I will it to appear on my phone.

> I have missed you too.

> Let's meet for a drink? Tonight? Tuesday means football, right? After?

> Yeah can do. That little pub halfway? 9pm?

> Yeah sounds good. See you there, then we can talk.

Oh my god. I just want to cry, scream, laugh, all at the same time. I had been numb from the pain. I feel the rush through my body. I'm giddy. The last seven weeks have been long and lonely.

The hurt of him leaving me, finding out I was pregnant, losing the pregnancy, knowing he was holding someone else, kissing someone else, touching her body, holding her hand, holding her as they sleep. I cried all my tears night after night as I lay unable to sleep, imagining the man I love being in bed with someone else, stopping myself from messaging him, knowing that I was blocked and that I could no longer reach him. No 'hello you' in the morning. No 'good night babe'.

Fuck! Just give him back, I would scream in my head. But I couldn't fight for him. Making it work was about bringing their family back together. I understood him trying again with the mother of his children, but being the collateral damage was goddamn painful. Who the fuck was I in comparison to her? No one. Just a woman who loves him. He didn't love me. He told me he had never loved anyone. He doesn't believe in love, only lust.

But I loved him and love him still. I just want to hold him again. I have been waking up to the vision of his ghost in my bed, hugging my pillow so tight, willing the space to be filled with his return for the last two months. Even the night I shared with Ferrero Rocher just couldn't defeat that feeling.

Yes, a long two months. My head has decided to shut the fuck up. It knows there is no way it will beat my heart on this. There's no point trying. My heart won't listen. I've cried far too many tears, unable to stop them. I just want his love back. His kisses. His embrace. I want to drive there now.

So, no, there will be no playing it cool. I won't throw my toys out of the pram because he has dared to contact me, expecting it to be OK to come back to my bed after what he did. The truth is, knowing I will see him in a few hours has made me the happiest I've been since he left.

We're both running late. I was held up with work and his football over ran. We're both flustered and rushing, just so we can make time to see each other, and have realised the little pub we usually go to will be closed soon. It's a weeknight and these quaint little country pubs aren't quite the same as the London bars, frenetic and full all hours. We look online for one still willing to serve us at 10pm and find The Players. As I pull up in its gravelly car park, I'm nervous. I'm actually shaking as I watch him walk around my car towards me. I'm not sure how to greet him. *Should I kiss him? Maybe kiss his cheek? Hug him? Oh God, I'm in total overthinking overload.* I grin from ear to ear, standing awkwardly in front of him with my hands in my pockets.

"Hi," he says sheepishly.

We walk side by side towards the pub noting how neither of us have been here before and head inside. The pub is tiny. It's run down and the lighting is really dim. It doesn't feel at all welcoming and everyone stares and falls silent as we head to the bar. *Fuck! This is weird. Very cliquey.*

Fruit and Nut whispers into my ear. "I don't think they like newcomers."

We laugh and it breaks the awkward atmosphere between us. *God, I have missed this man.*

He pays for our drinks. We walk across the room and sit on a musty old couch that's seen better days. *Jeez, the pub is not great. It's odd.* A group of people playing pool watch us. I'm pretty sure they don't get many newbies in here. Nor have they ever thrown any fresh paint on the walls. It feels old and sleazy here, but I am just so happy to be with Fruit and Nut, his gorgeous, cheeky face looking at me, that I can set the pub's failings aside.

Although we have been apart for what feels like forever, it doesn't take us long to feel comfortable in each other's company again. Our body language changes, softens. We face each other, legs lightly touching, allowing our hands to occasionally touch the other's arms or legs.

We're speaking more freely again as Fruit and Nut tells me what has been happening with him and his ex. She has told him they've grown too far apart, that she doesn't think they work. He says that they both believe now that the relationship is over. "We are both finally on the same page. We're happy to let each other go and we can remain friends."

Tell me you want me. Kiss me. My god I want to kiss you, Fruit and Nut. My heart screams out, battling my brain. *I can't let myself kiss him. Kate, he has got to make that move. You're too lost in him to make rational decisions.*

When the pub closes, it's too early for us to call it a night. We need each other. This night cannot end yet. We drive in our separate cars to my cottage. As soon as the door closes behind us, we're kissing, passion pulsating through our veins. I just need him naked, touching me, skin-to-skin. I need to taste him. I need to feel his body close. I pull his clothes off, hungry for his body. We stumble downstairs to my bedroom, both wanting each other more than we ever had before. The need to reclaim each other's bodies, to feel each other, is intense.

As I kiss him, I keep my eyes open. I want to make new memories. The old ones have been viewed in my mind continuously on repeat since he left. Now he is back in my bed, naked, kissing me, holding me, satisfying me beyond belief. I never want him to leave again. My heart, my head, my body cannot cope with anymore of pushing and pulling to and from each other's lives. My need for him to remain is all consuming. The man I love is back and I want to enjoy his body, his kisses and embrace all night long.

"Don't leave again, I have missed you so much. I just can't lose you again," I say quietly to him. I'm on top of his body, looking down at his beautiful face. "Have you missed me?"

"I've missed this!" he smiles and turns me over onto my back, to show me just what we have both been missing.

He stays the night. It's pure contentment and bliss. Any time either of us stir, we push into each other's lap and gently wake each other to start the fun again. *My god.* This man knows every part of my body and exactly how it works. I have longed so much for him.

As he sleeps soundly next to me, I look at him, his face so peaceful and beautiful. I lay my head down on his chest and feel him breathing beneath me. I look down to his belly, my eyes absorbing all of him. There it is. His birthmark. My birthmark. *Oh God, I adore this birthmark.* Before I know it, I'm kissing it. *Oh shoot, he is stirring.* I'm still. I pretend to be asleep. He rolls away onto his right side. I scooch up behind him and lay my head on the pillow, pushing myself up against his back with my arms around his waist, knees bent into his. The perfect spoon. Content, I fall back to sleep.

For the next two weeks we meet up regularly, enjoying long days in, cuddling on the sofa, evenings out at quaint little pubs (we avoid The Players), silly banter, and sex. Great sex. I'm making the most of the two evenings a week that he's all mine.

"If you lived next door, I'd be stopping in at lunchtime. It's rubbish you living an hour away. We'd be unstoppable if you lived here," he tells me during a call one lunch break.

"We are absolutely unstoppable," I agree. "We need to move to a little village that's all ours. That way we can be together whenever we want."

He has other ideas. "If we lived together, we'd just become complacent and not bother with each other. You probably wouldn't even want sex!"

"Well, you can fuck off with that shite right now," I say jokily, but with a tinge of insecurity at the back of my mind. "I like sex. I like it every morning to start the day and at night too, so don't be thinking any different my dear!"

"Promises, promises" he replies, laughing as we say our goodbyes, telling each other we can't wait until we see each other later.

We meet at a little country pub, The Coach and Horses, just outside of Dover. The barmaid has amazing hair, rose gold, lush. I chat enthusiastically to her about it while we order our drinks, then take our cider and wine and sit at a small table with a bench chair. We scootch in next to each other.

"I love her hair! It's been done really well," I say.

"I love her bum," says Fruit and Nut.

"Yes, she does have a cracking arse," I agree and we chuckle away together. I push a nagging thought to the back of my mind.

We people watch and chat about what's been happening with his ex and the kids. He says that now they both accept that there's no going back, he's going to look for a flat so he can get himself settled again and have the kids on set nights. He tells me about the festivals he wants to attend, and we start planning nights out to comedy clubs.

I can't shift my nagging thought. I turn to Fruit and Nut. "Can I ask you something?"

He looks at me inquisitively. "Ask away."

"Well, there are a few things that just don't make sense to me. The main thing, and please be honest with me as I really do need to know the truth here, is when was the crossover?"

"What do you mean, the crossover? Of what?" He looks confused.

"Well, people don't take a year off their relationship, meet new prospective others then get back together for the kids. Not after it took you so much strength to leave. Not unless you have been hooking up along the way. I'm asking you to be honest with me and tell me when you last slept with her."

Fuck me, that was brave. Straight to the point. Well done, Kate!

I continue, "You see, I think you might have been going back there at the beginning, when you weren't ready to be exclusive with me. Am I right? Please just tell me the truth. I'm not going to kick off. I just need all the answers."

Good question Kate. Nicely put so you don't scare him away.

He looks pale and shaken. "I was never officially single."

Silence. My throat is in my stomach, my heart in my lap.

"You're joking?" I say quietly, finding my voice, willing it not to be true. "Are you actually joking?"

"No. Look, I'm so sorry. I never wanted to hurt you, but I was in such a bad place."

He turns fully towards me, moves closer, places his hand on my thigh. "I didn't know this would turn into anything. I thought it was just going to be a hook up and then you didn't put out. Well done with that by the way," he says, smiling as he tries to lighten the mood.

"Fuck! I don't know what to say. I thought you were going to say you had hooked up a few times. I had prepared myself for that. But this? Who does this?" I ask quietly, feeling the pressure that we are in public.

I shake my head. I'm shocked by what I'm hearing and pull away from our shared body space. I can't believe he is for real, that this isn't some sort of stupid joke.

"I am honestly so sorry, babe. I liked you so much. I just wanted to keep seeing you. Then you were talking about relationship status and Facebook…"

I turn my body square to his. "Oh my god! I asked you about the profile picture. In fact, I asked you three times, you Judas. No, you Peter! Oh hell, I don't know who the fuck it was, but he was a liar. And you have lied to me over and over again. Wow! This is so shit!"

I laugh out loudly, bitterly, boldly, forgetting our public space. I call him out on his bullshit, eyes wide, my body rigid with anger. "You took me to your house. You told me how awful you had been to her. How it took everything you had to leave and all the reasons why you would never go back. Why do that?"

"I haven't lived with her for years. I sleep on the sofa when I'm there. We genuinely don't work living together. It's just that I've never been able to leave officially because she's never done anything to deserve that. I stayed to bring my boys up."

I have so many questions. Why didn't he just find his balls and tell her that he wasn't in love with her? If she is such a wonderful woman, then why treat her so badly? Why not just let her be free? And how could she live with that?

He continues, "I've never been in love with anyone. I don't even believe anyone could fall in love. People just get confused with infatuation and lust. Look, I get it if you want to walk out of here and never see me again, but I

178

really hope you stay. I'm one hundred percent single now. I promise you. Me and her are over now."

I'm silent. I sit still, staring ahead at the bar. "I won't leave. I can't. You've won. I'm in love with you."

As I turn to face him, to look him straight in the eyes, I continue. "I need to try this. I owe it to myself. You've finally opened your heart to me and bared your soul. I believe you when you say you're single and that you can be mine. But know this now, you don't get to do this to me again."

I'm willing it to work. As I tell Fruit and Nut the only way it can be, I hope to God that I'm strong enough to leave if he ever does this to me again. *Fool me once, shame on you. Fool me twice, well, that's shame on me.*

We continue to talk and somehow find ourselves laughing and joking together again, so naturally, as if nothing had happened.

But we head home separately. As I drive, I can't even bear to have music on. I'm numb. Thoughts race through my mind. *I can't tell anyone about this. The shame. The complete stupidity, naivety, the pure blindness of loving someone. He had told me to take my walls down, that I had no reason to have them up. Why do that? Why keep me when I could never really be his? Well, at least I no longer feel bad for sleeping with Ferrero Rocher during our separation. Fruit and Nut has no right to make me feel shit for that.* I consider telling him about it, but it feels like all too much. I'm emotionally exhausted. I just need to get home and go to bed.

When I wake the next day I decide to make a real go of things. I can't deny I have missed him. I love him. I know the whole truth now. He has been in such a bad place emotionally. I feel as if I owe it to myself too, to see just where this can go now. I asked myself if I was willing to give Fruit and Nut another year of my life. The answer is yes.

The last two weeks have seen us texting each other from first thing in the morning to last thing at night. He calls a lot more these days than before, obviously because he's free to. My heart is happy again and I light up when a 'hello you' text from Fruit and Nut pops up. It's so uplifting to have him back in my life. His little jokes, naughty fun texts. We make each other happy.

It's late in the evening and I'm getting settled in bed when WhatsApp pings. It's a picture message from Rhiannon.

> I am so sorry but I thought you would want to see this.

I open the image and my heart stops. Then it pounds, hard and strong in my chest. *Oh wow! This arsehole is something else.*

He's back on Tinder with a whole new bunch of photos.

Fuuuccckkk! This bastard of a man! Kate, Kate, Kate! Stop. Breathe for a moment. He may have uploaded after she left him. He might not be using it. Ugh, but how will I find out? Fuck it. I need to catch this shit of a man out. But to do that I need the right bait.

I regain composure and message Adira.

> Adira, I need your pics for a fake Tinder profile. I think Fruit and Nut is back on it and I need to know if he is using it.

> Hell yeah, use any of these. They fit the tinder box well. Let me know

> Thank you!!! xx

I upload five pictures to Tinder. Adira looks hot in them all. She's perfect. He always said he likes natural girls who are slim and pretty with olive skin and I always said to him that I could never understand how we matched. He'd told me he thought I was sexy even though I'm not his usual type. He never told me I was beautiful though.

Bastard. Just all about sex. Lust.

Adira fits his criteria perfectly. Lightened big curly hair and naturally tanned skin, toned build, skinny. *Aww I love her! She is so lovely to let me use her pictures.* I only put the basic information on her page, naming her Mary. Time is of the essence and it's only going to be there a short time anyway.

I need to get swiping and find him. The only issue is that this could take hours, or even days. On Tinder you swipe through everyone's profile, individually. Three hours later I'm still swiping. It's two in the morning and I need to sleep. I reluctantly close down the app. My body is drained of adrenaline and I fall straight to sleep.

The next day I swipe at every opportunity. I need to find him. I swipe first thing in between the school run and getting ready for work, then in between each client. Just before noon, I see him. His profile. *Wow.* I'm shaking as I take a look through his pictures. All five are new ones. There's nothing from before. *Little cheating, shitty man. Urgh!* I'm fucking fuming, hurt, embarrassed. I forgave his lie, the biggest lie you could ever tell, and he was my man for all of three weeks. *Oh Kate, you know what you have to do.*

I swipe right.

I was sitting in my car outside my client's house. It was time I went into her. Mrs Jennings is a respectable older lady who doesn't say much, but always asks about me and my life. I tell her all about the situation, venting away. I feel my phone vibrate in the pocket of my jeans and pull it out to see I have a match. *What. A. Twat.* I tuck my phone back into my pocket, take a breath and get back to Mrs Jennings' hair.

"Well?" she asks. "Did he swipe you?"

"Yes, he did."

"What a pillock," she says, sighing.

"Well, that's one word for him."

As soon as I leave and am back in my car, I open up the app and look through his pictures again. I'm shaking. Hurting. I am actually shocked that within an hour of Mary the catfish swiping him, he matches with her. He must be on it daily for us to match so quickly. *Fucking lies. Everything that comes out of his mouth is utter SHIT.*

> Hi ya, glad we matched.

Mary isn't here to play it cool. Mary needs you to message back Fruit and Nut.

> Hello you. Me too. You up to much today?

Hello you? Hello you? Oh Kate! That hurts. This whole thing is fucking awful. Let's see what else you have to say Mr Fruit and Nut.

Just at work ATM but it's quiet in the office today so I can message you now.

I work in marketing. What do you do?

Oh nice! You're just sitting down and getting paid to check out what's on the dating market. Good work, if you can get it! 😂

I run a general building company.
Nice in the summer, shit in the winter.

Argh, this guy is a real shit. I wonder how many other women he is chatting away to.

Oh yeah, I bet it is really nice outside all summer. Nice tan. 😊

How long you been single? x

Yeah, let's see what you say here? Three months I reckon.

Hahaha you gonna be perving on me this summer eh?

3 months, all a bit new to this type of thing.

And there it is! Hello Mr Cunty McCuntison! No other word will do right now. We are well past pillock. I am fucking fuming. *Played Kate. Absolutely well and truly played, played, played! What a joke!*

Fruit and Nut and Mary carry on chatting for the rest of the day. And throughout the next. With every message the pain in my heart lessons slightly and my anger builds. And the sick feeling of betrayal increases and makes me want to vomit.

I try to remember to message Fruit and Nut on WhatsApp (as me) and we chat away about him coming to see me this evening. He isn't sure if he can stay the night as he's starting ridiculously early on Wednesday morning and needs to be local. I play it cool and tell him that I really hope he can come over and hang out.

I want to punch him straight in the face, but I'm not a violent woman, nor am I strong enough to make any impact if I did punch him. I have come up with a different plan. A glorious plan. A date with Mary.

Adira is going to meet him for drinks at a pub near his. And I will be there waiting, ready to pounce on him, to watch his little face freak the fuck out as he squirms about what he has done. I want this moment, my Tinder moment. But first I have to bide my time until Sunday. Not long. I only need to see him this evening and play it cool. *I can do this. Come on Kate!*

I talk to Yorkie about the whole mess and my cunning plan. He is gutted for me and really wants to see Fruit and Nut's face when I confront him in the pub. Yorkie says he's getting the train down to come and film it all. We laugh and I'm grateful for the humour. I need to laugh. I'm terrified of opening the lid to the box of emotions that are sitting there, eagerly waiting for me to feel them. Laughter keeps the lid tightly closed.

Fruit and Nut is coming to the cottage that evening. During his journey down, he is messaging Mary on Tinder. He's telling her he's going to football. *Yeah Mary. He isn't playing football. He's on his way to see another woman, but we already know that because I am both!* I'm fuming. I shake as adrenaline courses through my veins. I need to calm down. Tinder shows how close you are to the person you match with and I'm worrying he will see how close he is to both Mary and me. I shut down the chat with Mary. He will be here in fifteen minutes. I need my game face on. I want my Tinder moment which means I have to get through this evening without saying anything. *Fuck. This is going to be harder than I thought.*

He knocks at the door. I take a deep breath and compose myself.

"Hello, you," I say, with an air of smugness, the moment he walks in the door. I smile, hug him, kiss him, trying to be my usual excited self.

He laughs and says, "Happy to see me, are you?"

"I sure am," I reply. I offer him a drink and we go to the kitchen. Before I've even put ice cubes in our glasses, he pushes up behind me. I can feel him hard beneath his trousers and against my bum. He lifts my skirt and while I pour our drinks his fingers start to work away beneath my knickers. I let him, emotions whirling. I wonder why this is not enough for him. I want to make excuses for him, telling myself he is just thinking with his dick when it comes to Mary.

But surely Kate, me, is very much satisfying that part of his life. Urgh, he is a selfish man. A complete prick! Kate, stop thinking about this. Think about how much you want to have that perfect moment to tell him that you played him right on back. Keep your head, put your game face on and let him satisfy you. After all, this is the last time you will have this.

We fuck in the kitchen, then I straighten up my clothing, hand him his drink and we settle down in the lounge. I'm at one end of my sofa and Fruit and Nut is at the other. I'm aware that I'm not as touchy feely, or as bubbly as I normally am, and I know I need to work on that. My glass of rosé will help me to relax. As we sit and talk, I ask him about how he is finding life without his ex. Is he OK? The kids? Is she OK?

"It has been difficult at times," he says. "But I know it's the right decision for us both. You know, I have nearly always had two women on the go. It is quite strange to only have you."

Oh, my fucking god! Is he going to fess up? This is definitely his moment to tell me. I probe him a little more, trying to see where this is going.

He says, "I mean, I'm just saying, what if we both had someone else? One person to have a bit of fun with? I want this to work between us. I know what I'm like and you told me that I'm not to lie to you ever again, so this is me. All of me. And I want you to know and understand that."

Holy fuck. I'm not too sure what to say. I'm not angry. I'm actually relieved he is talking to me and opening up about this. *Does it mean I have to tell him about Ferrero Rocher? No, Kate. It's a completely different thing. Isn't it?*

I take a deep breath and say, "I'm glad you're talking to me about this. I actually do understand where you are coming from. The thrill of talking to someone else, sleeping with someone else, is exciting."

I move over to him and climb on his lap, facing him. "But I need to know the rules before I answer you. There would have to be rules. I would want the other people to know that we are a couple."

As I play with the buttons of his shirt, he says, "OK, so you're saying they need to know about our situation, and they need to be OK about it? That would make it harder, but yeah I'd be OK with that."

He pushes himself against me. He is enjoying this. He's hard. He pushes again.

I grind myself against him in response and say confidently, looking him straight in the eyes, "OK. And what you need to realise is that while you are out there doing your thing, I will be over here fucking someone else."

"No way. I'm not OK with that," he responds quickly. "Forget it. Let's not do that."

He needs to know it will never be all his way again. I tell him, "The thing is, we're equally fun and adventurous and I really don't feel the need to look at others. I think we satisfy each other more than enough to not need naked fun elsewhere. But if you are fucking someone else, well, I'm telling you now, I will be too."

He shakes his head and tries to push me onto the couch, to take the top position. I distract him with a kiss and hold my ground.

"No honestly," he says softly. "I like what we have. I'm being an idiot. It's just a new situation that's all."

My feisty, domineering self has turned me on. I want this man naked. I want him to satisfy me one last time before Sunday, knowing I have my power back and I am in control. It's my turn to use him for sex, to manipulate him.

Once again, I am amazed at this man's skills. *How will I ever go back to normal sex after experiencing the great stuff that is the perfect combination of Fruit and Nut?*

As we lay cuddling on the sofa, his phone rings. He tells me to keep quiet. His ex is calling and he needs to answer. They have a brief chat about the kids and she is gone. Shortly after she sends him a series of text messages. She tells him she isn't stupid, that she knows he is with someone else and that he is an arsehole because they only broke up a few weeks ago. He tells me he needs to go, and I see him out.

Wow, this is so unbelievably fucked up. Three women in his world in one evening. His girlfriend who ended things just weeks ago, his previously unwitting mistress, and his new woman on Tinder. He thinks only of his needs and no one else's. He has absolutely no respect, or even a thought, for anyone but himself. He doesn't have the emotional depth or capacity to take anyone else's emotions into consideration.

I feel lost right now. Completely lost. I feel as though I am in a wind tunnel, fighting to move forward, unable to hear, see or think clearly.

I message him the next day as Mary, but he doesn't reply. Was his change of heart genuine? I'm unsure. I message a little from myself, but just the basics. Everything feels tainted now. I no longer want to see a 'hello you' text. After all, it's just a line to send to everyone, probably because he has no idea what our names are. Copy and paste, same name for everyone. You. It's easy and clear. We are all just a number to him. Insignificant unless we meet his needs. He knows how to play the ultimate game of Tinder. How to play me and everyone just like me who came before.

I call Adira and tell her what happened with Fruit and Nut, that he opened up and told me his concerns about being in a monogamous relationship.

"He asked me about having an open relationship with him, Adira! I know he will cheat if he can't have that. Any woman who chooses to stick with him will need to understand him. Maybe the right woman could. I wish, even now, that we had worked. I wish I was enough for him."

"Oh Kate, he doesn't deserve you. You are enough, but you're right, you just aren't the woman for him."

I tell her he has stopped messaging Mary, so the Sunday night date is a no go. I was all fired up for it, bringing him down and showing him that he doesn't get away with making a fool out of me. But now I just feel the sadness that we are over and that once again we are saying goodbye.

I text Yorkie and tell him Sunday is off. He's disappointed we won't get to make a viral video of the bad boy getting caught out in an epic way, but I tell him I just can't do it. I need to tell Fruit and Nut it's over and ask Yorkie if an epic long text will do instead. He says the video would be better, but as long as his favourite haemorrhoid (*God, I love Yorkie*) is OK, then I should do whatever I think is best.

Yep, I am going to text him a 'long' text. I do rather like those. I chuckle away. I feel that change in energy again. I no longer feel the need to make a show and dance out of it, but I want Fruit and Nut to know that I caught him. Yes, a nice long text should do it.

Hello you. I'm sitting here, reflecting and feeling foolish.

I fell in love with a man that didn't exist. He was a strong man, a little lost, but he was finding his way in a new chapter in his life. His kids meant the world to him and he still wanted to raise them with their mum. He was beautiful, funny and got what he wanted. I really liked this man, grew to love this man, to care for this man and wanted to grow with this man. He told me our 'non-relationship' had to end, even though he didn't want it to, but that he needed to be with his ex, that he needed to bring his boys up and can't do that if she stops him seeing them. I understood and even though I had all this love for him, even though I cried myself to sleep thinking I would never see him again, I agreed with what he was saying because I knew that sometimes you need to take a step backwards, before you can move forward. I thought this man came back. A new lease of life, wanting to live life and have new experiences beyond women. He was brave and told me that he had lied about the biggest thing of all, that he had never in fact been single. He told me it was only me he was talking to online and asked what I wanted. I said I wanted him, without the lies, and to exclusively see me. He knew I wanted more and was happy to work towards more.

I said to myself, fool me once shame on you, fool me twice, shame on me. You fooled me twice.

This is a message to ask you not to hurt us women who give you our hearts and who make room for you in our lives. This is to ask you to choose the path that is right for you, so you no longer choose the path you stray from. I would have grown with you because I loved you. You couldn't even stay off Tinder. Yes, Mary was a set up. 'Hello you'. Wow my heart dropped into my stomach. 'You need someone to cuddle up with'. What a line! And 'I've been single three months'. Hmmm, I knew all about that one.

You see I'm not your ex. I'm Kate. You can't do this to women. It's cruel. I have no idea how you could have treated me like this but then I have no idea how you have done this to all the women who came before me. Why would you put that much effort into a fuck? Think of the great things you could achieve if you put that much effort into your career.

So, this is a message to the man I hope you will become, the man you sold yourself as. Maybe it will fall on deaf ears or maybe you will do the decent thing. There's a little thing you haven't learned about women yet. We like to be told the truth. No one is perfect and we tend to forgive mistakes, but when you lie, and you lie well, we don't like that. You have lied so much the storyline is confusing.

Please just stop hurting us. X

Ten minutes after I hit send my phone buzzes. Fruit and Nut is calling. *Shit. Best answer.*

His words rush out. "Babe, I'm so sorry. I don't know what to say. Was it your mate or actually you that I was talking to on Tinder?"

"Me."

"Fuck. I had no idea. And I came round…" He realises I had played him. "We had sex! You said nothing!"

"I know. I had to play the game 'til you met Mary. I kinda wanted to get you to meet my mate and then I was going to pour a drink on you. All seems a bit silly now. I just wasn't sure how I was going to tell you I knew." I laugh ironically.

"Ah babe, this is all shit, isn't it?"

"Yeah, it really is." I almost pity him. "To be honest, I don't think you have any idea what you actually want. It wouldn't even surprise me if you get back together with your ex."

"We were actually talking last night. I don't know what to do. If we didn't have the kids, well, we would have been over a long time ago. But we do, and when she calls me back, I go. She's never done anything wrong to me. I feel so bad."

"For her to take you back time and again she must be so lost in you. I know how she feels. You seem to have something that keeps women coming back. I gotta say, she could have anyone. She is one hot chick and yet she chooses you over and over. But you never choose her. You never put her first. You stay and treat her so badly time and time again, using women like me who end up as collateral damage. It's exhausting."

"Urgh babe, I'm lost. It works to a degree being with her, the kids. I get to live at my mum's. We are separate, but together. If it was just about the relationship, I would be there with you right now."

"No you wouldn't!" I cry. "I can't trust you! The only way I would be with you now is if you rocked up with an engagement ring, ready to announce to the world that you are off the market. And that would be after you'd been single for a year! I love you, I do, but I need to love *me* more. My head has been all over the place with this shit, and it's not even my shit."

He laughs and tells me just how much he will miss me. Again. I tell him the same and we say our goodbyes.

Once again, I'm numb. I know the next few weeks will see me live through an array of emotions, but I will make it through. I'm sure of it. Just like I did the fifty million times before. How many times has my heart been broken by this man? A need a good boxset and some chocolate. Well, maybe ice-cream. I think chocolate is the problem here. Yep, 'Game of Thrones' from the beginning. Blood, guts, gore and a whole lotta use of the word *cunt*. That will see me thinking straight again, I'm sure of it.

The Mistress

I made it through nine weeks. I even found my way back on to Tinder and had a couple of dates. Neither made me laugh and all I did was compare them to Fruit and Nut. He's still there when I wake up in the morning cuddling my pillow, wishing it was his chest. *Ugh, how am I not over this?*

And I think I was addicted to the sex with him. It was absolutely amazing. I'm not sure I'll find anything like that ever again, even though I know I had some mind-blowing orgasms before he came along. The lack of it now is rubbish. I don't help myself to forget about him either, because every time I use my rabbit all I think of is him. Sometimes, I think maybe one quick session with him would fix me. It would help me move on slowly, like a drug addict being given something to help break off the addiction.

I get mad at myself when I want to text him. He might not even want to hear from me. He might be happy and finally have let his walls down and his girlfriend in. That is what should have happened. She has put in the years to tame that boy. Maybe she has finally won.

Oh, goddamn it! Now I want to know.

I battle with the two sides of my brain.

No, you don't Kate. Knowing will not end well. You will either cry because they are happy together, or you will cry because you will end up meeting him, sleeping with him and realising you will never be enough. You would have to leave all over again and be right back to where you are now. But you already know what you're going to do now the seed has been sown. My god, it's ridiculous.

> Hey I have just looked and seen that your Tinder profile is still up. You haven't deactivated it. Just deleting the app isn't enough. Unless of course you are actually using it and are single. Then that's my bad.

> Really???!!! Shit, better sort that out!

How's the Tinder search going?

I'm not really feeling it tbh. Made myself go on a couple dates but left as soon as I could. Feel like I should be out there but on the other hand I'm not bothered.

Everything else in life is great so I'm just plodding along with life.

I know what you mean. At least everything else is awesome.

Just same old, same old here. xx

Well, I'm glad it's the same old for you. Means you're being good. x

Yeah being good is great... not x

Even though the sensible part of my brain is crying out for me to stop, the texts just keep coming. I push further. I just can't stop myself.

I know I said that I regretted meeting you but that isn't true. I just wish you had been the man I thought you were. I miss your cheeky smile and our banter. Wish you were single and that I was enough for you. x

> Definitely not single. Fruit Salad has just got me on a long-term contract that I can't break. I'll pay heavy taxes if I do. As much as I would love to take the risk with you. 😁

He knows he's a chocolate bar after we had a silly conversation about it a while back. He loves the fact he's Fruit and Nut. The best one. He even started referring to his girlfriend as Fruit Salad. *How on earth did I get to this point? That boys are chocolate and I am being compared to a sweetie, along with the rest of his women? I wonder what sweet I am?*

And they are back together and staying together. Yep, this totally sucks. I need to keep walking away. I continue texting regardless. *Oh Kate! Stop!*

> Oh Mr...you do make me chuckle. 😁

> Glad I amuse you! 😄

> Can I ask you something?

> Hmm sounds interesting. Fire away.

> Do you miss our sex? The only thing that is really tough for me now is the lack of sex. Knowing what I had with you in bed, that doesn't come along very often. More than likely, getting someone new into bed will be a waste of time. It's a really shitty thing to have lost. I feel like you're a drug or something. That I'm addicted to you. And nothing I can do about it.

That's actually not the first time I've been compared to drug addiction.

Hahahaha!! Oh, you say all the right things, don't you! Big head! Although to be fair, it's true.

If there is one thing I'm good at, it's that!

Oh my god! He is so arrogant, but it's so true! I still can't help myself. I have to see where this is going.

Yeah, yeah. I have to agree with you there.

So how long you going to hold out then?

Hold out from what? 😊

Oh well, if you don't know then I don't know what I'm talking about.

I'm fishing this weekend. Maybe you fancy coming by and having this chat in person.

Shit! Am I really doing this?

> If I drive there, it
> won't be for chatting!

> Sounds very good to me.

Oh damn it. I feel like such a bitch. I'm going to sleep with him, knowing he is still with her, all just because I'm totally addicted to him.

I think about the shitty karma I will get from this selfishness. And the guilt. The guilt will be awful. My head is screaming at me. *Walk away Kate, walk away. Please! You know you can sleep with him and that will be great. But you also know you will never be enough.*

When you decide to start a diet you have a choice. Get rid of the last temptation in the box or gobble it up and start the diet afterwards. Well, I made my choice and the diet starts after.

I sit in my car putting the address for the lake he is fishing at in my sat nav. *I am just going to do this once. It will help me to move on. Never again,* I say to myself. *I'm sure of it!*

In fact, I have never been less sure of anything in my entire life. I know I am playing with fire. And I haven't used one match. I used a whole bloody box of them and a bucket load of fuel. *Oh Kate, this could be the beginning of something really bloody bad.* I start the car and put it into gear. I'm going fishing all the same.

I arrive and park my car next to his little blue van. *Ahhh. How I have missed this van. Stop it Kate! No feelings. Just sex. Only sex. Or go home. Do not let love be a factor here.*

> I'm here. I've parked next to your van.
> You sure I can leave it here? I feel sick.
> Think I should turn around and leave.

> It's all good babe, just walk up the
> path and you will see me at the lake.

Urgh. Don't call me babe. I don't want any niceties. Plus, it's just a name he calls everyone who came before me, like when he says 'hello you'. A safe substitute because I doubt he remembers anyone's name. OK, Kate, that's harsh, but good work. Keep thinking like this.

I walk up the path nonchalantly, trying to look innocent. It reminds me of when I was a teenager, sneaking into the Catholic school boarding house to sleep with the head boy. It was shameful, but bloody fun and exciting too. *This is not fun and exciting though Kate. Back when you were both single, it was fun. Now you are a willing player in this sordid affair, willing it on.*

Oh, there he is. His hot self in a t-shirt, shorts and flip flops. Oh, fuckity fuck! Bad idea. Fully bad. I'm going to open up my heart again. I can feel it. I just want to kiss him!

He sees me. "Hey babe," he says as he ushers me over to his tent.

"Aw, it looks smaller than the pictures. It's so cute."

"Yeah. You need to stay inside in case anyone drives up," he tells me. "I'm not supposed to have guests."

I sit on the little bed. This all feels strange. It's not like our time before, when we were hanging out legitimately, when I believed the stories and lies he was telling me. Now this all feels a bit seedy. It's all premeditated. I'm not so sure how excited I am anymore. *Kate, that's a good thing! It means you won't try and do this again.*

He sits down next to me. I feel his leg against mine and there it is. *Boom!* The chemistry. *Oh, this man, this man, this man. Everything I want is back next to me once more. But he's not mine.* The pang hits me hard. I want him. He wants me. But it doesn't make sense to me. We aren't together. *But then when he had you, you weren't enough. How can you love someone, have them want you and somehow find the strength to walk away? I'm not strong enough for this.*

I'm overthinking everything again. I know I shouldn't be here, but then he kisses me. Moving the kisses from my mouth to my neck and all I want is to be here. With him. His body close to mine, skin to skin. As I rush things, he slows me back down. Powerful Kate has gone. He's in control now, just how he always was before. I love this man and there is no denying it. He removes my dress, lays me down and his lips and hands explore my body once again. In his presence I feel like I'm home. The weight of his body on top of me allows me to reclaim back the security I've been longing to be returned. I feel him deep inside of me and I never want it to stop. I don't want him to leave me again.

My heart is craving this man whilst my head screams in anger, knowing that this man has disrespected me time and again, made a fool of me for over a year. My heart is begging to let him stay, hoping one day I will be enough, that one day he will only want me to be the one he laughs with, builds a life with, makes love to, allows through his walls. *My god, Kate! The girls before you all hoped the same, the girlfriend hopes for it now, and yet none of you will ever really be enough.*

We finish and I put my clothes back on, re-tie my hair into a messy bun and ask for a drink of his water. He gives me some. I need to leave. He knows it. I know it. I don't belong here. He makes a joke. "So, are you my mistress now?"

A shiver runs down my spine as I turn to him and say, "No. I'm not going to be your mistress. I need to forget you. This was just an itch I needed to scratch. You are a forbidden fruit and I am a complete nut for wanting to taste it."

We don't kiss goodbye. I can tell that he is nervous that someone might see. *Maybe he is worried about his girlfriend. Maybe he does have a conscience after all. OK, Kate. Stop that right now. You're not the first, you won't be the last.*

I walk away, determined not to look back as I ask myself: 'Can my heart win this?'

Over the next two weeks, we haven't got together but we have texted each other a little. A lot actually. I haven't told anyone, not even my closest friends because I know how it should be. I'm truly embarrassed at how much I like this man after the way he has treated me, disrespected me. The way I have disrespected myself.

I did this. Ultimately, I did this. I let him in, I fell in love. And then the bomb went off. I feel like I'm lost in the smoke of it all. I know it will clear but I can't move on with my life until I can see again, until I can clear the smoke with answers to my many questions.

I really believe that the key to letting this go is getting answers. Finally, I might understand just how I got so drawn in and why he picked me to do this to. This man convinced me to let my walls down and let him in. I feel stupid, completely foolish for being in love with him, even after I found out that he lied from day one, even when I questioned situations that just weren't adding up and he told bigger lies to cover his tracks.

Every time I see a text from him my heart kicks in though. It overrules my head and doesn't want me to leave his side. I know how selfish I'm being, how disrespectful this is to a woman who has no idea what's going on. I know that karma will pay me back for this one day. I ask myself why I continue to do this and realise that I matter too. I was brought into this mess, completely innocently. I had no idea what games he was playing and now I'm stuck in it. I'm caught in a horrible trap I can't get myself out of. He shouldn't have been on Tinder in the first place. He should have told the truth from the beginning. It should have been her he had the conversation with about an open relationship, not me. Then I tell myself she hasn't helped herself. *She forgives him time and again. She should have realised herself that she was in an open relationship.* I tell myself it's mean to think like that. *Yeah, Kate but come on! At some point we have to walk away from men who disrespect us. Wow, hypocritical now Kate. You could be her in fifteen years, if your heart has its way.*

We plan to meet during another fishing trip and this time I'm staying the night. During the last month of talking and texting, we've only met twice. The first time at the lake and another time he came to my cottage. But we haven't spent the night together until now. I will have him all to myself for twelve hours and think this is it. He has promised to give me all the answers I need.

I'm tucked up in the tent laying on the bed watching him sort all the fishing bits and bobs out. I feel strangely excited about seeing such big fish tonight, if he catches one. I've seen pictures of those he's caught before and they are huge. Music is playing quietly on the radio. I'm going to make this a good memory to end our relationship with. He is so damn handsome, manly with his rugged fishing gear and clothes. I love him. I accept that now and I understand that just because I love him, it doesn't mean he loves me, nor that he wants me. I'm tired of fighting the feeling. I'm at peace to just let it run its course. It will end one day.

"It's so beautiful here. Picturesque," I say.

"I love it here. There are some great fish to catch, a stunning view and complete peace where I can retreat from the world."

"I can see that… So Mr. Mister. You said I get answers. Can I have them please." I'm not messing about tonight.

"Other than everything, what do you want to know?" He's smiling cheekily, but I think he's nervous. "Ask away."

"OK, so you told me that you cheated before, over and over. Why do you go back to her time and again? Why can't you leave?"

There's no hesitation when he answers, as he repeats what he has said before. "Because she's never done anything wrong to me. She's honest and kind, and that means I have no reason to leave her."

"But it doesn't need to be for something she has done wrong for you to leave. You can't help how you feel. You're treating her so badly." He hadn't asked for my opinion, but I tell him anyway. "And why did you go to such great lengths to hide this all from me? I feel like such a twat. I saw the signs. I asked you over and over and you just told me such shit."

"No, I told you the truth. Everything about my past, how much I liked you. I didn't want it to stop, so yes, I lied about us being in a relationship. But I don't live there. I have no plans to ever live there. I love my kids. I love her as their mum, as my friend. She is a great woman, but we don't work living together."

"It's cruel. You should let her go. She is bloody hot and if she is this kind loving woman that you tell me she is, then she deserves to have a man in her life that adores her, loves her!"

He doesn't know what to say, so I carry on questioning. "Do you still have sex?"

"Yes, but rarely. And it's nothing like it is with us," he says adamantly.

"It doesn't really matter how you have sex, it's just the fact that you do."

I carry on asking random things about them not living together, the women that came before who then became the mistress. I start to get upset about the whole situation.

"You made me feel foolish."

"I know what women like, babe. I know how to play the game, don't feel foolish. This was me selfishly wanting you."

Like a fool, I ignore what he says about playing a game, hearing only that he is taking responsibility and he wants me. We start kissing, undressing, doing what we do best. A buzzer sounds. Not one in my head telling me to see sense. The one alerting us he has caught a fish. *Oh exciting!* We jump up, straightening ourselves out. I have my bra and trackie bottoms on. He is topless and has his shorts on. He is being dominant, telling me what to do and what to fetch him, to help bring in and weigh the fish. It's a massive catfish. *Ironic.* I touch it. It's all slimy, but beautiful. I really love it. I take a picture of him holding it then he puts it back.

Throughout the night more fish set off the buzzer. After each fish has been caught, photographed and released, we climb back into bed and cuddle up close, enjoying the fact we have a whole night together.

I leave at eight the next morning. As I drive home, I know nothing has changed. I still love him, but then I was expecting this. The questions I had for him answered, I now have many questions of myself. *Can I do this? Can I be the other woman? Will he ever leave?* He told me that he will when the boys are older. I'm not sure I believe anything anymore. Foolishly, I tell myself to stick with him, to let it run its course. Maybe if I allow myself to have him, then the strong feelings will all fade away. The novelty will wear off. Besides, I've been the mistress for the last year, albeit unknowingly, so why end it now?

I toy with the different ways to make this work during the whole journey home. I don't even have the music on. I just need to think clearly with no influence from love songs. By the time I reach my cottage I know I am going to stay with him. If I am honest with myself, I was looking for a way to convince myself to give it a try anyway.

Three months have passed since our fishing trip. We try to see each other once a week, or at least every other, on wet days when his work is rained off. We've named these days our Bubble Days. I live for them. I know it's crazy, but I change plans I have made just to make sure I can see him. He always arrives just after the morning school run and leaves just before the afternoon one. We lay together in bed watching boxsets, having sex for hours, and debating life (which always ends up with one of us telling the winner to shut up and ending the debate by taking the lead in having sex). We just laugh so much, and I adore being tucked up in his arms, dozing as I hold his body close to mine. I love the smell of his skin. I love the feel of his skin against mine. And his hair. I adore his hair and the way he never quite gets the cut he wants from his barber. Always a high fade, never a low one. It makes me smile. He's a pretty boy at heart really and not my type at all until now.

It isn't enough for me though and I always start to miss him before he has even left, in that last hour he is with me, knowing he will be gone again. He never tells me that he loves me. I think he does though. *This can't all be for sex, surely? Why come all this way when he could pick a girl who is local? He wouldn't fight to keep me in his life if he didn't love me would he?* I wonder if I am just talking myself into it, but the way he kisses me now is different. He has always had the moves, but now he wants to kiss for longer and draws out every embrace.

God, I wish we could spend a night together. We haven't spent a night together since our fishing trip. It feels like such a waste when I know he stays four nights a week at his mum's and that he only sleeps on the sofa at hers. I long for the time we can spend the whole night together again.

As time progresses, I begin to feel more and more frustrated with this affair.

"Happy Birthday to you, Happy birthday to you, Happy Birthday darling Kate, Happy birthday to you," my mother sings down the phone to me, her annual wake-up call.

"Morning Mum," I say with a sleepy smile filling my face. We catch up for five minutes until I hear the girls coming down the stairs into my bedroom. They arrive with an overloaded tray. There's a cup of milky tea, a bowl of chocolate cereal and a random pot of jelly with a jammy dodger biscuit on the side. *Bless them! This has made my birthday already!* They sing the birthday song to me and I check my phone. Birthday texts from The Nine, Adira, Sadie, Emily, family, Wonka. *Good old Wonka.* And Yorkie, who has actually sent me thirty-five happy birthdays to mark the occasion.

Then I get a birthday call from Fruit and Nut. "Happy birthday Babe. You having a good morning? I'm sorry I'm not there now, giving you a birthday morning treat!"

I feel happy at first and very quickly the emotions change to jealousy, sadness and resentment. *He could be here if he had wanted to be,* I remind myself. *He could have had flowers sent to my door. Hmmm, I may at last be feeling the correct emotions for this situation.*

We are using FaceTime while he takes a bath. "If you are heading over to your girlfriend's house, why don't you just go straight from work and have a bath there?" I ask.

"I don't have anything there, so I pop home, have a bath, get changed and then head over."

"I find that so strange because you always have a shower here." I pretend to be stern. "I'm telling you now Mister, there will be none of this rubbish when we live together."

We've started talking more and more like this. He does too, more jokingly, but I know he means it.

He raises his eyebrows. "Oh, you want to live with me, do you?"

"Well, yeah. And no sleeping on the sofa either. You will be in *our* bed overnight. Even if we argue."

"Well, we shall see. You gonna move here?" he asks.

"Nope. We can live halfway. In Deal."

"That could actually work," he agrees. "Well, I want dinner made for me and housework done. You will need to be a little wifey."

I laugh. He's too funny. "You have another thing coming if you think I am going to be the little wifey at home. I'm far too busy. I've never been the little wifey, not even when I was a wifey!"

He often tells me he will leave her. In time. Eight years, four years, next year. The time lessens every time we argue and I take time out from our relationship.

"If we could live together, would you honestly want to?" he asks.

I tell him he is the only man since Dairy Milk that I have honestly wanted to live with.

"But now is not our time. This whole relationship is a mess, built from lies and deceit. All the love I have in the world for you is not enough for us to fix this mess. You can't leave your relationship for me. You need to leave because you aren't happy and move out somewhere neutral. Live on your own for a while. Spend six months or so sorting your head out, settling the kids into a new way of life, supporting them. Only after that can we truly allow ourselves the time we need to grow in this relationship. I don't think we could live together until you have shown her that you left for you, not for another woman."

I overthink daily now.
What choices do I have?
I leave? This results in no Fruit and Nut.
I stay? No Fruit and Nut.
I date other men, but if I move on, no Fruit and Nut.

Whatever I do, I can't win. Nothing gives me Fruit and Nut.

It is such a waste. He's not even happy with her, but that's his story, not mine.

After weeks of conversations, back and forth over the same topics, we finally agree on what feels like our only real option. To walk away for a year. No contact. Then in one year's time we will go for a drink with clear heads.

By closing the door, but not locking it, I think I might finally set my heart free. No more clinging on to what doesn't belong to me. I love him, but not enough for the two of us, and we have reached the time for me to love myself more. I have spent too long at the ball and midnight is finally chiming. It's time to put this all on a shelf because I have lost who I am to it and so has he. I need to use this time to listen to the music, cry, scream, shout and fully figure myself out. I might date again, but without Fruit and Nut in my head. A year out will make me stick to this.

Fruit and Nut is the man I have allowed myself to get the closest to. He fought for me to take my walls down and succeeded. A chocolate bar with nuts and raisins. It was delicious enough for me to consume a whole sharing bar in one sitting, and to keep going back for more, but this just resulted in sickness. If I carry on eating too much it can only lead to heart disease.

It's time to walk away, go on a diet, then maybe treat myself to a holiday Toblerone.

Galaxy Smooth: Generation Gap

I'm leaving Adira's flat in London. We had a night out and I stayed over. I'm not quite ready to go home yet so I wonder what Yorkie is up to.

> Oi, Poo Face, Are you about? I want wine and I'm nearly at Kings Cross. Fancy a catch up before I head home as I don't have the girls until 6pm.

> Hello you little turd, yeah why not? I will leave now and meet you in half an hour.

Whoop whoop, he is on his way. Yay. I can't wait to see him. He really is a true friend. I hope we are always besties like this. I also really wish he was gay so that I didn't need to explain our friendship all the time. God, I wish people could accept that guys and girls can be just friends, even if they have seen each other naked.

We meet at a bar right next to the giant bird cage at Kings Cross station. I love this sculpture. There's a swing beneath it and it lights up at night. *So cool!* I tell Yorkie about my night out with the girls. I pretty much talk about myself for forty minutes before Yorkie begins to tell me what he has been up to.

"Erm excuse me," I interrupt jokingly, "But our little chats are about me, me, me!" We laugh.

I love that we have so much fun with each other and can tell each other everything. He's just broken off his three-month relationship with a girl he was seeing. He's a bit gutted, but not as gutted as he had been over She-who-shall-not-be-named. We drink red wine and laugh as we check people out and say to each other 'Oooh, they are sexy'. It's become a bit of a game. We are such pervs right now. *It is such a fun game though!* I can't stop checking out the barman. Tall, six feet tall at least. Slim, but muscular build and what a beautiful face he has. Very kissable lips too.

"I'm going to give him my number."

"Fuck off are you. If you do, I will be seriously impressed with you."

"I am!" I know I can. *You can do this Kate, come on girl!* Sometimes you need to be your very own cheerleader in life, and this is one of those times. I don't know what has come over me. Actually, I have had a few glasses of red wine so that could be helping, but I'm only tiddly and I'm certain I can do this. I write my number and my name on a napkin and add a little heart because I think it's cute.

"Change the heart to a classy kiss, not a naff heart," advises Yorkie. I do as he says and fold the paper napkin in half. I scan the bar, searching for the handsome barman's face. He's not on this floor. Yorkie doesn't think I will have the guts to hand over the napkin, but I really want to do it. I hop off my seat and begin my hunt.

This is actually quite a thrill! I spot him over the balcony working at the downstairs cocktail bar. I head down, willing him to look up so I can catch his eye. Nothing. Not once does he look up from his work. *Hmmmm, what to do? I've lurked for a few minutes now, very patiently. Yep, Kate, this guy ain't going to notice you. Fuck.* My confidence is dwindling. *Right, what can I do? What can I do?* I stop a waitress and just go for it.

"I fancy the pants off the barman. I've never done this before. Do you think you could help me out by handing him my napkin note?"

She laughs kindly and takes the note for me. I watch her walk over to him as I head back up the stairs. I see her talking to him and then they both look over as the waitress points me out. I shyly wave and he laughs in a shocked and shy way to his colleague. *Damn, why did I do that?* I feel a little silly, but also proud of myself for even giving it a go. I find Yorkie, sit myself back down and take a large mouthful of red wine as Yorkie congratulates me, or rather mocks me, for my attempt at handing out my number. I nearly choke on my wine as I laugh hysterically.

Anthony and my sister-in-law Emma join us for a short while before they head off to meet some other friends. I tell them how I'm trying to move on from Fruit and Nut and that Yorkie is helping me. They both like Yorkie and while he and Anthony chat away, I feel a strong sense of family. Yorkie would fit in so well. Sometimes I think life would be so good if we had fancied each other more and the relationship could have been more. I know that things happen for a reason, and I know we weren't meant to be more than this. Our friendship means the world to me.

When Anthony and Emma leave, we have one last drink before I need to catch the train. Day drinking has taken its toll on me a little and I need to get home. As we sit enjoying our drinks, the sexy barman suddenly appears right in front of us.

"You haven't text me?" I exclaim. *Oh, my fucking god, Kate! Where did that come from? Why have I just said that?*

"Do you have a girlfriend?" *Oh my god, stop talking! Stop talking now!*

He tells me he didn't hear me and is unsure what I said. *Oh my!* His accent is beautiful. Spanish. *Hot as fuck!* Even though I am cringing inside, my head mortified by what I have said, my mouth starts up again, repeating what I had said to this sexy, out of my league, beautiful barman. He starts laughing and looks over his shoulder to his fellow barmen. Even his laugh is big, bashful and blooming gorgeous.

"I'm sorry," he says. "I have a girlfriend."

Damn. I'm not surprised though. I think I would be more surprised if he was single. He seems quite embarrassed and moves to a different area of the bar. Yorkie and I laugh about what a let-down that was and try to see if we can find the girl he had fancied to give her a note.

By the time I am ready to leave, Yorkie is at the bar, chatting to the hot girl. I'm actually looking forward to getting home now. I have too many responsibilities for day drinking. I'm a little piddled and will need to use the time on the train to sober up a little. When I get home the girls will be at mine getting ready for bed. *Doh. How does Yorkie have the power to make me forget I have to do adulting and parenting? He is so damn fun that I forget life.*

The next day I receive a WhatsApp message from a number I don't know. But hang on, there's a picture. *Yay!* It's the barman.

It's definitely him from the bar yesterday.

Ahhhhhh! Whoop whoop, mini wave to me! The sexy, gorgeous, beautiful barman has sent me a message. I have the biggest smile on my face right now. *Hang on Kate. He said he has a girlfriend! I can't be doing with all that craziness again. Been there, done that, and well and truly over it!*

> Hello. I thought you said you have a girlfriend?

Sorry, I had to say that because I didn't want the other barman talking to the staff about the situation. I was shy and embarrassed. Sorry. x

Oh OK. Well this makes me very happy indeed!

I would have text you last night, but I was working until close.

No worries. So tell me a little bit about yourself?

I have just realised that I have no background information on this dude. Now I'm wishing for an online profile to read. *Oh Jeez!*

What would you like to know? I grew up in Spain and moved here last year. I work as a cocktail barman.

That's cool. Do you enjoy it?

Yes, most days! Some days are very long and I not enjoy them as much.

Do you live in London?

Oh, and how old are you?!

Oh shit, I have absolutely no idea about anything with this guy!!

Yes I live in London. I am
25. How old are you?

Oooh fuuuuck! Shit, shit, shit. I'm like a dirty old perv! I'm ten years older than him! Oh Kate! What have you done? Retreat, apologise profusely and walk away. Awkward!

Oh shit! I'm 35... Oh God! I'm so
sorry, you don't look 25. Damn!

Why are you sorry?

Because I am super old!!
And you are way too young
to date a 35-year-old.

I wish you were older.

Well, actually, if I'm wishing
things, then I wish I was younger.

So, so sorry. I should have asked
before I gave you my number.

I am very happy to have your number. Age is
just a number but in fact I like older woman
anyway. I would like to go on a date with you.

Oh, for fuck's sake! I am a 'thing' now? An older lady. That's weird. Oh man. This sucks. I really fancy him. If he was ten years older than me, I wouldn't have an issue, but the fact I am ten years older than him, has completely freaked me out. But I shouldn't feel like that. Maybe I should just go on a date with him? Maybe a lunch time date so that there is no wine and I can see clearly past his gorgeous face. *Oh, why is it that I pluck up the courage to give my number to a hot man and he ends up ten years younger than me? That is just my luck, damn it!*

I'm snuggled in a throw on my sofa, watching 'Don't tell the Bride', whilst nibbling the Galaxy bar I stole from my eldest daughter. It's her favourite chocolate, so I'm being very naughty, but she's not here to ask and my secret stash is empty. As I munch away, I wonder why I had dismissed it before. *I'll give it its dues. Galaxy is actually really quite nice and smooth... yum.*

> Evening Kate. I hope you enjoying your evening.

The twenty-four-year-old and I have continued to text for a week. He has tried very hard and has won me over, mainly because I really wanted him to win the fight. I like him. Not just his looks, but his personality too. He is super sweet, caring, kind and cute. *Because he is so fecking young Kate, you old perv of a lady!*

I am still shocked he is so young. He doesn't seem it at all. He has told me, quite a few times now, that I am just overthinking the whole thing. As our text conversation continues, I finally agree to a date with him, just a day-time date. I realise he needs a name and there's only one option. It's got to be Galaxy. Smooth and silky. *And so young he'd appeal to my eldest daughter! Oh my god!*

I've decided to get myself date ready before the school run mayhem, so I get up early to have a bath before waking the girls. This is a lot of effort for me. I'm never that organised on a school day. I am the kind of mum who drops her kids as close to the school as possible and watches them run down the path from the car because I'm still in my onesie and my hair is unbrushed in a messy bun! It's a perfect sight to see, my two little ones, with their big old rucksacks on their backs, bobbing against them as they run off towards their school entrance. The eldest just closes the car door on me as I yell 'love you, have a good day' then walks casually to join her secondary school friends. Then I return home to get ready for work in peace. Bliss! Long gone are the days when I had to walk them to the school door. I sigh as I reminisce, soaking in the warm bubbles. Now I'm like a taxi service to school.

Today is different though. I'm getting the train to London at ten so there's no way I have time to dry and curl my hair after the school run.

I think about what I should wear. I don't want to embarrass Galaxy by looking like an older woman. I want to look casual, but still nicely spruced up. I truly don't even know why he would want to meet up with me after learning my age. *Maybe he has issues? Maybe it's a fetish thing for the older woman? Oh, for fuck's sake, Kate. Overthinking it all again. Damn! OK. I just need to chill out.*

When the girls get up, I answer their questions about why I look like I'm going out somewhere when it's a school morning. I tell them that I'm popping to London to meet up with my friend for a date at lunch time and they are happy for me. They are so cute and tell me I look very pretty.

"What is he like?" they ask.

"He is a man I met when I was up in London before. This is just a first date, and I don't know too much about him just yet. It will just be a nice day out for me. I don't think I will see him again after today as I think we might be better off as friends, but I'll let you know the gossip this afternoon, after school."

We laugh and giggle. They are so funny, bless them. It's so sweet how they wish me well. Not in a 'pimping out their mum' way, just a sweet, excited 'caring about their mum' way.

I use the time on the train to respond to my clients' booking enquiries for the next week or two. I'm pleased I'm going to be busy. As the train pulls into the station, I pack my phone away and check my makeup. All good.

We're meeting at a café bar close to the station, so I don't have far to go to get the train back at two. I need to be home for the school run. I sit down at a table for two, order my tea and wait for him to arrive.

This is actually really nice, I think to myself. *I should do this more often. Jump on the train and head up here for lunch and cups of tea in trendy cafés. I love the fast train too – so quick!*

I'm beginning to think I've fallen in love with London rather than the men I've met here over the last few years. Although still not enough to live here. *Well, maybe I could have a house here and a house in Kent. Wow, I had better meet a man who can afford that then. I can only just afford my rent!* I chuckle as I continue taking bookings in my diary, dreaming of a lottery win, while I wait for Galaxy.

In he walks. *Wowzers!* He's even better looking than I remembered. The image of him I did have wasn't just drunken memories. So tall. Definitely over six feet. He's so confident. He walks over to me, kisses each cheek and sits down at the table. He is wearing a white casual shirt, skinny jeans and trainers. And he is wearing plain silver rings on three of his fingers. I don't know why, but my attraction grows further with the rings. He is so stylish.

He had told me he was shy, but he doesn't seem to be to me. We talk and talk over a light lunch. I thought with English as his second language, we might not be able to communicate as easily as we do. After all he has lived in London for less than a year and I, embarrassingly, can only speak English. No Spanish for me. I can't even speak French and I live so close to France. *Yep, I really must learn another language.*

I'm really enjoying my first date with Galaxy, and I don't feel the age gap at all. I don't even think I look too much older than him either. I tell him, and he says, "Your eyes are the only thing that gives your age away."

I laugh loudly. "Wow, ever so tactful!" *He is a funny man. Oh wait, young man, boy? Oh, for fuck's sake. Now I'm thinking about the age gap again! This really is ridiculous. He is smart, funny, gorgeous, into me. And if he was the one who was ten years older, I wouldn't give it a second thought. But no, because I'm the cougar, I'm overthinking it.*

It's time for me to leave for my train and we walk to the station together. He walks me to the platform. *Aww, he is so scrummy.* The chemistry is building even more. He has his arm around my shoulders, making me feel tiny. We both lean in for a kiss just before I get my train. *Oh, the boy can kiss! Damn it!* We say our goodbyes and I head for my train, texting the moment my train departs.

Galaxy texts me so much. It is really helping me to move on from Fruit and Nut. It's not a healthy way to help me, but just what I need. My phone had felt empty since we parted. It is really refreshing knowing the man texting me is fully interested, and only in me, investing his time and attention in getting to know me.

I think he must be crazy wanting to hang out with me though. I mean, this man can have a gorgeous, spritely, twenty-something who hasn't had any children, let alone three of them! To be brutally honest, in ten years it would be more appropriate and more acceptable for him to date my eldest daughter. *Oh my god.* I realise there are ten years between them too. *Oh, for fuck's sake, Kate!* I do know three women who have a big age gap with their fellas who're younger than them and they are really happy. Plus, most of The Nine's fellas are a few years younger. I need to stop dwelling on the age gap. I cannot figure out if I am trying to self-destruct, or if the age gap is actually a problem. A second date is needed – and wanted. I'll see how I feel then. I don't need to rush into anything. I can slowly get to know Galaxy.

Our second date is dinner and cocktails in London, the following Friday. I meet Galaxy just outside the restaurant. A waiter shows us to our table, and we order drinks. We mull over the menu, chatting constantly. We are having a great time together again, enjoying the start to our evening. We place our orders and get back to our conversation.

We learn all about each other's families, work life, past relationships. It feels like we are back in the school yard. *Although Kate, if that was the case, you would have been finishing primary school as he was being born!* I cringe at the thought. The age gap again. A light shiver runs down my spine. Galaxy takes my hand from across the table. He is tender, loving. I know he genuinely likes me.

We finish our meals and order a couple of mojitos. Galaxy leans over the table and kisses me. He asks if I am his.

"I don't want anyone else to kiss you," he tells me.

Wow. This should make me run away. Date two and he doesn't want anyone else near me? Instead, his desire to claim me and my kisses really turns me on. He genuinely likes me and is man enough to want to make me his. *No secret girlfriend.* Knowing I have kids doesn't even bother him. He has told me that he does want one of his own though. *Hmmm, this is something we will need to talk about another time. Not on this date though.*

We leave the bar and walk to the train station. Galaxy towers over me. He leans down to kiss me goodbye and I am lost in his arms as they scoop me up. The chemistry between us is insane. It's clear that we want to take things further, but I'm just not sure I can. I'm not sure that I'm ready.

We're on our fifth date night and this time Galaxy is coming to me and he'll be staying the night. I'm excited to see him again but I'm a little worried he will be here, staying over and that I'm not one hundred percent sure I'm ready to sleep with him just yet. He is making such an effort with me though. I believe that he genuinely likes me, and I do really like him, but... But, but, but. There just seems to be something in the way. Other than the age gap, I just can't think what it is.

After he arrives, we go into town for a few drinks in one of the local pubs, far from the swanky cocktail bars that he is used to, but he says he prefers pubs to bars.

"At least the company is good and worth the journey down here," I say as I tilt my head up at him trying to look innocent. *Nothing about me is innocent!* We both laugh. I know we are both thinking about what might happen later. We chat away, laughing, joking and enjoying flirting with each other. I find myself touching his arms, his thigh, his hands whenever I get a chance. He does the same. The chemistry continues to grow between us through the evening. Somehow, the conversation becomes about sex.

"Women like it up the arse, no?" Galaxy announces.

"Erm. No! What the fuck? Bloody hell! What a question!" I cannot stop laughing as I declare, "That's it. That's the generation gap. You youngsters learn about sex through on tap porn. My generation had 'More' magazine with a few tips and Position of the week!"

We laugh about our age gap and kiss again. We kiss all the time, from the moment we see each other, during every break in conversations. He just makes my knees weak.

We return to my cottage in a taxi and go straight downstairs to my bedroom. The chemistry is out of control now. As we kiss, undressing each other, there is no longer an age gap between us. Despite this I can't help but blurt, "I have mum boobs and a mum belly, and you are fit as fuck!"

Why Kate? Did you need to draw attention to your belly and boobs when you're completely naked? No. No you did not!

He kisses me. "You are sexy too."

I laugh shyly and say, "Trying to please me again, but I'll take it."

We climb into bed. The sex is all new and exciting and I haven't had sex in such a long time that I am eager to please him too. I take the lead, something I never have the confidence to do. I want him so badly. He explores my body and tells me he enjoys being with me. He knows the moves. I have been with more partners than him, and have been married too, so I was unsure what he would be like, but bloody hell, this is passionate and hot. I think because he has spent the time investing in us to get to this point, well, I trust him with my body. He isn't a pull my hair and slap my arse kinda man. He's a making me feel beautiful, sexy and wanted kinda man. I enjoy every moment.

When we're in the moment, enjoying each other's bodies, I don't think about the negatives: his age, the fact he doesn't have kids yet but does want them, that his whole new life is in London since moving from Spain, or (and this is the most honest one that I couldn't quite put my finger on before) I am just not emotionally available yet. But now, as I lay here after he has fallen asleep, I feel guilty for sleeping with someone new. Would I be feeling this way if I was truly ready to move on? Maybe I would? Maybe this is just part of the process of letting Fruit and Nut go?

In the morning, I decide to talk to him about the age gap and children. I ask him how it could work.

"If we have a relationship and it ends after five years, I will be pretty much forty and starting over. You will just be the hot guy in his late twenties who doesn't have any children, with plenty of time to start over and settle down when you're ready."

I continue, "And what if you want to party every weekend? I love going for a night out, but all-night dancing in a club? Hell no! I've had those nights. I loved them, but not now. Then what happens if we do fall in love and decide that this is definitely the right path for us and you want a child of your own? What if you don't want children any time soon, but want them with me later? By then I might be too old to give them to you."

There's a bomb of questions exploding in my head, firing out of my mouth. This poor guy is just happy that we made it to the bedroom. Now I'm acting like a crazy woman, asking him where this is all going after one night together. I blurt the million questions out, all at once. All before a morning cuppa. I just cannot stop overthinking this whole situation.

Galaxy is so chilled out though. He takes my hand and kisses my cheek. He seems to have an answer for every one of my questions and concerns. All his answers completely contradict each other though. Just wanting to please me and get me to chill the fuck out. One minute he says he wants a child, then when I say I don't, he retreats and says he can live without children of his own.

"I know that that isn't true," I say.

"I want a relationship with you. I would marry you, if you would want that later down the line," he says.

"That is just the lust speaking, not your true thoughts. You don't know me well enough yet."

Then he tells me he doesn't want to ever get married. "We can just have fun then. If you would like? I have never in my life just had fun before because I like to be in relationships."

He is like a puppy, so eager to please me. He is happy just to make me happy. Not at all selfish.

I feel like Cinderella after midnight, the magic slipping away into the night. He sees himself finding his Sleeping Beauty, waking her from a peaceful slumber to live happily ever after. As I think about it more, I feel less like Cinderella and more like the Fairy fucking Godmother, giving other people what they want! I laugh sadly to myself. *Can I even have a happy ever after with so much baggage. Soooo much baggage.*

I have absolutely no idea if I am having a moment of clarity or if I'm self-sabotaging. I can't help it though and I will more than likely regret it, but I'm just not over Fruit and Nut enough to think clearly. Time to let this Galaxy get back to his twenties, to enjoy his youth and not live the life of a thirty-something just yet.

Galaxy is new to me, uncharted territory. I am choosing to leave before I get the chance to taste it fully and to stop anyone getting hurt. What I have learnt though, is that Galaxy chocolate is smooth, sweet and incredibly moreish. Walking away will be extremely hard because it is ridiculously tempting, just waiting to satisfy my every need.

Dating Overload

I decided to take some time out to get my head together, but it didn't last longer than a month. I missed having someone to message, chat with, spend time with. After all, the chase is so much fun. Yorkie told me, "You're like a kitten with a string, Kate. The moment it falls to the floor and you've caught it, you no longer want it."

Every date, well, there have been four dates, four men, none of them are Fruit and Nut. *Bloody hell.* I'm bored of still missing him. Tired of still saying his name.

Date one: Lion Bar. All talk, no real chocolate involved.

Date two: Terry's Chocolate Orange. Solid slices that fall apart when dropped, and he had definitely been dropped. Tastes yummy, but no way he would get on with Dairy Milk.

Date three: Cadbury Turkish Delight. My mum would love him. Totally into the arts, darling. All a bit too soft and chewy. Not much chocolate. Definitely not solid.

Date four: Supermarket own brand. Basic at best. No taste, with a texture like plastic. Totally depressing after spending a two-hour first date crying over his ex, sobbing into a napkin whilst I downed the bottle of wine.

I even ended up kissing a Starburst just to mix it up a bit. Turns out that I'm just not into women!

"You've been staring for ages!"

I'm at the corner shop pondering my love life.

"What do you like Neil?"

"I'm a Haribo kinda guy myself."

"Kids and grown-ups love it so...?"

"We do indeed. You know what I think you need?"

"What?"

"A bacon sandwich."

"I'm a vegetarian!"

"Then make it an egg sandwich. Or a packet of crisps. Go savoury. Sometimes we get so fixated on what we are craving, we forget to listen to what our bodies really need."

"Maybe you're right."

"Or maybe just buy them all and get the hell out of my shop so I can serve my other customers." He grins. There are no other customers.

But I like this idea. With a tip from Mrs Jennings burning a hole in my pocket, I buy the lot. The restock of Kate's stash. A trip down memory lane. I buy a Dairy Milk, a Bournville... and a packet of Starburst. This is it. The ultimate trip down memory lane.

"Do you want to try the Haribo?" asks Neil.

"Thanks Neil, but I've enough to process right now without adding more into the mix."

"Right you are," he says, scanning each item. "Do you want a bag with that?"

I feel sick. There are too many empty wrappers on the floor and the cats are going crazy for them. I can honestly say there isn't a single one I want more of. None of these dates were what or who I am looking for. *Oh, for fuck's sake, there is just no easy way to do this.* Adira said I will feel better in the winter. It's still the summer. "Enjoy the sun and allow the autumn to come along," she said. I know she is right. Texting and dating men isn't working. I just need to date myself and my friends. Give myself time. Oh, and the sun. I enjoy the sun. The sun is a great date.

I hear of this strategy working out for people all the time. Don't look for the boyfriend and he will find you. Stop trying to get pregnant and bam, you're up the duff, bun in the oven and baking yourself a baby. The only issue is 'time'. *Urgh.* It's all very dull, this healing process. I know I am boring anyone and everyone who will listen about the man who tricked me. There is only one bar left untouched. The perfect purple wrapper and silver foil is staring up at me. Mine, and yet somehow untouchable. Fruit and bloody nut.

The man who had the girlfriend. The man who, in all truth, I just want to be right here with me, right now, cuddled on the sofa, telling me it was all a mistake, a funny joke and that we are meant to be together. Telling me that he is back and my life with a player can continue. I would do his washing, cook his dinner and make sure his every need is catered for because I have missed him more than anyone would ever believe.

But nope. It's just me, tumbleweeds (no, sweet wrappers) blowing across my floor. Sexy undies going unworn and far too much pizza and wine being consumed.

OK. Time. I am calling time on this bullshit. In fact, it is time to make a stand against my poor me attitude. It's time to fill my evenings after work when I don't have the girls to occupy me. I need to get to the gym that I pay £55 a bloody month for and haven't been to for weeks on end.

Yes. It's time to kick start the diet and get the fat gone and the mind clear. After all, it won't be long until I want to get back into a black Bodycon, date-night-favourite dress and head out again. Heels and all.

STI Hell!

Unprotected sex. Thirty-five years old and I'm that stupid. I had unprotected sex. I was caught up in the moment and have had three weeks of freaking out thinking I'm dying, that I've contracted all sorts of diseases, most probably HIV, and will never have sex again. Despite the fact I have googled the hell out of HIV. *It's absolutely mind blowing the advances being made in HIV treatment.*

I have finally made my way to the local sexual health clinic. I am told to fill in a form that I have collected from the lady at the counter. Name, address, gender. All the usual stuff. And then, 'Are your sexual partners male, female, both?' *Wowzers! That's a little intrusive. Does a kiss with Starburst count as a sexual partner?* I chuckle to myself as I tick male and continue with the form.

I take a seat in the rundown, grey and blue-walled waiting room. I look around the room and there are six other people waiting. We're all spaced out around the room in the battered old chairs. Only two women are sitting next to each other and I'm pretty sure they came along together. There's some really hideous, naff dance music playing somewhere. I think it's coming from a teenage girl sitting a few chairs down from me. I briefly look up and see she has her phone in her hand. It's coming from that. *Why would you sit in an STI clinic and draw attention to yourself? I mean, I'm sitting here wanting the world to swallow me up.*

I've been here before, but just for a routine check. On those occasions I've felt quite smug because I'm being responsible, having a full sexual health check. I usually feel confident the results will just be confirmation of the all-clear because I use condoms unless I've got to a stage in a relationship (of sorts) where we are happy and we've both been checked out. These last few weeks, I have been reckless though. Now I feel like a kid waiting to walk into the confessional at church. *Well Father, I have had unprotected sex, outside of marriage and I am probably going to go to Hell, but can I take fifteen Hail Marys instead? I would really appreciate the Hail Marys right about now.*

Shit. This is horrendous. I wait for an hour before I am called through to the small side room. I sit down in the chair and the nurse asks me if it is OK to let the trainee run through my checks and questions? *Oh my god! You couldn't write this shit. Why me? Why now?* I feel every inch of my body curling up in embarrassment as I answer politely, "Yeah, sure. Why not. I don't mind at all."

But you do bloody mind Kate! Why didn't you just make your excuses and apologies and say no? The twelve-year-old trainee who I swear goes to school with my middle child thanks me and sits in the chair by the desk, while the nurse stands behind her. Both are looking straight at me. *Oh, for fuck's sake, this is mortifying. How can you know anything about sex? You should be asking your mother to sign a sex ed consent form, not asking me the ins and outs of my sexual history.*

Mortifying. No other word will do. She asks me all the same questions that were on the first questionnaire, I have literally just filled in, to make sure the answers that have now been input onto the computer are correct.

"Why are you here today?"

"I had unprotected sex with a new partner," I say sheepishly. *Fuck it! Own it, Kate. You messed up. People do all the time.*

"Who I am unlikely to see again." I add completely unnecessarily. *Oh, do shut up Kate!*

"I am fully aware of my stupidity, and I am really quite anxious."

The young girl is really kind. "I'll keep an eye out for results. They should be back by the end of the week, or Monday by the latest. I'll make sure the text gets sent straight out to you, or if the test results show anything then I will give you a call."

Great. Now I'm crying. Fucking empathy from the twelve-year-old. She hands me a tissue. *Oh, bless her heart.* She turns and looks up at the nurse behind her and asks, "I can do that, can't I?"

The nurse says, "Yes of course," looking at me with a face that says 'she'll get over this quick'. She hands me the swabs to take behind the curtained bed and tells me to follow the instructions. I do what I need to do then wash my hands and hand the swabs back over. Then she takes a blood test.

All done, I get up to leave and joke about hoping I never hear from them again and that I'm greatly looking forward to receiving my text on Friday.

Friday comes. As I'm driving between clients' houses, my phone rings. It's a withheld number. *Sales? You've been in an accident people? Not answering that. Oh shit! No! It's Friday. Bollocks!* I pull over to answer.

"Hello. Is that Kate?" I recognise the voice. It is indeed the sweet girl from the clinic.

Shit. I'm dying! I bloody knew it! AIDS. I have AIDS!

"Yes, hi. It's Kate. This is bad, isn't it. I so badly did not want a phone call! I was hoping for a text."

"Can I just ask you to confirm your full name and date of birth, please?" I do so.

"Thank you. Yes, I'm so sorry. It's chlamydia. You have chlamydia," she softly tells me.

"Oh my god. Thank God! At least it's not AIDS!" I blurt out, shocking her slightly with my reaction. "And as I would have only had it a few weeks it shouldn't have done any damage! Antibiotics, right?"

My dyslexic, boggled brain is somehow able to recall word for word the contents of the chlamydia page I googled a week ago.

"That's right, not AIDS!" she laughs, lightly. "Yes, antibiotics. Any chance you can pop by today?"

"Damn no, I'm stuck working. I'm sorry. Can I call the doctor? Would they be able to prescribe the medicine?"

"Yep, that shouldn't be a problem. If it is, come and see us on Monday."

I hang up and ring my GP to arrange a phone call appointment for later that day.

He calls just after 5.30pm. He has a kind, friendly voice and asks how he can help me. I explain that I received the results of my sexual health check-up and I unfortunately have chlamydia. I ask if he can prescribe me the antibiotics.

"Why didn't the clinic issue them? They should have," he says.

I tell him I can't get to the clinic and he agrees to send a prescription over to the pharmacy for me to collect within the hour.

"I'm so grateful. Thank you. You are an absolute angel," I exclaim.

The doctor laughs, and says, "Oh, I'm good looking too! And you are very welcome indeed."

Did he just say that? I can't believe what he has said. *Has he actually come on to me?* I'm so shocked I can't help laughing at this completely inappropriate thing to say.

And in true Kate fashion respond equally inappropriately. "You can't come on to me! I have chlamydia! You won't want me with that!"

I hang up, laughing. *You have to laugh Kate. You absolutely have to laugh, or you would cry. Only you Kate! This kinda crap, only happens to you.*

I chuckle to myself as I compute the day I've just had and thank God that it was something curable. I know just how lucky I am, after such a stupid mistake. *You're a grown woman with three kids! Don't you ever do this again, Kate! Learn from this and put it all behind you. Once you have contacted the guy! Oh, fucking great!*

> Hi there. Sorry to tell you but you have given me chlamydia. I have regular health checks and after our random night together I now have it. I suggest you get yourself checked out and take the right medication.

> Oh

Oh? Are you kidding me? Oh! What does 'Oh' mean? Hmm, it means, he more than likely knew. The bastard! Right. I know I have issues with doors, but not this one. This one doesn't deserve a spot in the secret stash. Block and delete.

Condoms without fail and wiser decisions from now on.

Kinder Bueno: Only Joking

Finally, winter is close enough to taste. The time in the sun was short-lived but refreshing, and the longest days of sunshine came strangely when the kids were back in school. Work picked up and I was suddenly inundated with clients, all of them wanting to chat. It's a real privilege to be a hairdresser sometimes. So many people let you into their lives, opening up about things. It was nice to talk about someone else's dramas for a change.

I am feeling clear headed now and ready to end my dating famine. I'm finally feeling like I'm ready to get out there again. I know what I want. I know that I cannot play the multi-dating game. It's too overwhelming and confusing. I want to date one man at a time. Even if only for coffee dates and lunches. I am going back to taking things slowly.

Nothing gives me what I had with Fruit and Nut and unless anything changes with him, nothing ever will. I am finally ready to accept that, and I know I'm wasting my life thinking he could change. I know I'm worth more than what he can ever offer me too. To be Mrs Fruit and Nut I would have to accept an open relationship. And I don't believe he is even capable of loving me anyway.

So, at long last, I am moving forward. This time, there's no looking back. I'm straightening out my crown and finding myself a king. A man who knows what he wants, has a job, some kids and is happy to get to know me before we go to bed together. I doubt I will be lucky enough to find the mind-blowing bedroom fun I have had in the past, but if he shows willing, and the crown jewels are OK then I can work with that.

I'm signed in and all uploaded to Bumble, a new dating app I found. I like Tinder. It's my old favourite. But it's time to try something new. Bumble is similar to Tinder with swiping, but girls chat first. It means I have more control over who I chat to. I like the sound of Happen too, a dating app that is all about who you cross paths with, but as I live in a village, I doubt I will match with anyone.

I feel chilled out about dating again. I'm taking my time to find the right sweet treat. If someone comes along that I think could be suitable, then I won't meet him until we have spent a couple of weeks texting and calling each other. Just to make sure he's a fit. There will be no more bad date situations, no more rushing and making bad decisions.

It's not long before I come across a match that seems very promising. *Ha-ha, don't get carried away with yourself Kate. You've thought that about so many times before!* He has blonde hair, he's six feet two inches tall, big built, butch. He looks a real man's man. Yeah, I think I will say hello to this one.

> Hello. How's the world of bumble treating you?

Hello Kate. Well as we matched, I'm going to say very well indeed. How are you? You look very pretty and have a cute smile.

Even better. He has messaged me right back!

> Aww thank you. You look very nice yourself and loving how tall you are!

Yeah I get that a lot 😆 And you're only 5ft 2. You're tiny! Surely you can have your pick of men shorter or taller.

> Well, most people are taller than me! 😆

We spend the next couple of weeks texting. I enjoy myself. It's a fresh start and I'm happy to be back in the dating world. He is such a softy. He has a career in engineering which he is really dedicated to, working long hours. He's from London and I'm amazed he has a car and drives! Everyone I've dated from London before has used public transport. He owns his own house too. *Oh, wow.* Boxes are being ticked all over the place. We chat on the phone regularly. He is funny, sweet, romantic. I feel like a grown up, once and for all. This is just what they say: you give up and then you find the one. Or the one finds you.

Our first date is three weeks after we first connected. I excitedly set off in my little car to him meet at a pub in Bromley. I sit in my car, texting my friends, to let them know I have arrived safely and wait for him to arrive. I see him before he sees me. He looks exactly like his pictures: friendly, kind, good looking. He has such an honest, gorgeous face. And I love how tall he is. He's bigger built than most men I have met, and he makes me feel tiny. Like I could eat ice cream and pizza, gain a stone and still seem like the 'tiny little woman'. He isn't all muscles though, which is even better, just big and toned!

I hop out of my car and we say hello to each other really easily. There's no awkwardness at all and we go inside to find a table. Conversation flows well and we laugh non-stop. He has such a great sense of humour. He asks if he can take a picture of us together. We take a few and choose our favourites. They look nice. We look like a real couple that suit each other.

When it's time to leave, he scoops me up in his arms and kisses me, a kiss I was really hoping for, and we say our goodbyes. We each set off on our journeys home and five minutes later he calls. I put him on speakerphone.

"I loved meeting you," he says.

I agree enthusiastically and can't wait to arrange the next date.

As I continue my drive home, I think about what I need to call this man in my phonebook. *Hmmmm what could your name be Mister?* I'm just not sure what chocolate bar suits him best. I think about what I have dated in the past. *Cadbury, that's a good old, life-long favourite, but also each Cadbury bar has hurt my heart. I don't want to jinx this. Nestlé? There are lots of varieties there! Lindt? No, no. Only one man will ever be my Lindt bar and he is in a league of his own.* My first love was Lindt, but that's a whole other story and Lindt is far too showy and flamboyant for this poor little church mouse. I want a bar I haven't sampled before, a new beginning, a fresh start.

Oh, I have it! This new man should be a Kinder Bueno. I had bought a pack of four from Neil's shop the other day. *Yay to me and my multi pack purchase.* I took one away so that the girls wouldn't squabble (*or commit murder*) over who got the fourth bar. I enjoyed it very much. It's a very grown-up bar. Sophisticated. Fitting for this man of many layers, sweet and smooth in the middle too. *Yes, I shall name him Kinder Bueno.*

Over the next week, we spend hours on FaceTime. We speak on the phone every night before we fall asleep too. Once we actually did fall asleep on the phone to each other. We text throughout the day, every day, and a smile is permanently fixed upon my face. There are no games being played and I feel I might have actually found somebody on my wavelength.

Aww, this is dead cute. He has just sent me a video of an elderly couple in love, with a text.

> One day this might be us. Xx

> The way things are going, I agree. xx

He's a Frankenstein of all the men I have met before: all their best bits. I enjoy his company immensely and really think I could cope if the sex was bad. *Not shit though. Let's not be silly here, Kate.* Well, I guess I could work with a bit crap. I chuckle as I remember all the situations I've found myself in before.

Kinder Bueno is a true family man. He gets on really well with his ex, the mother of his girls, and her new husband. They even go on holidays together like me and Dairy Milk. He totally understands the importance of me raising my children in this modern way and why I feel the need to make this modern family work. He's even told me he is looking forward to meeting the girls and their dad. *Wowzers!* I do not think there are any must-have boxes left to tick. I just cannot believe my luck. Life really does have a way of working out. Maybe my happy ever after has found me now, at long last.

Dates to pubs, dinners and drinks. I don't want to rush this. We are both more than happy to take things slowly. My friends all think he sounds fantastic and I'm looking forward to the day he meets them. Things couldn't get better. I feel like life got the memo and sorted me out a good'un, someone who is in the right stage of his life and who likes me back.

This evening we are enjoying a good old-fashioned date at the cinema. It's so nice to reach this point where we can just chill at the cinema, all relaxed.

Kinder Bueno takes off his jacket and puts it over the front of him, telling me he is chilly. We tuck up together, all intimate and cosy. This is sweet.

As we get into the movie, I hear an annoying noise. A food noise. I shuffle away slightly, thinking he must be eating or drinking something. I cannot stand the sound of someone eating right next to me. Even if it's the kids. I googled it once and it's 'a thing'. Misophonia. The hatred of certain sounds.

I chuckle as my train of thought steals my concentration away from the film. I turn my head and glance at him. *Oh shite!* He's not eating at all. *No. I must be wrong.* I glance again. *Oh! This is tricky!* This is a new one on me. He is sucking his thumb! *Oh, my fucking life. This must be a joke to wind me up, surely?* I take a moment to compute this. I can't believe it. I just cannot fathom for one second that this six-feet-two-inch, big, butch, manly man, father of two daughters, at the age of thirty-nine is a thumb-sucking man child! *I will ignore it. Can I ignore it? OK. I have to! Well, I will try my hardest to ignore it.*

The film is completely lost on me now. He is openly sucking his thumb, trying to talk to me while his thumb is in his mouth. I feel like telling him off, like he's one of my children. I want to tell him he has germs on his hands, but thankfully stop myself.

Oh, I just want to leave, I think to myself, completely disheartened. *Have I found a baby man? Will I go to his house one evening and find him wearing a nappy asking me to cradle him?* I can't think of anything else. I feel so mean for wanting to laugh, but, oh my god, I feel as though this is a Channel 5 documentary. *What if this might even be a fetish in bed. I might be happily exploring his downstairs and look up to him sucking his thumb. Or worse, it might become a 'Bitty' moment from Little Britain. Oh, Kate! Only you. This crazy shit only happens to you!*

I shudder at the thoughts flying around in my mind. Physical contact with this man now gives me the ick. I know it's mean, but I just want to leave. Leave and never look back.

After the film we leave separately. I kiss him on the cheek and explain that I am not feeling too well. We drive home, in our separate cars, and head to our separate houses. I don't even want to call a friend and ask for advice. Rightly or wrongly, I am done. I have had my babies. I do not need another one. I need a bottle of wine and a packet of crisps, so I stop off at the corner shop. Neil smiles as I enter.

"Hey there. I've found a chocolate bar you've never tried before!"

He reaches down beneath the counter, but I stop him. "Crisps Neil. I want crisps and wine. And you are the only person open who can give them to me. Now."

"But I thought..."

"I'm done. You're right. I'm listening to my body. And my body says deep fried fatty potato crisps with mono-sodium glutamate and a very alcoholic bottle of wine. If you don't mind. Please."

My Kinder Bueno turned out to be a Kinder Surprise. It's sickly-sweet chocolate when you think about it. And no one wants the crappy toy once you reach adulthood. It might be fun when you're a kid, but there's a point when you need to let go and grow up.

Damn! I feel like life has said, "Here you are, we found him Kate. Just what you were looking for!" before pausing then saying, "Only joking!" to the sound of raucous laughter, a big old fat Cheshire Cat smile on its face!

Yes, my Kinder Surprise needs a fellow surpriser, and I am not that. I will get back to my chocolate hunt. Or maybe a diet? I am unsure at the moment. This one may take a while to digest.

This is Kate, over and out.

Stop, Breathe, Regather

I lie in my bed. I have just woken up. The girls are with Dairy Milk, so I've had a nice lay in. I have a new appreciation for my bed. It really is quite a comfy one. Terribly squeaky, but nice all the same. A white, king-size bed with lots of pillows and blankets, throws, and a big fluffy quilt. I like to sleep right in the middle. And I flipping adore my heated blanket, my best buy ever. I don't know why I feel the need to fill this bed with a man. Although I do love cuddling into and hearing the heartbeat of the man I am with, my head laid on his chest whilst his arms embrace me. *Yeah, I like that part. Cuddling into my pillow isn't quite the same, eh.*

I think about the last few years. *Wow.* Almost five years have passed since I signed up to online dating. What long years they have been. I admit that I have loved meeting these boys. These men. We did have some laughs along the way. Great nights out, cuddled nights in. I learned about so many different ways of life. I heard a lot of relationship stories. I gave far too much advice, but then I can never really help myself with that. Whether it is wanted or not, I do just tend to advise. They all opened up to me, but that's because I am an over-sharer, so people tend to share right on back.

I learnt so much about myself too. I have realised I don't need to change who I am. I just need to be honest about who I am. I know my own mind and I need to claim my own bullshit. I am far from perfect, but I love me, scars and all.

I need a cup of tea and a wee. *Right. Time to get up, Kate.* I go upstairs to my bathroom. I look in the mirror, look at me reflection, and begin to reflect on my life again. I'm drawn back into the nostalgia. *Wow. Yep. A lot has happened.* I have been through the mill, left to scramble out the other side. Each time I met someone, I would take on their emotions. I became caught up with their way of life, what they need, what they don't need, what I can do for them. But what about me? I feel like I am remembering something. Someone. Me. I'm tuning into me and I find I'm bloody exhausted.

In the icy kitchen I put the kettle on. I fancy the kids' chocolate cereal. Truth be told, it's not the kids' cereal at all. They don't even like cereal. I buy it for them, but I am the only one who eats it. *Why did I call it the kids' cereal? It's only me here and I love chocolate cereal. Own it, Kate!*

I mooch through into the lounge, the Christmas tree in the corner, lights twinkling, still on from the night before. It's beautiful. I chill on the sofa for a bit and reflect some more. I can see now. My eyes are open. I don't want to sit here with a cup of tea feeling sad about what I don't have. I need to look at what I do have. Lots more than just tea and a pink sofa.

And actually, my house isn't a cold, dark dungeon. It's beautiful. It's twinkling with Christmas lights…

The thing is, I don't *need* a man. I *want* a man. That's a very different thing. I can do many things for myself and anything I can't do, I can just ask a professional. I run my job, my home, look after the girls, see my friends. I even have a rabbit for the times in my life when quite simply a rabbit is just what's needed.

I don't want to become hardened to the world of dating though. A bit tougher, yes, but not closed off. The truth is, over the last few years men have brought me adventures and taught me so much about myself. They've reawakened my heart and allowed me to love again.

I have had my heart broken though, over and over. *My heart.* Why on earth did I open it up and fight to allow my walls down time and again for men who have never really deserved it? Why did I think so little of myself that I accepted the little these men brought to the relationship? Why did I feel the need to make them feel the security within our domain when they gave me none? All bar two of them forgot my birthday, and if they didn't, I received a late evening birthday text, or there was a note on social media. That hardly counts as remembering my birthday. It was just an afterthought.

Kate, Kate, Kate. Please hear yourself and truly listen.

None of them ever bought me flowers. *Wow. That's a heavy realisation.* If I was seeing anyone when they had a birthday, I always bought them a gift, not because I felt obliged to, but because I wanted to. Green and Black's was amazingly thoughtful though. He bought me little gifts, sweet ones, when he would work away. And then he spoilt it by sending me, a vegetarian, a picture of his dead lunch. *Rookie error that one.*

I think of all the failures. *Homophobia, not meeting me, not wanting me until I'm gone, not coming to visit my hometown, not trusting me, little willies, bad sex, having a secret girlfriend, not leaving a girlfriend they say they don't want. And thumb sucking! I mean, Kate? Come the fuck on! This behaviour is downright ridiculous. In fact, the most mature and loving was the twenty-four-year-old. And the issue there was me!*

I am a strong woman and none of these men have brought anything real to my table. *Thank you all for the wonderful dates, the laughs, the company, and some of the most amazing orgasms I have ever had. I adore you all, but I have realised that I love me more.*

I am a bonkers, short, tubby, over talkative, over-sharing, loving, kind, caring, always running late woman. I have only wanted, and still want, the best for each one of my past lovers. I have always found it hard to close doors and I really do believe that there is absolutely no need to hate people. I have cheated and been cheated on. We all make mistakes. What is the use of carrying around bad feeling? I prefer to talk things through, accept the rights and wrongs that have been done and move forward.

I am learning from the mistakes I have made. It annoys me when people judge people for past mistakes. Like when people say 'once a cheater always a cheater'. *Really?* If someone is cheating, I believe it's because they are not fulfilled within that particular relationship. It doesn't mean they'll do it every time. Unless, of course, they just believe that they can enjoy an open relationship like Fruit and Nut. And that is fine and healthy as long as all parties know and understand the rules. *If not, that's cheating!*

I think about how I have been made to feel so guilty by someone I have been dating when he learns I cheated in a past relationship. If we are walking together side by side, talking to each other, and more importantly actually hearing and taking in what our partners are expressing, then that will all lead to an open and honest, healthy and loving relationship. One with mutual respect. Why would anyone cheat then?

I don't think anybody should be so naive to think that you will reach sixty years of marriage without someone else trying to get in your pants, or even you wanting someone else to get in your pants, even if it is just a fleeting thought. Nobody should be scared of that. Couples should talk about it. Those conversations make lasting marriages and relationships. Forgiveness and understanding is key to making it work, and honesty is the best policy, even when you fuck up. And trust. Everyone is innocent until proven guilty, not guilty until proven innocent.

I chuckle ironically at this thought and smile at myself. *Time to move forward, Kate.*

I head downstairs to my bedroom and start to get ready for work. I have a full diary of clients today. Saturdays in December are always busy. As I get dressed, sort my hair out and put on a little makeup I go back to my thoughts. It's time to do some soul searching. My future relationship will be a full and beautiful one because it is with myself. I will walk alone happily in the knowledge that I am choosing to, and that I am happy to. Only when I am completely fulfilled in myself will I again open my eyes to the world of dating.

I may or may not wish to be in a relationship with anyone other than myself. *Ahh, who am I kidding? I love to love!* Next time around though I won't be looking for validation from others. I already know my worth. I won't be discounting myself to make the other feel better, or to get a quick sale. *I am full price baby, and proud to be.* I make myself a promise to take nothing less than a man who walks along the same path as me, with me, side by side. When we stumble or fall, we will lean on each other, but not smother or derail. Love is a rare and magical emotion. To love and be loved right back, is mind-blowing.

I want to meet a man who respects, loves and admires my achievements and nature. A man who finds me beautiful before he finds me sexy. A man who buys me flowers 'just because'. Someone I can support and grow with. *Yes, that's the man for me. Oh, and if I'm doing this cosmic ordering right now, can he please be tall, dark and handsome. Just saying.*

The last few years have been a blast, full of ups and downs and a whole lot of craziness in between. *I mean I even became confident with the mum tum and boobs! Who knew that would ever happen?*

I am finally right where I need to be. Single and surrounded by wonderful friends, family, little people, three gorgeous cats and a tortoise. (We have a tortoise now. I bought it as an early Christmas present instead of another dating app subscription. *Go me.*) Here's to being a strong, single, independent woman, standing on rubble-free ground, walking proudly on her own for a while and absolutely loving life.

I head back up to my warm and cosy front room, the cinders of last night's fire still sparkling. I walk over to the Christmas tree and turn off the lights. I look around me, content with life. I realise just how much I love living here. I pick up my kit bag, head for the door and as I pull it open feel the fresh winter air hit my cheeks. Time for work. I close the door gently and it clicks locked behind me.

28th December, 8.02am

> Happy Birthday beautiful Kate. x

It's Wonka. I smile. Sometimes it's nice to leave a door on the latch. You never know when the timing might be right to let it open.

Acknowledgments

Where do I start? I have been so lucky to have had help and support from so many wonderful humans: Carly, Lucy, my Mum, David, Peter. The read-throughs and creative ideas from my dad, Amy, Seb, Charlotte, Lucy, Lucy, (so many Lucy's), Rachel, Hannah, Katie, Kate and Clem.

My brother Andrew has been my cheerleader throughout this entire process and his creative flair and ideas helped my book to grow. His encouragement when he read the first chapter of the book led to where we are now. How he laughed at the many different ways I wrote the word 'orgasmums' when he read the first draft! Oh no, Kate, that would be 'orgasms'!

And so, thank God that Nic Evans, a true perfectionist, came along to be Bernie Taupin to my Elton John. She found her way through my dyslexic mind, gave some ideas for development, and a little bit of constructive criticism to make the book readable. What a difference grammar and spelling makes!

My dad and his wife made publication of this book possible as they believed in me enough to dig deep in their pockets for the publishing costs. Thank you.

Then that brings me to the cover, the original drawn by Ellie, the digital tidy up from Kelly, and the creative cover by Craig. Here's to my family, from my blood to my honorary sisters. I am one lucky woman to have had the support and constructive criticism from them all.

The guys who let me share our stories and to the ones who I drew inspiration from.

Thank you to my Megan for lending me her laptop for the countless hours it took to actually write the book in the first place.

Lastly, thank you to all my daughters and stepdaughter, for not telling me I couldn't write a book with naughty scenes, nor disowning me because I have!

Love and humongous hugs to you all,
Mary xxx